*continued . . .*

"A dynamic gripping plot, excellent characters, smooth writing, and enough action and palpable suspense to keep you turning pages well into the night." —*Mystery News*

"Imaginitive, fast-paced, and gripping . . . thriller in the true sense of the word—white knuckles, rapidly turning pages . . . the tension is off the charts."
—*Deadly Pleasures*

"This is nail-biting suspense at its finest."
—*Romantic Times*

"Danielle Girard is a superb thriller writer who never disappoints her audience. . . . *Cold Silence* will appeal to fans of Barbara Parker and Jeffery Deaver."
—*Midwest Book Review*

"*Cold Silence* has all the makings of a compelling revenge drama." —*Publishers Weekly*

### Chasing Darkness

"Swift pacing and high tension . . . a compelling thriller." —*Publishers Weekly*

"[A] real thriller, a tantalizing story with an ending that packs a punch. Ms. Girard spins a tale that will surprise all." —*Romantic Times*

"For a riveting read, chilling and heartrending at times . . . I highly recommend *Chasing Darkness*."
—Romance Reviews Today

"Danielle Girard is a name to watch because she's rapidly reaching the level of Nancy Taylor Rosenberg or Sandra Brown." —*Midwest Book Reviews*

### Savage Art

"Chilling and suspenseful. But [it] isn't just about jeopardy—it's also about hope and resourcefulness and perseverance in the face of terror. [A] compelling tale." —Stephen White, *New York Times* bestselling author of *Missing Persons*

## Also by Danielle Girard

*Cold Silence*
*Chasing Darkness*
*Ruthless Game*
*Savage Art*

# THE
# ROOKIE CLUB

Danielle Girard

A SIGNET BOOK

SIGNET
Published by New American Library, a division of
Penguin Group (USA) Inc., 375 Hudson Street,
New York, New York 10014, USA
Penguin Group (Canada), 90 Eglinton Avenue East, Suite 700, Toronto,
Ontario M4P 2Y3, Canada (a division of Pearson Penguin Canada Inc.)
Penguin Books Ltd., 80 Strand, London WC2R 0RL, England
Penguin Ireland, 25 St. Stephen's Green, Dublin 2,
Ireland (a division of Penguin Books Ltd.)
Penguin Group (Australia), 250 Camberwell Road, Camberwell, Victoria 3124,
Australia (a division of Pearson Australia Group Pty. Ltd.)
Penguin Books India Pvt. Ltd., 11 Community Centre, Panchsheel Park,
New Delhi - 110 017, India
Penguin Group (NZ), cnr Airborne and Rosedale Roads, Albany,
Auckland 1310, New Zealand (a division of Pearson New Zealand Ltd.)
Penguin Books (South Africa) (Pty.) Ltd., 24 Sturdee Avenue,
Rosebank, Johannesburg 2196, South Africa

Penguin Books Ltd., Registered Offices:
80 Strand, London WC2R 0RL, England

First published by Signet, an imprint of New American Library,
a division of Penguin Group (USA) Inc.

First Printing, June 2006
10  9  8  7  6  5  4  3  2  1

Copyright © Danielle Girard, 2006
All rights reserved

The Edgar® name is a registered service mark of the Mystery Writers of
America, Inc.

 REGISTERED TRADEMARK—MARCA REGISTRADA

Printed in the United States of America

PUBLISHER'S NOTE
This is a work of fiction. Names, characters, places, and incidents either are
the product of the author's imagination or are used fictitiously, and any resem-
blance to actual persons, living or dead, business establishments, events, or
locales is entirely coincidental.
    The publisher does not have any control over and does not assume any
responsibility for author or third-party Web sites or their content.

*For Helen Breitwieser,*
*for guidance, untiring support, and friendship.*
*This one is all yours!*

## ACKNOWLEDGMENTS

As always, I am indebted to so many generous people who took the time to keep this book on track. I hope I have done them justice. Any errors are wholly mine.

The San Francisco Police Department has continued to be incredibly generous. Thank you to Lieutenant Richard Corriea of the sexual assault division for access to the department and to Inspector Dan Everson, now of the homicide division, who took me through a day in the life of a sex crimes inspector. I am especially grateful to sex crimes inspector Dolly Casazza who has answered every question and then some as *The Rookie Club* came to being. For DNA information, I would like to thank police inspector and DNA expert Pam Hofsass. For coroner information, I am indebted to Andrea Wagner of the Santa Clara County Medical Examiner-Coroner's Office. I appreciate the help of Anthony Toby O'Geen, Ph.D., Soil Resource Specialist in Cooperative Extension from the Department of Land, Air & Water Resources at UC Davis.

In addition to wonderful professional resources, I am also very fortunate to have an amazing cast of friends who were involved in *The Rookie Club*. I am extremely grateful to Tony Kelly, who spent many lunch hours walking the streets of San Francisco, talking about New York City and trying to make sense of 9/11. Thank you to Dr. Rachel Lewis for the mockups of medical diagnoses for my victims, to Brian Grossenbacher of Grossenbacher Guides for fishing terminology, to David Wanderer of Ridgeline Computer Solutions for endless technical support, and to

Dr. Tracey Hessel for setting me straight on San Rafael geography. Thank you to Inglath, Monica, Lisa
H., Lisa B., and Jean for reading and commenting on
all stages of the manuscript and for the moral support
only other authors know how to provide.

I'm also deeply indebted to the editorial staff at
New American Library. To Claire Zion and Kara
Welsh for making this happen and especially to my
brilliant editor, Kara Cesare, for the incredible time
and energy she has invested.

Lastly, I want to thank friends and family who know
when to tiptoe around me and when to drag me out
into daylight. Especially Marcie, Ixtla, Albee, Tiffany,
Dani, and Julia. And to Leigh Anne, for Tuesday
lunches.

Finally, my sincerest gratitude and affection go to
my husband without whom any achievement would be
diminished . . . and especially for this latest chapter.
It's one worth writing.

# 1

Emily Osbourne stepped out of the darkened sex crimes department and closed the door behind her. The station was deserted. Everyone was already at the awards ceremony. It was the last place she wanted to go. She'd been up since five a.m., in the lab for fourteen hours. The cases were so backlogged that evidence in even the most time-sensitive ones were taking up to three months.

Any crime less serious than murder was backed up six months or more. At least she'd finally finished the initial findings on Jamie Vail's latest serial rapist case. It was more than six months old. Vail had been on her hard. Now Emily just had to stay awake for two hours of acceptance speeches and she'd be able to catch a few hours of sleep. Maybe even seven. A record.

She entered the bright hallway, blinked away the spots. Her eyes burned. She punched the down arrow on the elevator. She propped herself against the wall, closed her eyes. Man, she could sleep right there.

Forcing herself up, she jabbed the button again. Nothing. She'd take the stairs. The walk might wake her up a bit. She leaned against the long metal bar and the heavy door creaked open.

The cold, steel handrail stuck to her clammy hand. The soles of her boots scraped against the cement stairs. She passed four. Three more, she thought. As she reached the landing, a door creaked open above her.

Her stomach tensed. She looked up but saw no one. She took a breath and shook it off. She'd never liked the police station. She preferred the bright open space of the crime lab at Hunters Point. She picked up her pace, almost out.

Footsteps clunked above her. At the second floor landing, she eyed the door. No, she was almost there. One more floor. The footsteps neared and she hesitated. She glanced back, then moved forward again, her heart pattering.

The footsteps stopped. She halted, like a rabbit with ears perked, poised to run. A door opened and then shut and she was alone again. With a deep breath, she began down the final flight of stairs.

Now alert, she jogged the last steps. She reached for the door. Felt the cool metal graze her fingertips when someone grabbed her from behind.

The strap of her purse yanked her backwards. Something hard struck her square in the head. She stumbled forward. He shoved her into the wall. Hands out, she tried to brace herself against the impact.

Her face struck the wall. Bone snapped. She screamed out, saw black. Fighting to shake it off, she reached to claw at him. Her wrist throbbed as it knocked against him. She groaned, cupped it to her chest.

Hands gripped her shoulders, swung her away from the wall. The room raced across her vision. She couldn't focus. He pushed her to the ground. She landed hard. Her wrist collapsed and red pain rocked through her. She tried to lift herself, but he slammed her down on her back. His head was covered in a white hood that was cinched around his neck.

She gasped. "No."

Jagged eyeholes and a larger mouth were cut in the fabric.

She started to scream. He covered her mouth. "Not a word," he hissed. Spit struck her cheek as he spoke.

"I've got a knife." He jabbed the point into her side. The blade struck a rib. Warm blood dripped down her side. She closed her eyes. Fought to breathe. God, no.

Fabric covered her face. She opened her eyes to blackness. Panic filled her lungs like water. She coughed and choked, reared her head.

He struck her again. She toppled to one side. He pinned her down with his legs. She bucked her hips, cried out.

He punched her face. Her head crashed against the cement floor. She heard a pop in her skull, nausea rose in her gut. She gagged.

She blinked, struggled to stay alert. She heard the crisp sound of her shirt ripping, felt cold air. A button struck the wall behind her. She flinched at the cold blade of the knife under her bra. Choked on a sob at the raspy sound of the blade cutting fabric.

She heard a rip of something like tape. Oh God. She twisted to her side, struggled to get away.

A sweaty palm wrenched her injured wrist over her head. Vomit rose in her gut. She gasped, choked.

He clasped the tape over her hand. Pulled the other one over her head. Bound them together. He shoved her hands to the floor above her head. Pinning her, he sank his hips down into her stomach.

She flinched as moist hands palmed her breasts. He rubbed them hard like he was molding clay. Squeezed and pinched her nipples. She turned her head, tried to escape her own body. He wrenched open her zipper. Helplessly, she struggled to reach for her pants as he jerked them off her hips. He slammed her down, back-handed her.

Pain closed in like darkness. She stopped moving. She touched her tongue to her bloody lip. Struggled to control the panic. She considered whether she could break free. He had a knife.

She prayed it wasn't what she thought. Not that. Then she felt the hardness. Jabbing at the bare skin of her thigh.

She wanted to move, didn't dare. Eyes squeezed shut. Oh God. No. No. No.

The head of it stabbed her. She tensed as the whole of it tore her open.

Bucking against the pain, she screamed. With bound hands, she clawed at him as he jammed inside her.

He grabbed her neck, squeezed.

She stopped fighting. Sobbed.

He rocked on top of her. Rammed her into the floor. The buckle on her purse strap was caught beneath her. The hard metal ripped into her back with each violent thrust.

And she did nothing—nothing. She turned her head into her arm and cried. Silently. Shamefully. Listened to the click, click, click of the building's old heating system. She pushed her mind away. Imagined a beach, sand, and ocean. God, drowning. She tried to inhale the water, to make this stop. Anywhere but here. She wasn't here. This wasn't happening. Not to her.

It got faster. Blood dribbled along her cheek. She didn't wipe it. Couldn't. The flesh around her eye ballooned, throbbing. Please let it be over. Please let it end. Please.

She was being—No, she couldn't think it. Wouldn't let the word enter her mind. It was just too terrible. She searched for the ocean again, struggled to imagine cool water or soft sand. The images that came were dark and horrible. Blood. Pain. Searing heat. Fire.

Then he groaned and slumped into her. There was a stretch of silence. It felt like forever. Breathe. She counted. Prayed. Please let it end. Please, God. Please leave.

He shifted. Something sharp scratched her thigh. It stopped, then she felt it again. The knife or a zipper. Then the weight was gone.

She heard him stand, the rustle of clothes.

She didn't move. She listened to the aching thud of her wrist, her head. Ignored what she felt below. Ignored the fluid that seeped between her legs. Knew from the viscous warmth that it was her own blood.

She heard him growl. Flinched as his foot struck her side. Howled. She lost her breath. Fought to draw in air. She was ready to die. Please. No more.

Then she felt his face beside her head. Terrified, she turned away. The next blow didn't come.

Instead, he said, "Tell the inspector hello for me."

She didn't move. Didn't speak. A hundred thoughts flashed through her mind. What inspector? Jamie Vail came to her mind first—Jamie Vail of Sex Crimes. Sex crimes. Oh God. Rape. She trembled, shudders rocking through her.

She heard him stand. She held her breath. His shoes squeaked against the cement as he walked. The door whined open, hissed closed, and clicked as the lock engaged.

She waited. Counted to three. Then waited some more.

Shaking, she pulled the hood off. She blinked hard. Her focus was blurred. She couldn't separate her hands. Held them both to her face and ran her fingers across her skin. She felt the swollen mass of her left eye.

She sat up and looked down at herself. A single drop of blood struck her shirt. She watched as the white fibers drank in the red.

Collapsing, she sobbed.

# 2

From the far corner of the convention center ballroom, Jamie Vail cupped the perspiring glass. She tugged up the waist of her pants, shifted them across her flat, bony hips. Underneath, nylons pulled the fabric in strange places when she moved. Did women even wear nylons anymore? She adjusted her jacket, then realized nothing would help. It wasn't the suit or the nylons or the pants. The problem was her.

She took a tentative sip of Coke and watched the officers mingle. Natasha Devlin stood talking to Bruce Daniels of Internal Affairs. Devlin tossed her hair over one shoulder and kicked her head back to laugh at a joke. Jamie felt ill.

She imagined her own hair, the blunt cut just above her shoulders. Her light brown strands had no rich color, no blond highlights, no sexy curls. Just a weird wave she could never quite control. Her green eyes were dull and pale, faded against her light skin and hair. She'd had people tell her she could accentuate them with makeup. But for what? Or whom?

Someone touched her elbow. She turned and found her ex-husband.

He clinked his glass to hers. "You okay?"

"Great," she lied. She didn't even try to smile.

He smiled. "Good."

They stood awkwardly. She made no effort to fill

the air. There was silence as his eyes traveled across the room. His attention piqued by something more interesting. More likely it was someone. Perhaps even Devlin, though Jamie no longer saw her. "See you, J."

She didn't answer. Screw this, she thought, and turned for the door. She walked ten steps before she saw the women sitting at a small table. Women she couldn't just walk by—members of the original rookie club.

Fifteen years ago, when Jamie had been a rookie cop in her early twenties, a group of women had bonded together. It had begun as a drunken night back in the days when Jamie still drank. They'd spent hours in a bar, bitching about the assholes who held them back because of their gender. After years of being isolated in the predominantly male department, suddenly they'd had a network.

That first night had felt so refreshing, the gathering had become a monthly ritual. It still went on, but Jamie hadn't been in years. Not since she found one of the other rookies in bed with her husband.

The women glanced up and Sydney Blanchard waved her over. Jamie eyed the door longingly as she approached them, wishing she hadn't left her quiet corner.

She took the seat between Inspector Hailey Wyatt of Homicide and Sydney, who headed the Crime Scene Unit (CSU) and managed the crime lab.

"I haven't seen you in ages," Sydney said.

She nodded. "Been buried."

"I heard about the latest case. Did Emily get you the results?"

Jamie shook her head. "She said she'd drop them off before she came here." She glanced around the room. "I haven't seen her yet."

Sydney shook her head. "Me, neither."

Jamie looked back. "You know the results?"

Sydney frowned. "No swimmers, no cells."

Jamie slumped back into the chair. It was the same as the last one. "Damn." Two percent of the male population naturally produced semen without sperm. A vasectomy produced the same results. But this rapist produced no semen. Even without ejaculating, a man normally released some semen. Not this guy and Jamie had no idea why not. A condom would explain it, but there was no evidence of latex to suggest condom use. No semen meant no DNA. And no DNA meant no way to match the rapist with the FBI'S Combined DNA Index System (CODIS).

Sydney touched her arm.

She opened her eyes.

"I'm sorry."

Jamie nodded, thinking she was referring to the case. But when she glanced up, she saw Natasha Devlin saunter toward them. An inspector with the Crimes Against Persons Department, Devlin wore a black pantsuit that hugged curvy hips and fell straight down over long, thin legs. Her jacket was cropped, and when she raised her hand to touch her thick dark hair, a tiny strip of navel showed.

When Devlin returned her hand to her wineglass, cleavage hefted out of the top. Somehow, though, it was never quite enough to be obscene.

"Will you excuse me?" Sydney said. "I'm going to try to find Emily."

Jamie nodded, steering her gaze away from Devlin, who walked right toward them.

Sydney stood, greeted Devlin briefly, and left.

Devlin laughed at something Sydney had said and Jamie felt the room silence as all eyes turned toward the beauty.

"Hi, ladies," she said, then glanced at Jamie. "Vail."

Jamie nodded to her. "Slut," she said just loud enough for the group to hear.

Devlin glared. "Did you say something?"

Jamie stared back. "Nothing newsworthy."

"Sit down, Natasha," Cameron Cruz said.

Devlin glared at Jamie and sat.

Hailey Wyatt leaned in to Jamie. "She does it to get your goat. Loves the reaction."

Jamie shifted toward her. "She got my husband already. You'd think that would be enough."

"You doing okay?"

Jamie looked over at her. "Fucking dandy."

Hailey smiled softly. "Glad to hear it."

Jamie laughed, then relaxed a little. "I just found out my rapist isn't leaving any DNA. I'm in a lousy mood."

"Condom?"

"No sign of that either. Just no semen."

Hailey frowned. "I'd say you've got reason to be pissed."

Jamie nodded. "How are things with you?"

She winked. "Murder."

Jamie watched as Tim approached the table. She shifted awkwardly as Tim stopped beside Devlin. He glanced at her, then quickly shifted his gaze away. Though Jamie had never suspected it would last, Tim and Natasha had been on again, off again for more than a year and a half.

Devlin glanced over her shoulder coyly, then looked at Jamie and grinned.

"Knock it off, Natasha," Hailey Wyatt said.

Devlin's eyes widened. "What do you mean? I'm not doing anything."

Jamie stood. "Don't bother, Hailey. I'm leaving."

Tim touched Devlin's shoulder again. She waved him off.

Tim's expression stiffened in anger. "I need to talk to you."

"Not now."

He grabbed her arm. "Now."

Devlin turned in her chair, set her wine down, and stood slowly. "I said no, Tim."

He pulled her toward him. He spoke softly, frowning.

Devlin stared over his shoulder.

Tim jerked her arm to get her attention.

When she turned to him, her face was set in fury. "Get the hell away from me."

He grabbed her shoulders with both hands.

Suddenly everyone was watching them. Jamie was embarrassed—for them, for herself.

"Stay the hell away from me," Devlin said and shoved Tim with both hands.

Hailey stood.

Jamie froze.

One of the assistant district attorneys, Chip Washington, stepped in and grabbed Tim's arm. "Is everything okay here?"

"It will be if he leaves me alone right now," Devlin said.

Jamie watched the pain in Tim's face, the cruel smirk on Devlin's.

"Don't do this," Tim whispered.

"God, stop with the drama already," Devlin said, her voice commanding the attention of the room.

Tim reached for her.

She winced. There was a momentary flash of fear. Then she regained herself. "Stay the fuck away from me."

Tim didn't let go. Instead, he yanked her closer and spoke through gritted teeth. "You'll be sorry, Natasha."

Jamie shuddered at the emotion between them. Unable to stand another moment, she turned away. She took two steps and felt her phone buzz on her hip.

She didn't recognize the number. "Vail."

"Inspector Vail, this is Officer Hamilton. You're needed on a scene."

Christ. She pulled her notepad from her jacket pocket and flipped it open. "Where are you?"

"Eight fifty Bryant, ma'am."

"The station? You got a suspect?"

"No. A scene, ma'am. Main building in the stair-well, bottom level."

Jamie stiffened. "You've got a rape scene at the Hall?"

"Yes, ma'am. We've got medical response on the way for her, but they told me to call you."

Medical response. "How bad is she?"

His voice cracked as he spoke. "Real bad, ma'am."

"I'm on my way." She started to hang up, then added, "You have an ID on her?"

"She's with the department."

Jamie closed her eyes.

"The name's Osbourne, ma'am. Emily Osbourne."

Jamie looked back as Chip Washington stood between Tim and Devlin. Jamie turned for the door, didn't look back. She was on her way to another rape scene.

Another police officer raped.

# 3

They stood at the closed office door. He pressed her against the hard surface as his tongue explored her mouth. His huge hands gripped her breasts, then trailed downward, cupping between her legs. She pulled back for a quick breath. Her insides fluttered with the feel of him. She had a buzz, heightened by alcohol and the fight.

She gripped the knob and pushed the door open. With his tie in her fist, they stumbled into her office. She glanced at the room. He came up behind her, pressed his erection against her. With a sweeping motion, she cleared the papers off her desk and turned toward him, propping herself on the edge. Spreading her legs, she pulled him between them. Crossed her feet on either side of his buttocks and gripped him between tight thighs.

"You're so hot," he whispered, kissing her neck.

She let her head fall back, hair cascading down her back. She knew what this looked like. She'd practiced in a mirror. It was good. Irresistible. And he was no different than the others.

His mouth trailed toward the mound of her breasts. She pulled his head into her, pressed his nose to her flesh. His fingers fumbled on her buttons. She leaned back, drew her feet onto the desk. One at a time, she let her heels drop to the floor. His expression grew fierce as her jacket came off. She unhooked her bra, let it fall off her shoulders.

He cupped her breasts, rubbed her nipples. She arched her back, set her feet on his shoulders, rammed her hips toward him. He unzipped her pants. His breath rasped in the silent room. She moaned, watching the reaction it caused. His hands fumbled. His mouth dropped open. He could hardly contain himself.

He yanked at his tie, yoking himself. She laughed and sat up to help him. She moved her fingers slowly, drawing out each motion until he was clawing at his buttons. He tugged the shirt from his pants. A button popped off and struck the hardwood desk. He grunted.

She laughed. He swooped down and grabbed her mouth in his, swallowing the snicker that rose in her throat.

She closed her eyes. Her pants slipped off her legs. Her underwear tugged away from her hips. Warm fingers fondled her. She arched, moaned.

Suddenly, he was inside her. She gasped as he filled her. The motions grew frantic. She clung to the desk. He gripped her thighs.

He struck into her as though he were punching through her spine. The pain was welcome. It was always welcome. She lolled her head up, watched the frenzy. A minute passed. Then several. His expression tightened into a grimace. His fingers dug into her buttocks. He stopped, drove again, and she felt the pulsating inside her.

He smiled, proud as he slumped over her.

She ran her hands through his thick hair like she might a child, held him against her.

"Oh God, baby," he whispered.

She smiled. She waited until the pulsing had stopped and pressed him up gently. "You should go."

He lifted his head and kissed her lips. "When can I see you again?"

She held the smile, softened her brow. "Soon, sweetie. You can call me tomorrow."

He kissed her lips. She pursed them, let him search for the passion he'd felt. He thought it was still there. It was gone for her. He pulled himself out, grabbed a fistful of tissues, and wiped himself before handing her the box.

She glanced at the red in his cheeks. He looked like an overgrown schoolboy. But didn't they all?

She slipped back into her pants, found her bra, pulled the jacket back over her shoulders. Turned her back to button it.

She saw his button on the floor and pointed to it. "Don't forget that."

He cupped it in his palm. "Maybe I'll leave it here as a souvenir." He set it on the edge of the desk and kissed her again. Then, after taking his coat off the chair, he left.

He turned back once at the door and winked.

She smiled, thinking he was an idiot. They were all idiots.

When the department door clicked shut, she scooped the button up and tossed it toward the secretary's trash can. Missed. Next time, my ass, she thought.

Back at her desk, she ran her hands through her hair and pulled her compact out of her purse. The brown eyes in the reflection were wide, flat of emotion. She smiled, watched them light up. Control, she thought.

She clicked the mirror closed and dropped it in her purse. She glanced at the mess. To hell with it.

She heard a creak behind her. She spun around, startled.

His frame filled the doorway. His eyes narrowed.

Her pulse raced. A rush of heat filled her belly. Seeing him created a bigger buzz than the last ten minutes. She thought of the other man inside her. Secretly reveled at the thought of another lay. She stepped forward. "Hello."

He crossed the threshold and shut the door behind him. Locked it.

She reached out for him, but he thrust her hand away.

"What is going on?"

She frowned, tossed her hair. "You should leave." She moved to pass him.

He clamped his hand into her hair, wrenched her head back.

Tears flooded her eyes. A wave of panic swelled up around her. She fought it back. "Let me go."

"What the hell game are you playing?"

"Let go now."

He lifted her by her hair. She felt his ragged breath, so much more powerful than the one before. It made her excited. She tried to touch his face.

He shoved her away.

She tumbled to the ground, slammed her face on the edge of the desk. She cried out.

She sat up, felt the fury rise inside her. "You pathetic moron. Did you really think I'd be satisfied by you? You don't even know how to fuck."

He bared his teeth, sank them into his lip.

She smiled, soaked in the pathetic expression on his face. "We're through."

"You c-c-can't."

Power streamed through her. She stood, smiling. Touched her lip, licked the warm blood. Shoulders back, she let the power buzz through her. She moved past him, reached for her purse. She turned back, raised an eyebrow. "I just d-d-did."

"You whore!" He spit the words, launched himself at her.

She backed away.

He was too fast.

He knocked her down. She tried to roll over, but

he straddled her. Using his hips and thighs, he pressed her to the floor.

She felt fear.

She'd never seen him angry. Not even a little. He raised his hand to strike her.

She reached out, gripped his balls. She squeezed and twisted as hard as she could.

He fell backwards, cupping them.

She used the break to push him off. Scrambled to her feet. She reached for the door, but he caught her foot.

Standing, he whirled her to face him. Anger burned in his cheeks.

She struggled to speak. Shook her head as his fingers dug into her shoulders.

Felt the intensity as he launched her across the room.

She caught her foot, tumbled sideways. She saw the desk come up at her. She reached to brace herself. Too late.

She struck the corner of the desk. She saw a swell like a giant wave crashing down on her head.

Then everything went black.

# 4

San Francisco General Hospital was a series of square brick boxes, stacked and connected like a child's LEGO creation. No symmetry. No interesting architecture. The building screamed functionality. Many of the city's worst injuries came here. Maybe the architect thought an attractive structure would be hypocritical for the building's grim reality.

Jamie Vail gripped her cigarette. Steeled herself for the worst part. This was always where she considered a transfer to Homicide. It would be easier. They got grieving, angry families, but no victims. Jamie knew how long the victim's road to recovery was.

This first day, only hours after the rape, the victim had yet to realize how the rape would change her life. Jamie did. She had witnessed her best friend raped when they were young. Been there, watched helplessly. Every time she stood in front of S.F. General, she was back to that day, watching that man . . .

She sucked the last drag off her cigarette, dropped it in the ashtray outside the emergency entrance, where thousands of others had gone before. She opened her purse and found a pack of spearmint gum. Then she squeezed out a dollop of antibacterial lavender-scented lotion and rubbed it into her hands. Smelling like flowers and spearmint, she walked through the emergency room entrance to the back hall, where the rape exam room was located.

When the door opened, she stared at the same eyes she always saw on a victim—wide, red rimmed, terrified, humiliated. Perhaps it was penance for not being attacked all those years ago, but Jamie took the gaze head-on. Only today it was a face she knew. Today it was her fault.

She blinked hard. "I'm so sorry, Emily."

Emily Osbourne shuddered. She ran a hand over her bare arm. Her right hand was wrapped with an Ace bandage. The bandage was just a temporary hold until evidence was collected. The arm was probably broken.

She balled a fist and sucked in a breath. Bastard.

Jamie was tempted to look away. Instead she studied Emily. Her left eye was swollen closed, the rim a purple that had begun to pool above her cheekbone. Blood stained her upper lip where her nose still bled. Sitting in the pale green hospital gown, she looked no older than twenty.

Jamie's cell phone buzzed on her hip. "Vail."

"It's Klein. I checked the records on Marchek."

Marchek was her serial rapist suspect. He'd been in jail for six years, convicted without the help of DNA evidence. He had a penchant for women in authority. Two officers of the court and a judge had been his victims. He'd used condoms, but finally one woman identified him. Now his DNA was on record and Jamie thought he was good for these new rapes, too. It was his MO, but so far she didn't have any evidence to run against his DNA.

An anger retaliatory rapist, Marchek loved to beat his victims. Head and face, especially. They'd brought him in yesterday afternoon for questioning on an attempted rape in the police station parking lot. A traffic officer, Jill Muhta, had gotten away unharmed. She'd been unable to ID him and they'd had to cut him loose.

Marchek was also suspected in two other police officer attacks. Though targeting police officers was inherently risky, Jamie knew the police represented an attractive target for more violent, anger-motivated criminals. The police represented power, and for someone like Michael Marchek, a woman police officer was the ultimate prize.

"Yeah. I'm at General. What time do you have?"

"He signed out at 7:58 p.m. You think he's your guy?"

"I do."

"You want me to send for him?"

"Yeah. Thanks." Jamie snapped the phone shut and blinked hard. Emily Osbourne had been attacked at 8:19 p.m. The bastard had literally gotten out of jail and headed over to the department in search of a new victim. Jamie had gotten him riled up. She knew he had been angry when he left. She should have followed him. She'd let him walk right up to another officer. Christ. How could she have been so stupid? She drew a slow breath to calm herself.

Turning her focus to the interview at hand, Jamie announced the time, date, day of the week, and location of the rape, for the tape running in the room. But she wrote nothing. Her job was to watch for anything the tape would miss. The nurse would record important details, including victim's race and gender. 99.5 percent of the cases she saw were female, but she'd had male victims, too. It was no easier with them.

"For the purpose of the recording, I'm Jamie Vail. I'm an Inspector with the San Francisco Police Department's Sexual Assault Unit." She lowered her voice. "Have we contacted your family?"

Emily started to cry.

The nurse, Maxi Thomas, patted her shoulder ever so lightly. "We called her parents. They're back in Connecticut. She has an aunt coming down from Stockton. We called her boyfriend, too, but didn't reach him."

Parents. Aunt. Boyfriend. She was a daughter, a niece, and a girlfriend. She wondered how the boyfriend would handle it. From her experience, a rape either made a couple indestructible or it flat out ruined them. Unfortunately, odds favored the latter.

"Thanks, Maxi." Jamie turned her focus back to the victim. To Emily, she told herself. "I'm here to catch this bastard."

Emily choked out a sob, her nose red from tears that streamed down her face.

Jamie set a box of tissues between them. Pulling one out, she handed it to her. "For the record, will you state your full name?"

"Emily Kathleen Osbourne."

She gave Emily another tissue and paused. Felt the familiar tightness in her own chest. Watching the victim became tougher each time. It grew harder to block it out. Bits of their pain seeped into her more easily now than when she'd started. She wondered if the same were true of the rapists. Was some of their evil seeping in as well?

Emily wiped her cheeks, tried to look brave.

Jamie nodded her encouragement.

"I'm ready," she whispered.

"Okay. I'm going to ask a lot of questions. This is all the standard stuff. If you need more time, tell me. If you think of something else, interrupt me. Anything you can tell me will help. Okay?"

"Okay," Emily squeaked out with a deep breath and a shudder.

There were nearly sixty questions Jamie had to ask. Most of the victims begged to leave more than once before the interview was over. Jamie understood the desire. More than once, she'd wanted to tell them, "Yes, you can go."

They'd been beaten, violated, shamed, and within hours of the attack—as soon as possible—Jamie's job was to make them go through it again in as much detail as possible.

When the answers took too long, Jamie waited. She offered water—once a mouth scraping was completed in case of semen or other evidence. But mostly, she stayed quiet and let the victim have her time. Ninety-nine out of every hundred spent it crying. Jamie knew about that, too. That's what her best friend had done. It had lasted for weeks. And Jamie thought seeing the victims in these first moments, before the shock and pain had settled in, was probably the easiest job in the recovery process. A few weeks from now, the painful reality of what had happened would be deeper and more difficult.

She started with the easy questions. "Did you see your attacker?"

Doe eyes flashed as Emily shook her head. Her bottom lip trembled. "He wore a hood."

"Did you see any part of him? Any skin?" Jamie pressed.

"His hand," she whispered. "I saw his hand."

"Can you guess at his race?" she asked.

Emily started to cry again. After a moment, she sucked in a breath. "White. His hand was white."

Jamie met Maxi's eye. The nurse nodded. The first piece of something.

"Okay. That's good. Emily, really good." She paused as Emily nodded, her gaze down. A tear dropped from her cheek onto the green hospital gown she wore. Her clothes were already on their way to the lab.

Jamie squeezed Emily's shoulder, moved on. "Were they white like mine?" Jamie put out her own hand and slowly twisted it up and down, so Emily could see both sides. "Or more olive, like Maxi's?"

Emily lifted up her own hand and looked at it as though she'd never seen it before. "I only saw the palm. It was white—like yours."

"Okay. Good." Jamie moved on. "Can you guess at how big he was? Height? Weight?" Jamie always said "he." Guidelines said never assume, but Jamie had never had a female rapist.

Jamie moved quickly through questions on appearance since Emily had seen only his hands. Still, she asked them. She'd discovered that sometimes a question would unleash an image a victim didn't think she had.

"He bound you?"

She nodded.

Jamie knew he had used duct tape. Pieces of it were still stuck to her forearms. It would have to be removed for evidence, but that could wait. "Anything else besides the tape?"

She was never amazed at the extents these assholes went to—tape, plastic bindings, handcuffs. It wasn't to prevent escape. Duct tape alone was enough for that. The overkill was all part of the fantasy.

"No other binding?"

Emily shook her head.

Jamie waited for a moment before moving on. From an earlier scene, evidence suggested her serial rapist had used some sort of restraint across the victim's chest, too. She didn't want to plant ideas in Emily's mind, but she wanted to ensure nothing was missed. "How about a strap across your middle? Anything like that?"

"No. He sat on me."

"Can you show me where?" Jamie asked.

She touched a rib. "Here."

Maxi prodded softly along Emily's ribs until she located the most sensitive spot. The dark edges of a bruise were already forming on the skin. With Emily holding her gown up, head turned, Maxi photographed the bruises. Maxi marked the chart before retying Emily's gown. She would have to be photographed again in a day or two when the bruises were fully formed, but Jamie didn't mention that now.

Next, Jamie walked Emily through how the rape had occurred. Every question helped to create a map of the rapist's MO. How did he attack? Con, blitz, or surprise? Was anything stolen?

Some of the best cases were the ones where the perp took a piece of jewelry, then gave it to a girl-friend, or one time, to his mother. In that case, his mother had known it was too nice for her bum son to afford and she'd called the cops. A bold move for the mother, but as she said, "If he's stealing from some-one else, what makes me think he won't do it to me? Or worse."

In Emily's case, it was a blitz approach, which made sense since she hadn't seen him. Nothing stolen.

"Did he wear gloves when he touched you?"

The victim paused at that. "I saw his hand."

"Without a glove?"

She nodded. "I think so." Then she shook her head. Tears fell faster. "Oh God. Now I'm not sure."

"Emily, it's okay. This is hard. It's a lot to digest. Are we moving too fast?"

"No. No, it's okay."

Jamie turned to Maxi. "Try for prints." They'd dust for prints on her skin. Maybe they'd get lucky.

After a moment, Jamie continued her questions. Did he use a condom, did he talk, threaten, bribe? No condom, she didn't think. Shawna Delman had said the same, but they hadn't gotten any DNA from Del-man's exam. Jamie wondered if Osbourne's would be the same.

The next part was the worst. "Can you tell me where he touched you?"

Emily choked on a sob.

"We're just going to walk through it slowly."

Maxi pulled a fistful of sterile swabs from a drawer.

"Maxi's going to take a swab from each place." Jamie paused. "This is going to suck, Emily. It's the worst part. We'll do it as fast as we can. As soon as it's over, I'll buy you a soda, okay? You're a Coke drinker, right?"

Emily nodded, tried to smile.

Jamie touched Emily's arm again. She never touched her victims, but Emily was different. She was a colleague. The third one she'd interviewed. It got worse every goddamn time. When would it end?

Jamie stepped back. "Can you do this?"

Emily's back straightened. "Yeah. Let's do it."

"Anywhere he came into contact with you—his hands, his skin, his penis."

Tears streamed down Emily's cheeks.

"I know this is tough. We're almost done."

"You know what they don't ever tell you?"

Jamie waited, her gut tight.

Emily wiped her cheeks with the backs of her hands. "You get all that defensive training, you know? I wasn't even going to be a police officer and I got it. And I paid attention. I thought it was important." She shivered, some memory stirring her.

Jamie winced, wished she could make this all go away.

"But it didn't help. I didn't do any of the things we learned. I couldn't even think. I just shut down." She looked up, tracks of tears like stripes on her face. "I just laid there and let him do it."

Jamie felt her own tears well and fought them back. "It's not your fault, Emily." Jamie searched for something more to say but came up empty.

Emily straightened her back. "Let's get this over with."

Jamie stood. "You're sure?"

"Positive. I just want it over."

Jamie slowly began the process. "Let's start with his hands. You think he wasn't wearing gloves, so where do you remember his hands?"

"He touched my—" She caught her lip in her teeth. "My neck. He grabbed it."

Using clear tape on the skin, Maxi tried to lift prints off of her neck. The process took ten minutes and in the end, Maxi shook her head. No prints. They printed her hands, arms, and inner thighs with the same result.

"Okay, Emily. The last thing we have to do is talk about the sexual assault. Did he put his penis in your mouth?"

"No." Emily cupped her face and started to sob. "Thank God, no."

They'd already taken a vaginal swab, so the physical collection was done. "I think we're ready for that Coke now."

"I'll go," Maxi said.

"Thanks." Jamie pulled money from her pocket and offered it to Maxi, but she waved it away.

"You want diet or regular?"

"Regular," Emily said.

"You?" she asked Jamie.

"Regular's perfect."

Maxi left and Emily turned to Jamie. The tears had momentarily subsided when Emily said, "God, I wish I was just regular again."

Jamie exhaled, the knot in her gut heavier than ever. "Me, too, Emily. Me, too."

When Maxi returned, they drank their Cokes while Maxi photographed Emily with a highly sensitive film designed to pick up any marks that were emerging on the skin. Aside from the obvious injuries, Emily had a series of bruises that had yet to fully form and a jagged mark inside her thigh that Jamie suspected may have been caused by the knife during their struggle.

"We're done with the physical evidence. I just need to ask about anything he might have said."

Emily's mouth dropped open. "God, I almost forgot." She paused. "He said to tell the inspector hello."

# 5

Jamie arrived at the station at 1:10 a.m. The assistant district attorney, Chip Washington, was seated in an interview room, drinking bottled water. Jamie set her things down, poured a cup of thick, overcooked coffee, and brought it to the table.

Chip wore navy sweatpants and a gray Cal Berkeley sweatshirt and dress shoes. "Nice outfit."

He glanced at his feet. "They were the closest to the door when the phone rang."

"Sorry."

He shook his head. "Don't be."

"Any word on what CSU found?"

"No hood, no blood. They're doing a sweep for fibers, but you've been in his house."

"He's clean."

Chip raised a brow. "That's an understatement. He's obsessive."

Jamie dropped her head. "Christ."

"They did find a single blond hair on a jacket in the closet."

She looked up. "Emily Osbourne is blond."

Chip nodded. "I sent someone to General Hospital to pick up her sample." He glanced at his watch. "That was an hour ago. They promised to run it ASAP and call me." He patted his cell phone.

"You want to wait for the call?"

Chip shook his head. "Let's bring him in."

"Try to shake something loose?"

"Here's hoping."

Jamie called the guards to bring Marchek in. The process took him out of jail custody and into hers. It looked good for the record, that they'd treated him respectfully.

Though the interview room was barely large enough to fit a table and four chairs, it wasn't where they'd interrogated him before. She hoped a new venue might make Marchek more agreeable.

She wanted him to think he was about to leave. The closer to freedom he felt, the more apt she was to get something out of him. This was just a little chat between old friends.

Marchek wore jeans and a T-shirt, shoes without socks. They'd dragged him from home without any notice.

She thanked the officers for bringing him over and motioned Marchek to a chair.

"Please, Michael."

"Don't call me that," he said. The words came out a long, low hiss like a tire losing air.

His carefully kept appearance was now bedraggled. She knew he wasn't happy about it. Of the few things she'd learned about Marchek, the clear one was that he had great contempt for slovenliness. His home was like a technology-manufacturing clean room. The floors were hardwood. A small black tray at the door held his work shoes. In the bottom was a half inch of liquid bleach.

He had few material possessions. No books or music, no TV, which seemed odd for a guy who worked in a video store. A small hobby bench sat in the center of the living room. From what she had seen, he built mostly small planes. She'd seen one floater plane, too.

Marchek owned only a half-dozen pairs of pants and

that many shirts. They were clean and folded, stacked on two single shelves in the bedroom closet. Underwear and socks shared a separate shelf. He owned only two coats—one of heavy wool that looked like it had come from an army surplus store and the light brown denim Carhartt work jacket he wore now.

Marchek had short curly dark hair and it covered him. It spilled out under the cuffs of his jacket and down the backs of his hands. This morning he was unshaven and he looked like he could grow a beard in a few days. She wondered if the hair bothered him. He seemed like someone who might shave himself from head to toe to be rid of it. His eyes were dark. In certain light, she'd seen green in them. But usually, like now, they looked flat and brown. He narrowed them, scanned the room.

"Would you prefer Mr. Marchek?"

He glared.

"I'm not trying to make you angry. Please tell me what I should call you."

He didn't answer.

"This won't take long."

"Then I leave."

It wasn't a question. She didn't answer it.

He kicked the chair out and sat, scooting it in with his feet. His hands were in his lap. He hadn't touched anything. He was a neat freak and the tendency not to touch anything could be part of that. But she also thought he was wary of leaving prints. Criminals tended to create wonderfully elaborate conspiracy theories about how police entrapped them.

"It's amazing what science has done for forensics. Tests can show that two pieces of duct tape came from the same plant and how close in time. We can actually prove that two samples came from the same roll even if they're not successive pieces."

She watched him. A corner of his mouth turned up. A smile. She paused, let that sink in a bit.

He lifted a hand, focused on his thumb. Ran a finger across it like he was petting a tiny animal.

"You're in trouble, Michael."

One cheek bounced in and out like he was chewing on it.

She continued. "This will be three strikes. No chance of parole next time."

He ran his finger along the thumb more slowly as though considering an offer. Something about the motion was childlike.

She felt close to something, considered her options.

"It'll be easier if you cooperate with the investigation," Washington added.

Marchek glanced at Chip. He turned his gaze to Jamie. "I've been reading up on serial rapists."

Chip Washington raised a brow.

Jamie was silent.

He nodded. "Since you seem to think I am one, I thought I'd brush up on how they work. All sorts of different ones, aren't there?"

She didn't respond.

Chip's phone buzzed on his hip and he left the room to answer it.

The motion didn't seem to disturb Marchek. He rubbed his finger more slowly. "I've been reading about what they do to their victims. Modus operandi and signatures. Truly, you have an intriguing job, Inspector." He drew out her title.

"What kinds of things did you read about?" she asked.

Marchek smiled. Not the tight, fake smile, but a real one. Joy.

Her gut tightened.

"I read about men who bite and then cut pieces of skin from their victims. And, of course, the ones who take things—mementos."

"What kind are you?"

Marchek's smile vanished. His eyes stayed flat. He

was playing. "Silly inspector. I've already explained I have nothing to do with any of this."

Chip returned to the room, frowning.

She nodded. "Okay. If you were a rapist, Michael . . ."

"What type would I be?"

She nodded.

His finger moved more quickly across the knuckle. A smooth, repetitive motion—up, back, up, back. Then it stopped. He rested his hands in his lap. "The difference between your rapists and me is that they consider this an art." He frowned. "You and I, we see it as an atrocity, a crime." He focused on the far wall. "If I were a rapist, which, of course, I'm not, I'd have to be one of those people who saw it as art."

"And if you saw it as art?"

He shrugged. "I'm sure I'd sign it."

Jamie watched his expression. His eyes neither widened nor narrowed; his lips remained passive in a flat line. "You'd sign it? Like one of your little models, Michael?"

His gaze shifted back to her. Nonplussed. Almost bored. "If there's nothing else we need to discuss, Inspector, I really should be going."

"I'm going to catch you, Marchek."

"You're making a mistake," he whispered. His shoulders shifted up, his spine straightened. He focused on her.

She held his gaze. "I don't make mistakes."

The air in the room stopped. Somewhere someone shouted, but Marchek didn't blink, didn't look away. He leaned forward, hands hovering just over the table. His eyes widened and she saw the flash of green. Without ever touching the table, he pushed the chair back with his legs and rose. "I'm leaving now. Unless you can charge me with something."

Gone was the awkward child.

She rose as well, put her hands in her pockets. Kept her voice calm. "I'm going to let you go today, Michael. But watch these last steps. I'll be on your every move. And when I catch you again, you're going to jail for life."

He stared.

"You know it, don't you? You'll rot there."

He smiled, shook his head, like a parent listening to the nonsense of a child. "You should be careful, too, Inspector." His smile disappeared, but his voice remained even, almost friendly. "Whoever attacked that woman is still out there. It's very dangerous."

She grinned back, feeling the tremor in her cheeks. "I look forward to seeing you again soon, Michael."

"Not as much as I do, Inspector. It would be a real pleasure, I'm sure."

With that, Marchek turned and walked from the interview room.

She turned to Chip.

He shook his head. "The hair doesn't match Osbourne."

She had nothing to keep him on. Crime Scene Unit, or CSU as it was called, hadn't found anything in his place and the blond hair didn't match.

She sank back into the chair and dropped her head in her hands.

Chip touched her shoulder. "You tried."

She didn't answer.

"Call if anything comes up. I'm heading home."

She nodded to him. When the door clicked shut, she crossed her arms, replaying what Marchek had said. He'd sign her. If he were a rapist, he'd sign her.

She thought back to the first police officer who had been assaulted. Shawna Delman. She'd been the single caretaker for a younger brother. Only two months on the job, she'd been brutally raped. A month later, she overdosed on heroin.

A signature. The image kept flipping in Jamie's brain. Michael Marchek. A logo to claim his victims. She sifted through the memories for a signature.

Back at her desk, she lifted the file of pictures and took it back to the interview room. Slowly, she spread them out, studied them one by one.

There, twenty pictures in, she found a photograph of the small, rough cut on Emily's inner right thigh.

Jamie stared at it, squinting. It was almost like a crude W.

Her heart pounding, Jamie rotated the picture one hundred eighty degrees. She gasped.

If Emily Osbourne looked down at it, the cut would look like a child's M.

"Bastard."

# 6

Mackenzie Wallace emerged from the car and shed one of the layered fleece tops she'd donned, still searching for an ounce of predictability to San Francisco weather. She'd spent the whole summer freezing and now in November, she was hot. The only thing worse was being hot *and* stuck inside the nine-hundred-square-foot apartment she shared with her husband, Alan. Even asleep she felt crowded. Alan, on the other hand, loved it.

Despite the charming crown molding and wide-plank hardwood floors, the apartment paled in comparison to what they'd left in Montana. Two thousand square feet on over an acre for less than half what they now paid in rent. The thought made her long for home. She palmed the ache in her chest and focused on the task ahead.

She entered the silent department building and took the elevator to the fourth floor. Alan hovered at the front of her mind. For more than three months now, she'd searched for a way to tell him how she felt. She wanted to be happy with him, for him. He was writing, working a dream job at the *San Francisco Chronicle,* which was a big step up from the freelance writing he'd done in Montana. Never a morning person, Alan now rose at dawn, brewed a big pot of coffee, and set to work on his book before going to the paper. The only extra space in the one-bedroom apartment was a closet fewer than three feet wide and ten feet long. They'd had to rent a small storage space in the basement to house their extra things so there would be space for Alan to put a tiny desk in the closet.

Mackenzie didn't know how he could stand it. In her opinion, the fact that the closet's single, small, rotted window lacked bars was the only thing that distinguished it from a prison cell.

Between the hours Alan spent at the paper and the ones on his book, they were lucky if they had two hours a day together. They'd had conflicting schedules before now, but in a foreign place with no family or friends, Mackenzie was more than a little lonesome. And somehow, she had yet to gather the courage to tell him.

Down a hallway lit with the pale yellow cast of halogen lights, Mackenzie found the door marked "SFPD Evidence" and reached for the knob. It was locked. She stepped back, knocked. It was the middle of the night, but Captain James had said someone would be waiting.

"What?" a man called out.

"Captain James sent me down to pick up a file on the Harrison assault." She waited for the door to open. "My name's Mackenzie Wallace," she added when there was no response. Then, "I've got a case number." She dug in her pocket for the slip of paper she'd written the case number on.

"Wait."

She stopped and stared at the paint chipping on the door, resisting the urge to pick at it. She pictured Alan in his closet, pecking away on his laptop. Sighed. She had to tell him she hated this.

A full minute passed without another sound. Mackenzie raised her hand to knock again when the door swung open. A man wearing an ill-fitting tweed blazer over a plaid flannel and khakis held a package in one hand. He held the other out to her, palm up.

She stared at it. "Uh—"

"ID."

"Oh, sorry." Flustered, she patted the pockets on the coat she wore in search of the thin leather wallet that housed her photo ID and badge. It wasn't there. She looked at the man, who simply blinked, and tried to offer a smile. "I—"

He started to close the door when she remembered the fleece tucked over her arm.

"Wait. I've got it." She fumbled to find the wallet and flipped it open before passing it to him.

He wrote her badge number down on his clipboard and then handed it back, gave her one second to tuck it away, and passed her the clipboard.

"There," he said, pointing to a line for her to sign.

She reached for his pen and he handed it to her as though annoyed she hadn't brought her own. "Thanks."

When she'd signed, he handed her the package. "It's sealed for your captain. Don't break the seal."

It was the most he'd said to her since she arrived and he still hadn't met her eye. She nodded as he closed the door.

She blinked at the door, biting back frustration before turning and leaving the building. So rude. It burned her. Weren't they all on the same side?

Finding friends in the police department was like landing a tarpon with a Royal Wulff lure. Nearly impossible. It didn't help that Alan was more gregarious than she and had already established a niche at the paper. Though he'd feel terrible if he knew how bad it was at the station. Maybe that's why she hadn't told him.

Sweating, she yanked the other fleece over her head and marched outside. The low, dark fog surrounded her like a chain-link fence, slowly closing in.

She stared up, into the thick, gray blanket of sky. She longed for a Montana night, for stars as close as the lavender she picked from her yard.

She knew it wasn't the stars, or the weather, or even the jerk behind the door. Mackenzie was out of her element and it wasn't a feeling she was used to. She'd been a confident kid—tall and athletic, smart. She'd excelled in school.

After college, she'd worked for the park rangers' service at Yellowstone for eight years. There, she'd tracked bears, rescued injured climbers, and hunted the occasional poacher of the park's protected game. She'd been good at it. Probably great.

Searching for the next rung on her career ladder, she'd trained with the sheriff's department in nearby Gallatin County. And then Alan had gotten this job in San Francisco. And she'd had little choice but to enter the local police academy at thirty-one. Nothing since had convinced her she wasn't a whole lot better off back in Montana.

She blew out her breath and thought about the end of the shift. In five hours, she'd be out of her uniform and on a run. She ran every morning. She hadn't missed a day in three years—even feverish, a run always made her feel better. Afterwards, she would buy a scone at Café Baby Cakes, a few blocks from their apartment, and head to Golden Gate Park. Tramping through moist grass, she often stopped to watch the small herd of buffalo that lived there. Sometimes, the sight of them eased her homesickness.

She turned to glance at the other cars in the lot, trained to scan for trouble. The single streetlight cast a bright circle on the parked cars, reflections bouncing off chrome fenders and windshields. As she walked, shadows moved and twisted. She saw the shape of a person sitting up in a Ford Taurus. She halted, stared. A trick of the light, she thought and moved on.

At her car, she pressed a button on her key fob to illuminate the sidelights and unlocked the driver's door.

She climbed into the Blazer, locked the doors. Glancing in the backseat, she tried to temper her pulse, which was now beating a little too fast. If she couldn't stand a few shadows, how could she ever manage to be a cop?

It wasn't a question she was prepared to answer. The seat belt fastened across her chest, Mackenzie shifted the car into reverse. Maybe she wouldn't be a cop here. Maybe she'd never be a cop anywhere. She let her foot off the brake and eased the car backwards. As she looked down to shift into drive, she caught sight of the shadow in the Taurus again.

The dark form remained. She waited, watching it the way as a child she had watched the shadows in her bedroom at night. She expected it to transform into something else the way the monsters of her childhood had changed back into a hanging jacket or a stuffed animal.

She reversed and stopped. The shadow was someone's head. She blew her horn twice. The shadow didn't move. Her pulse drummed in her ears as she glanced at the clock. Why would someone be out here at three o'clock in the morning? She leaned across the seat, released the glove box. It fell open. She pulled out the Beretta, released the magazine. Eleven bullets.

She slid the magazine back, felt it click in place. She chambered a round, waited. She stared again. It was the back of a head for sure.

Adrenaline coated her stomach. She gripped the gun, no longer hearing her heart. Her ears filled with the whoosh of nerves. She remembered why she loved being a ranger. She could do this.

Out of the car, Mackenzie crossed in front of her car, blinked at the headlights shining into the dark. A

heavy mist like rain spit from the sky. She wiped her
face with the sleeve of her shirt, cold. She crouched
around the Taurus, gun leading.

Quickly, Mackenzie peered into the driver's window. Her pulse thundered. She saw a nest of dark,
wavy hair—a woman. She wore a black jacket that
exposed the cleft of full cleavage. A red beaded neck-
lace decorated her slender neck. A professional
woman. Why would she be sitting in the parking lot
at this hour?

Mackenzie rapped on the window. There was no
response. She took a quick breath and tugged open
the door. Stale air struck her.

It was followed by a smell she'd heard described
but never understood until now—lack of breath, emp-
tiness. Maybe it was the process of decomposition
starting. Mackenzie knew without touching the woman
that she was dead.

Still, fingers trembling, Mackenzie forced herself to
test for a pulse. She pressed the flesh of the woman's
neck, felt cool skin. The head lolled back. Mackenzie
jumped, smashing her own head on the doorframe.

She gulped air. She wanted to rub the ache in her
head but didn't. She stared at the woman's face. She
was attractive, maybe ten years her senior.

Mackenzie leaned forward into the car. A curl slid
off the woman's neck. It left a track of red. Jesus.
Blood. Her scalp was covered in it.

Mackenzie jumped. Stepping back, Mackenzie spotted a thin leather wallet like the one Mackenzie carried sticking out of the woman's purse. She reached
across and slid it out. She stared at the leather in her
hand. It was a police badge.

Mackenzie flipped it open and glanced at the woman's picture. Alive, she'd been gorgeous. She saw the
bolded word beneath her name and the San Francisco
Police Department shield.

Inspector.

# 7

Cigarette in hand, Jamie hung up with her surveillance team. She blew smoke out the open bedroom window. It was three o'clock in the morning and she had no good news. They had followed Marchek from the station and he'd done nothing of interest for the past two hours. No secret hiding place, no sign of a car where he could ditch his rape kit. Nothing. Surveillance had confirmed his presence twice in the last hour through a window. She had twenty-four hours to catch him—ten percent of her allotted surveillance already up. Marchek wasn't dumb enough to get caught like this.

And there was no way to link him to the cut on Emily Osbourne's thigh without more evidence or a confession. She knew she wasn't getting the latter. She had to focus on the former. She pictured Marchek's thin frame bent over one of his models. Maybe he was already in bed, resting up for the next attack. She shuddered, forced him away.

She sighed, stared at the thrashed bedcovers. A messy bed always reminded her of Tim. He never slept straight. Facedown, he wiggled deep into the bed until his feet hung over the end, head buried somewhere in the middle. Jamie slept up at the top, on her back, hands to her sides like a soldier at ease. Her head raised on two pillows, she molded the sheet across her legs, smoothed it on either side.

For a lot of police officers, sleep, if they could get it, was a well-guarded secret. The process was a ritual. Or they went without. Tim hadn't understood. He slept easily. Kicked and shifted in the bed. He had never disrupted his own sleep, only hers.

In the swell of the wrinkled bed sheets, Jamie pictured Devlin and Tim. Curled up under the covers, two sets of feet hanging over the end. Jamie dragged on the cigarette, stared at the bed like the enemy.

She wanted a drink. She dropped the cigarette into a glass of water. The flame snuffed out with a hiss. She sprayed the room with deodorizer, left the window open to air it out. She refused to let herself focus on the alcohol. Don't think, just sleep.

In the bathroom, Jamie walked through her nightly routine to ward off the smell of cigarettes. She showered again, brushed her teeth three times, painted them with the Crest whitening paste, and put her molds in. Some nights she thought she should just quit smoking. Not tonight.

She glanced in the mirror at her tired eyes. Eyes Tim had once told her were like mood indicators. Blue when she was calm and peaceful, sea green when she was feisty or angry. Now they always looked a flat steely gray-green to her. She wondered what mood that was. Depressed?

She made the bed with military precision, changed into generic gray sweats that had once fit but were now two sizes too big, added a long-sleeved T-shirt from her police academy days. Near her left breastbone a hole cut between the yellow N and C of Francisco. Through it, she felt the tail end of the snaking scar from an old knife wound. A routine traffic stop gone bad.

Restless exhaustion overcame her as she sank onto the edge of the bed. The sheet corner, carefully folded back, awaited her. The desire to sleep had waned.

Eighteen months Tim had been gone. Eighteen

months and she still missed his fidgeting in bed, the way his hand sought out her thigh in the dark. The way he met her with a cup of coffee after a bad night at work, the way he always seemed to know which nights had been especially rough. Her life remained suspended in the months after he left. After she'd thrown him out. She'd bought this house but never really lived here.

Outside she could see shadows of the overgrown yard. The windows were still bare of blinds or curtains. Inside was no better. The living room stood empty but for a couch and a TV without cable. The kitchen had only a small worn oak table with an older model Gateway desktop at one end and a tattered place mat where she ate at the other.

Most of her clothes were unpacked into the bedroom closet and a single dresser, but full boxes of things from her life with Tim still littered each room. Things she couldn't remember now, didn't want to.

She plumped the pillows, tucked her feet under the covers, and lay down. Stared at the ceiling.

From the floor, Barney whined.

She patted the bed and he jumped up and after spinning twice, settled down beside her.

He tucked his head on her shoulder and she scratched it. He whined, sniffed her ear. At least she had Barney. He had been witness to her first serial rapist case. He'd been dumped with a broken leg and the worst case of fleas the vet had ever seen. One part German shepherd. Ninety-nine parts mutt. He was the size of a large hound with the same basic shape. With pointed ears, he was a muddy brown except for a few spots of caramel behind his ears and on his belly.

Jamie, still drunk from the night before, hurting like hell, had brought him home. She'd bathed him every three days with a special prescription dog shampoo, covered his front right leg with plastic for the four months it had been in a cast, and spent three thousand in vet bills. But he was as good as new. Sometimes she'd wake with his head resting on her arm, the sound of his breath like the rumbling of a far-off train. Sort of like Tim, but more loyal.

Barney's breath shifted into sleep. Jamie felt herself relax into the sheets. Her eyes fluttered closed. Maybe she would sleep.

The doorbell rang.

Barney lifted his head.

"Forget it," she said.

The bell chimed again, and he let out a whine.

Jamie yanked off the covers and got up. Grabbing her gun from its holster, she stomped down the stairs. "What?"

"Jamie? Is that you?"

Tim. She halted. Held her breath.

He pounded on the door. "Jamie? It's me. Please."

What was he doing here? She shook her head. She didn't care. Not her problem. "Go away," she hollered. She pictured him. Warned herself to keep her distance, go back to bed.

She imagined his green eyes the way she remembered them in kinder moments. Wondered how he was. She didn't care. Still, she crept to the door to look. She saw his eyes and her stomach sank.

The first time she'd met Tim had been at a Bay Area police event. He'd been making small talk with a group of officers, drinking Budweiser from the can. She'd been standing alone, as she almost always did at those functions, until someone came and ushered her back into the mainstream. She watched as he ran his finger under his collar, then adjusted the waist of his pants, all the while looking like he'd never worn a suit before. She'd felt the same in a skirt suit and hose. When he'd looked over, she'd been smiling. He'd made his way over to her and asked straight out, "Are you laughing at me?"

She hadn't realized until he was beside her how attractive he was. Greenish gray eyes half cloaked under a mane of thick, dark hair. He was trim, average height—maybe five ten.

Now, standing on the front porch, a bluish black ring under one eye, he looked like he'd been in a bar fight.

Why had she looked? She started to turn away from the door and stopped. Chest tight. "You're an idiot." He screwed around. But even as she said it, her fingers gripped the knob and turned.

She opened the door and saw Tim's right eye was swollen and black. "What happened?"

He stepped into the light and she caught sight of dark blood on his white shirt. She guessed by the quantity that the blood was from a broken nose, but his looked intact. "What the hell happened?"

His gaze flat, he stepped into the house.

"Are you hurt?"

He didn't answer.

"Was it a fight?"

He closed his eyes. His head lolled back.

She grabbed his shoulder, shook him. "What the hell happened?"

"I went to see her, to talk things over."

Jamie let go. "Who?"

He opened his eyes. "I would never have hurt her, Jamie. Never."

Jamie's stomach clenched. She tightened her grip on the gun. "Tim."

He shook his head. "She was there. I leaned down to touch her." He looked into the distance.

Her heart hammered in her chest.

"I was hit in the head."

"She hit you?"

He didn't answer.

"Tim, answer me. Are you hurt?"

He touched his head absently. "Someone hit me in the head. I fell forward and hit my eye." He shook his head. "I don't even know on what."

She fingered the spot on his scalp. She felt blood but not enough to explain his shirt. "Whose blood is this?" She heard the panic in her tone.

He met her gaze. "It's hers."

She clenched his wrist. Blood covered her hand. She cringed at the thick coolness of it. "Who, Tim?"

He shook his head. "I didn't do it."

Oh God. She stepped backwards.

He followed.

She put a hand out. "Stay there, Tim."

His gaze snapped to hers. He walked toward her. "I know what it looks like. That's why I came here. I didn't do it. I went to see her. She was already dead.

"You have to help me, Jamie. You have to. I didn't kill her. I swear I didn't." He wiped the back of his hand across his face. He left a smear of bright red blood on his cheek.

Heart racing, Jamie spoke slowly. "Who is dead, Tim? Tell me who is dead."

He choked out the name. "Natasha." As he said the name, he collapsed to the floor, sobbing.

Jamie looked down at her darkened hands. Devlin's blood. Natasha Devlin's blood was on her hands.

She gasped for air.

Natasha Devlin was dead.

# 8

Hailey Wyatt stood at the perimeter of her children's room and watched them sleep. Camilla was almost five, a head full of brown curls and the untamed personality to match. Ali was three, straight dark hair, an even temper, and a smile as bright and as quick as a bolt of lightning. Both had their mother's brown eyes. Camilla lay sideways in her bed, facedown. Curls covered her face. Ali was on her back, arms straight beside her. So different. Hailey leaned into the doorjamb, gripped her coffee cup. God, she loved them. Felt her heart expand like a balloon when she watched them. Especially asleep. No bickering, no whining. Just her sweet beauties.

It was nearly seven fifteen. She'd been up since five. They'd be up soon. Thankfully for them, they had their father's sleeping genes. Hailey turned, walked into her bedroom. She passed her husband still asleep in bed. A larger version of Ali. Calm, sweet, peaceful. She was the restless one.

In the bathroom, she swallowed the last of her coffee and set the cup on the white tile. She started the shower, glanced in the mirror. Let the robe slip off her shoulders and stepped into the steaming water. She could never pick one. No one would ever suggest it. She could love them both. Different but equal. Camilla for her cunning, Ali for her sensitivity.

She let the water run down her back. Hoped the steam would clear her head. No one ever said you could love only one child.

She shampooed, soaped. So why did they say you could love only one man? Because Hailey Wyatt loved two.

Just then, the shower door clicked open. John stepped in, naked. He wrapped his arms around her waist. Kissed her neck. Groaned.

"You're up," she said.

"Not by choice. Your phone rang."

"Sorry."

He tucked his face into her neck, held her from behind.

"The dinner go okay last night?"

He groaned again. Sounded like a yes.

"You answer my call?"

"Uh-uh."

She turned around, kissed his cheek. "I'd better go find out what's up."

He pulled her close, held her, ran his palms across her breasts. Coddled them. "How about a sick day?"

She smiled, relaxed against him. The water sprayed over their shoulders. "Rain check?"

"It's not raining."

She kissed his lips, softly. "How about an early night tonight?"

He pressed back. "Deal."

She stepped out of the shower, toweled off, and put her robe back on. Her phone was on the bedside stand. It started to ring again before she reached it.

"Wyatt."

Her captain's voice was as groggy as John's had been. "Homicide at 850 Bryant."

"The station? Did dispatch call *you*?"

He didn't answer. "Need you ASAP—CSU is already there."

She glanced at the clock. "I'm home. It'll take an

hour." At least the Crime Scene Unit would secure the scene.

"As soon as you can."

The line broke and Hailey frowned. Homicide worked in rotation. If her name was next, she got the next call, whatever it was. Normally, though, the call came from dispatch, not her captain.

She dressed quickly and when John emerged from the shower, she was nearly ready.

"You got one?"

She nodded.

He frowned but didn't speak. John didn't understand her job. Sometimes neither did she. It just felt right to do something, to make some difference. Even when the odds were stacked against her.

He crossed the room, stopped in front of her. He fingered a lock of hair, tucking it behind her ear. "Early night, right?"

"Promise. Have the girls call when they're up." She pocketed her phone and unlocked her holster and gun from the safe in their bedroom closet. She peeked in the girls' room one last time and was in the car by 7:40.

Traffic coming in on Highway 80 was already bad, so she used her lights to warn people aside. By the time she reached the bridge, she had a caravan on her tail, like racing cars trying to take advantage of the leader's tail wind.

Her phone rang again as she was crossing over Treasure Island.

"Wyatt."

"Hey." The voice she heard now had been up for hours.

"You already at the station?"

"Not much to do at my house alone."

She knew it was a dig. "Buck—"

"I know. Asked and answered."

She switched lanes, passed a slow-moving Mercedes.

"When can I see you?" he asked.

"I got a call. At the Hall. Know what's going on?"

"No idea." He paused. "Any chance for tonight?"

Guilt. "I don't think so."

Silence. Disappointment.

"I wish it could be different," she said. It was true, but she wasn't sure how.

"It could be," he countered.

"Bruce."

He laughed. "I always know I'm in trouble when you use my given name. Like my mother."

"Thanks."

"Got to tell it like it is. Call me when you get in." He hung up without saying good-bye. His sullenness made him seem like another person to take care of. She'd fallen for him because he was strong, unwavering, but he wasn't. No one was, really. Some people just looked that way from the outside.    She crossed the bridge under gray clouds and a shroud of guilt. Always guilty. For John. For Buck. For Camilla and Ali. For everyone except herself. She had it all. If only there was a way to make it work. But there wasn't. She knew there wasn't.


At 8:20 Hailey exited the freeway at the Civic Center. When she reached the street entrance to the police parking lot, it was cordoned off with bright yellow crime scene tape. She pulled to the edge of the tape, scanned the faces.

Her stomach clenched. Christ. A murdered cop. There were too many people for anything else.

The police captain of the district that included the station was there. Captain Linda James stood with a younger woman Hailey didn't recognize. The other woman was thin and tan with long legs. Something from a Lands' End catalog.

Linda waved. Hailey looked past them, making a mental list. A couple of people from CSU. She saw

Jamie Vail standing alone, smoking. Jamie looked even worse than she had the night before. Rail thin as ever, the cropped cut of Jamie's hair that had once seemed manicured now looked shaggy. Her hair had fewer highlights, and the cheeks Hailey once remembered as being covered with golden freckles now looked sallow.

Jamie stood ramrod straight, the veins in her neck taut, one leg behind the other like a runner ready to take off.

Hailey got out of her car as Linda James approached, the younger woman behind her.

"Who was it?" Hailey asked, looking over at the two uniformed officers who guarded the car.

"Natasha Devlin."

Hailey's gaze immediately traveled to Jamie Vail.

Linda nodded. "She showed up less than an hour ago. I told her."

Hailey looked back. "Surprised?"

Linda shrugged. "I think so, but I wouldn't put money on it."

Jamie Vail was known as a loose canon by some of the higher-ups, but not the ones she worked for. Hailey had heard rumors about how Jamie's captain, Ben Jules, had fought for her. Jules was no pushover and Jamie was no kiss-ass. Hailey knew that no matter what anyone thought, Jamie was as dedicated a professional as they came. And she was damn good at her job. If she wasn't, she never would have lasted after the shooting incident.

Linda James stepped aside and motioned the other woman forward. "This is Mackenzie Wallace. She found Natasha. She's one of mine—a rookie—came to get an evidence file from upstairs."

Mackenzie nodded, said nothing. She had long straight brown hair that hung in a clean line across her shoulders and a shorter line of bangs that covered the tops of arched brows. Her eyes were a dark brown with flecks of gold. They appeared large against her olive skin. Despite her height, she looked young to Hailey, especially her eyes. Like a child taking in all new sights, most of them terrifying. Hailey wondered if it was just because of the body she'd found or if Mackenzie Wallace always looked a bit overwhelmed by the world around her.

Hailey flipped open her notebook. "What time did you find her?"

"Just before three. Maybe two fifty-five."

It was almost eight thirty. "And no one's been out before me?"

"There was someone else," Mackenzie said. "A tall man with blondish gray hair. Nice-looking."

Hailey searched for a match in Homicide but failed. "In uniform?"

She shook her head. "Suit."

"What did he do?"

"Made a few calls on a cell phone and then when CSU came, he left. I never talked to him." She glanced at Linda James. "I tried to, but he sort of waved me off."

Hailey couldn't make anything of it. She focused back on the crowd. "Can you hang around a bit? I want to hear more, but I need to check in."

"Sure," Mackenzie said.

"I've already gotten a call from the chief on this," Linda added. "It's going to be ugly. Everyone knew her—she was popular."

Hailey thought about Natasha. They'd been friends once—sort of. They'd joined the department around the same time. Not in the same academy class, but close. And there hadn't been many women. Hardly any, actually. Hailey had tried to get Natasha to hang with the women.

Natasha had mostly passed. Said she preferred male company. Rumor was, Natasha had had plenty of it— from the seniors in the department all the way down to the newly initiated rookies. Married, divorced, single, it hadn't much mattered. And she'd pretty much gotten away with it. Even when she'd been caught in bed with Jamie Vail's husband and Jamie had unloaded her weapon, Natasha had emerged unscathed. At least until now.

Hailey wasn't one to pass judgment. The thing that bothered her about Natasha's lifestyle was it made for a long list of suspects.

She ducked under the yellow tape and studied the car Natasha had been in. A crime scene tech was still photographing the inside.

Hailey found Cassie Jones, a senior tech with CSU, and waited while she gave directions to a man holding a small handheld vacuum used for sucking up hair and fibers from the scene. When Cassie looked up, she gave Hailey a wide smile.

"Looks like a blow to the head," she said brightly, a short blond curl falling into her eyes. She pushed it away with the back of her forearm and then turned and started pointing. "But the real mess is upstairs."

"What do you mean?"

"Primary crime scene is her office."

Hailey frowned. "She was killed in her office, then moved?"

"Yep. Not nearly enough blood here for a primary site. She'd stopped pumping blood before she was moved. I'd say at least ten minutes before based on the blood quantity, but that's a guess." She pointed to the building. "Roger Sampers has a team up there. Down here we've got some tire tracks. Maybe eight sets of good ones. We'll cast them.

"Also, we found prints in the car—a lot of them, actually. Some are clean—they might belong to the deceased or to the perp. The rookie touched some stuff. I need hers to rule them out. I've got fibers and hairs—it's a heyday of crap in that car."

Hailey looked at the vehicle Natasha had been driving. It was a gold Ford Taurus, department issued. She frowned. "Cassie, it's a department car."

She raised gloved hands. "I know. It's going to be a nightmare to sort out. Can you get us a list of who's been driving it?"

Hailey nodded. "No problem, but it'll be a dozen people in the last two weeks, easy. We'll need to go back further to rule them all out. These cars don't get cleaned much."

"Go back a month. Most of the good prints will be newer than that. We'll find as many as we can. You're the one who's got to find a suspect to match them."

"No prints on the skin, then?"

Cassie smiled. "One very nice index finger."

Hailey looked over at the tall, thin rookie. "Hers?"

Cassie nodded. "Pretty sure. We'll check it, of course, but it's on the neck, right at the jugular."

"Checking for a pulse," Hailey thought out loud. "Anything else?"

"Not yet."

Hailey nodded. "We'll get him."

"It's why we do this."

Hailey smiled, excused herself, and pulled one of the uniforms away from the scene. She read his name badge. "Officer Grossen—"

"Grossenbacher," he said. "Means 'big river' in German."

"Okay, Officer Big River, I need you to compile a list of everyone on the scene right now. Get full names, phone numbers, when they arrived, and what they saw. Get your partner to help."

He jerked his right hand into the air as if starting to salute. He caught himself, stopped, and turned away quickly. She glanced down at his shined boots. Army, she guessed. Law enforcement was a natural succession for people who'd served in the armed services. Always took a while to get the military out.

Hailey scanned the crowd until she found what she

wanted. Get the worst over first. As Hailey crossed
toward her, Jamie fumbled with her pack of cigarettes,
shook one loose. Under the smoke, Hailey smelled a
mix of something she thought was peonies and
peppermint.

"I figured you'd want to talk to me," she said as a
flame flared from her lighter with a hiss. When she
opened her mouth, Hailey noticed that her teeth were
still clean and white. A sign of vanity, Hailey took it
for good news. Deeply depressed people often had no
regard for hygiene. Despite some of the signs, maybe
Jamie wasn't as bad off as she could have been.

"Just what you saw."

"Nothing. I got here about quarter to eight. I was
just stopping through on my way down to the lab
building to check on some evidence from the Osbourne assault last night."

Hailey frowned.

"Emily Osbourne was attacked and raped in the
stairs last night."

"Is she—"

"She'll live," Jamie said flatly.

Shit.

"When I got here, I ran into Linda James. She
told me."

Hailey shook her head. "Where were you last night?"

"You have a time of death?" Jamie asked.

"Not yet."

"I left the station at almost two. We pulled our
suspect in after the rape exam. Washington was with
me."

"You nail him?"

She shook her head, looked away. "On the way
home, I stopped for gas and cigarettes."

Hailey was poised to write.

"The one with the tiger."

"Exxon."

Jamie nodded. "Exxon. Off the Central San Rafael

exit. On Irwin, maybe. I paid cash. Marlboro Lights. Kid behind the counter had red hair, skinny with a little square of hair under his lower lip. What do the kids call that?"

"Soul patch."

"Right. Stupid-looking thing."

Hailey nodded. The details were good. Any cop knew that details were what made a story believable. Some things would be hearsay, but details like that could be checked. "And before the interview?"

"I was at the awards thing with you until I got the call on Osbourne. It was—what—close to nine o'clock? I went straight to the hospital and from there to the station. Came back this morning. In between, I was at home."

"Alone?"

Jamie paused, drawing a deep drag on her cigarette and blowing it out over her shoulder. "Alone."

"You sure, Jamie? If you weren't alone, it would make it easier. I can be discreet."

Jamie smoked a moment, then dropped the cigarette to the ground and stamped it out.

Hailey waited. "You were alone," she prompted again.

"I've got a dog named Barney. Don't know if he'd be convincing in cross-examination."

Hailey crossed her arms. Sighed. "This isn't fun for me, either. You think I want to interrogate a friend? But everyone's going to be asking the question. I get you out of the mix early, I can find the killer."

Jamie picked up the cigarette butt and put it in her pocket. Then, turning, she faced Hailey for the first time. Jamie was taller than she by a good three inches, and she looked like hell. Dark circles, no makeup. She'd been up most of the night with a rape case, back early. From her appearance, Hailey would have guessed she'd been dragged out of bed a few days ago.

Jamie paused. When she spoke, her voice was soft

and void of humor. "We're not friends, Hailey. Feel free to bring me in if you have more questions. Sorry I couldn't provide a better alibi." Then she turned and walked away.

Hailey didn't watch her.

The defensiveness made her suspect, but Jamie didn't fit the MO. Though Natasha was found in her car, the evidence indicated that she had been killed in her office. That meant that the perp had killed Natasha, then moved her. It would take strength to move Natasha's body. Plus, not many people would move a dead body—the very act indicated that whoever killed her also cared for her. Maybe the killer was trying to save her; maybe he was going to hide the body. Either way Jamie didn't fit.

As far as Jamie was concerned, motive was lacking, too. Jamie had found Natasha with her ex a year and a half ago. Why let all that time pass?

Hailey was also confident the killer wasn't anywhere near here now. Every cop knew to look in the crowd first. Jamie wouldn't be that stupid. It didn't change the fact that after the shooting incident, people would point to her first.

Hailey would have liked to rule her out early. An alibi would have done it. Barney the dog wouldn't.

Hailey searched for Mackenzie Wallace in the crowd. Propped against a black Chevy Blazer, the rookie stood stretched out, arms crossed, one ankle hooked across the other. Her lean legs were like the neck of a violin, strings taut.

Hailey approached and waited until the woman's gaze shifted to hers. Fear was stark in her eyes.

"You're new?"

Mackenzie nodded, looked down, ashamed. "My first dead body."

"I'm sorry."

Something like gratitude flashed in her expression. "Thanks."

"Captain James could arrange for some time off."

She shook her head, stood up straight, and rubbed her hands together. She dwarfed Hailey. Over six feet tall. "I'm sorry. I've tried to remember everything."

Hailey drew her notepad out, poised her pen. "No need to apologize."

Mackenzie nodded, like it was a criticism. "It was still too dark to see clearly and only one thing stands out."

Hailey waited.

"Another car. I saw it only from a distance. The rear left brake light might have been missing a small section. The bottom right corner looked broken." She glanced away and then back. "Like I said, it was just a glimpse."

"That's helpful. Anything else? Type of car?"

"Only thing I saw were the taillights. Domestic, I think, and square. Made me think of an older model pickup. Ford, I'd guess."

Hailey made notes, then looked up. "That's a lot of detail to remember about a car you only saw for what—"

"Less than thirty seconds. I used to work for the rangers' service in Yellowstone. We tracked poachers and hunters in the park at night. Helps to be able to recognize cars by their taillights."

"Nothing about the color?"

She shook her head. "No good light, so all I saw was black. Could have been any color."

"Reflection from the taillights didn't help?"

Hailey smiled softly. "Always makes the car look red. I'm guessing this one wasn't."

"Red's pretty conspicuous," Hailey agreed.

"Not what I'd choose if I were going to murder someone." She seemed to swallow the last words, shook her head. "God, I'm sorry. That was inappropriate."

"We all do it," Hailey said.

The rookie didn't answer.

Hailey asked a few more questions, but the taillights were the best clue Mackenzie could offer. Hailey figured the description narrowed it to about a twenty-five thousand cars in San Francisco alone. Better than the almost three hundred and sixty thousand she'd have otherwise.

Hailey thanked her for the help.

Mackenzie's gaze drifted back to the empty car. The body was now en route to the morgue for autopsy.

"It gets easier."

Mackenzie looked at her. She furrowed her brow. Intense. "Does it?"

Hailey saw Jamie leaving the scene. Considered where she was in her career. How far up she'd climbed. How far she'd fallen back down. She sighed, shook her head. "I don't know. Maybe sometime." Probably not, she thought.

Mackenzie seemed to understand the elusiveness of the answer.

As Hailey walked away, the rookie's gaze swung back to the crime scene. Hailey guessed she'd see Natasha's body in her mind for longer than she could imagine.

# 9

Stepping out of the car at Hunters Point Naval Station, Jamie zipped her flimsy jacket to combat the hostile wind. People milled around in front of the building. She'd suffered enough talk this morning. And last night. Damn Tim. He swore he'd turn himself in first thing this morning. And not mention being at her house. But there'd been no sign that he'd spoken to anyone. And then she'd lied to Hailey Wyatt. Why hadn't she just ratted out the bastard? Damn, she was dumb. Dumb. Dumb. Dumb. Not as dumb as Tim, though.

She just hoped he didn't do anything stupid. Anything else.

Blowing the last breath of smoke out her nose, she dropped the cigarette. She stamped out the butt, picked it up, and threw it away. She'd save a hell of a lot of time if she'd just litter, she thought. Hell, if she didn't smoke.

But that wasn't going to happen. She'd already given up drinking. If she was going to quit smoking, too, she might as well just jump in a hole and start shoveling the dirt on.

The lab was down a hallway to the right, but Jamie turned toward the bathroom. On the women's room door hung a sign that read, "Temporarily closed for maintenance."

"No way," she mumbled, shoving the door open.

"Closed," a male voice called back.

Jamie walked in and found a gangly teenager on his hands and knees in the far corner of the bathroom.

"What are you maintaining? A mouse hole?"

"We're closed," the kid said without turning around. "Use the one upstairs."

In answer, Jamie headed for a stall.

"Jesus Christ," the kid said, getting to his feet. "What a bunch of bitches."

She locked the stall and heard the outer door slam closed. When she was done, she came back out, washed her hands, and walked over to where the boy had been kneeling. A section of maybe thirty-two-inch tiles had been newly laid. Grout was slopped all over them. She touched it. It was nearly dry.

Just then the door opened again.

"Get away from that."

Jamie didn't move. "You're doing it wrong."

"What the hell do you know about it?"

She glanced up, scanned the boy's face. Early twenties, maybe. "Obviously a lot more than you," she said without rising.

"My father owns the contracting company."

"My father was a firefighter. Doesn't mean I know anything about putting out fires."

"Well, I know about this. I've been dragged along on these fucking jobs since I was nine." He looked at her with his eyebrows up, as though testing her with his language.

She just stared. If he thought language was going to shock her, he needed to spend a day in her job.

He pressed his shoulders back. "If people would stop interrupting, I'd be done already."

"You'd better get back to it before that grout dries and you've got a bigger mess."

Frowning, he slumped his shoulders. "Yeah."

She looked back at the floor and picked up the bag of dry grout.

He tried to snatch it from her hands.

"Let me show you a little trick." She grabbed a fist full of the dry powder and sprinkled it on a small section of wet grout.

"What the hell are you doing? You're just making a bigger mess that I'm going to have to clean up." He sighed. "Come on, lady."

Jamie found a rag and rubbed it across the area where she'd strewn the dry grout. The dry grout stuck to the wet stuff and acted as an abrasive to clean the grout off the tiles themselves while leaving it in the grouted areas.

The kid dropped down beside her. "Huh."

He sounded so shocked, Jamie actually laughed. Then she caught herself. When was the last time she'd laughed? The boy looked at her like she was mad.

"Well?" she said, offering the bag out to him.

He reached in and filled his fist with grout and repeated what she'd done.

Still kneeling, Jamie handed over the rag.

He wiped it across the grout, then leaned down to survey the area. "It works."

She nodded.

He scowled. "How'd you know that?"

She shrugged. Her father had redone every room of the house they'd lived in. Helping was about the only father-daughter bonding time they'd ever had. Jamie stood up and washed her hands. As she headed for the door, the kid said, "Thanks."

She looked back.

He grinned at her.

"No problem," she said, turning back for the door.

"And, lady?"

"Yeah?"

"You've got grout on your pants."

She glanced down at her navy slacks. Both knees were covered in gray mud. She swiped at it, then decided to hell with it. She didn't like these pants anyway.

She crossed the main entrance, walked down the hall to the lab. She stopped to write her name on the sign-in sheet.

A group hovered by the door. The head of CSU, Sydney Blanchard, stood with three other lab techs. Two had their backs to her. Voices were low, bodies crossed and closed.

Hailey Wyatt stood with them. She met Jamie's eyes, her gaze cool. Jamie knew they were talking about Devlin. Sydney glanced over and saw Jamie. Her red eyes widened. She'd been crying.

Jamie scanned the other faces, her gut tight. She searched for anything appropriate to say, failed.

"I'm here on Osbourne."

Sydney wiped her cheeks. "It's under the second scope."

Jamie passed them and peered down into the eyepiece. Immediately, she knew something was wrong. "Shit." It was the same something as before. A normal sperm sample showed white and red under the scope. The red denoted the nuclei of the cells. Jamie exhaled. No red in this sample. "No cells at all?"

Sydney nodded. "Doesn't look like we got any semen."

Jamie shook her head. "She swore he didn't use a condom. It's just like Shawna Delman. No prints, no DNA. Guy walks."

Two police officers raped and she had absolutely nothing. "Have we processed anything else from the case?"

Sydney shook her head. "We're working Devlin full force."

Jamie looked at Hailey, who stepped toward her.

"Tim came forward just after you left."

Jamie didn't respond.

"You knew, didn't you?"

She nodded.

"And you protected him."

Jamie had no answer for that. Sheer stupidity was the only thing that came to mind. Hailey could come to that conclusion on her own.

"That's a hell of a risk, Jamie." Jamie didn't answer. "He's lucky you care so much about him."

Jamie met her gaze. "I trusted him to come forward."

Hailey nodded. "It would have been better if he'd done it before he cleaned up."

Silent, Jamie turned to leave. Her surveillance on Marchek was due to expire in a few hours, and she had no evidence to keep him. She knew better than to think she was going to get any attention on Emily Osbourne's case now.

Even dead, Natasha Devlin would steal the fucking limelight.

# 10

Crouched inside his shed, Zephenaya watched the lady through the window. When she sat on the bed, he picked up the jagged rock. He held it tight in his fist, made a notch in the wood. Same as every night. He'd been watching her for thirty-nine plus ten days.

When he got to thirty-nine, he started again because he couldn't remember what came after that. At first he'd tried to count superfast, hoping the next number would spring into his head. It never did.

Maybe he never knew what came after thirty-nine. He'd only been in school till kindergarten. He had a few weeks of first grade, but it didn't seem much different than kindergarten. Then his father lost his job and they'd had to move. After that, he remembered three different houses, but maybe there were more. He'd never really gone to school in those places. Oh, they made him show up a few days. But he sat in the back and didn't listen. Now he wished he had. He could have used some more counting. His sister could count higher and she would have told him, but she wasn't there. He didn't know where she was. They told him she was dead, that she took drugs, but Zephenaya didn't believe it. No way Shawna would leave him.

That's why he was here. This lady knew Shawna. He remembered her from when Shawna got hurt. And someday, he'd gather up the nerve to ask her about Shawna. But not yet. He kept waiting for her to be hanging around the yard or something, but she never did. So he kept waiting.

All he had to do to pass the time was watch the lady. It wasn't like he was trying to. He knew that wasn't polite, but he couldn't help it. He had to wait until he could talk to her, and the lady didn't have blinds or nothing. Her big windows looked right out on the yard.

At first he thought it wasn't going to work, him staying there. How could she not see him, no shades and all? But the lady didn't seem to even see through that glass. She didn't act like she had a yard. She went out the front every day. At all sorts of hours, too. She'd leave at three in the morning or not until two in the afternoon. That was mostly weekends, he thought, though it was hard to keep track of the days. The big window upstairs was mostly where he saw the lady.

He didn't have a calendar or anything, just his notches in the wood. And his letter. He kept the letter in a secret place in his shed. When his sister got back, he would make her read it. He'd carried it in his pocket for a while, but it had gotten so worn, he could barely see her writing anymore. So, now he kept it inside a grocery plastic bag he'd found flying around the yard. Sometimes he took the letter out, just to see her writing, just to remind himself that she was real.

She loved him. That was the first line. She'd read him that first line and he knew it said, *I love you, Z.* That's what she called him. Z.

When he went for food or whatever, it was always early in the morning or at night just before he did the notch. It was best when it was dark and no one could see him. He couldn't read or count, but he was smart enough to know a lot of things—like that people would call the police if they saw a little black boy in this neighborhood. Then he'd have to go back to one of those homes. So Z kept in during the day, watched the house for signs of the lady.

He mostly knew if anyone was home or not because he always heard the garage door open and close. He could tell by the motor sounds if she was coming or going.

He never saw the men this lady was with, but he knew about the coming and going. His father had been like that, too, especially after his mother left. Z could think about his mother now and it didn't even make him too sad. He used to miss her. He didn't miss her so much now, but he missed having someone to talk to. He wished he could find Shawna. After she had the work accident, she'd been in the hospital. She told him he would have to go stay in a foster home for a while. She didn't think it would be long, but he should have asked how many days long was. He stayed in the first house for fifteen days before he went to find her. That had seemed like long enough to him. When they'd taken him back, those people didn't want him. The second home was even worse. They told him Shawna was dead. He stayed there for a long time. Until that man hit him. Then he left to find Shawna.

The lady treated him pretty good by not noticing he was out there, and he knew better than to mess things up. It had been that way living with his dad, too. If he was quiet and blended in, made like he wasn't there, his father didn't seem to mind having him around. But if Z started to be loud, or ask for something, well that's when the trouble started.

Same with his lady, he figured. If things disappeared, she might start to look around. It wouldn't be too long before she got to the plastic shed in the backyard. The yard was on a hill and filled with trees and bushes, so he had good shade. No one bothered to cut the trees or anything, so it was peaceful.

The air started to get cold and he'd made his notch, so Z had only one last thing to do before bed. He walked across the yard to the hole in the far corner that he'd dug to do his business. He passed the tree where he sometimes sat and counted stars when he couldn't sleep. Got just past it when he heard a loud crunch.

He dropped to the ground. Heart pounding. Squinting in the dark, he saw a man circle the back of the house. Z held his breath, pressed his body flat.

The man stared up into the windows. Z didn't see the lady now. In the dark, Z couldn't see the man's face. He was just a shadow as he climbed up the hill toward Z's house.

Z let the breath hiss out of his lips. Took another breath and held himself perfectly still. He had to pee bad now.

The man stopped at Z's shed. He slapped the side of it as though to see if it might fall over, peered inside.

The man was dressed like a regular guy—jeans and a brown jacket. He didn't look like one of those people who had made him go to school and taken him to a foster home.

The man squinted into the dark. He seemed to aim his gaze right at Zephenaya.

Z blinked fast. His nose tickled. He ignored it, breathed slowly. The ground was wet on his legs. He longed to shift but didn't dare. The man turned back toward the house, started down the hill.

Zephenaya itched his nose quickly.

The lady crossed in front of the window upstairs.

The man halted, watching. He watched like he was studying her. It gave Z the willies.

The bedroom light shut off and the yard went dark. Z blinked hard, couldn't see. He reached down and squeezed his penis to hold it. He didn't want to wet his pants. They were the only ones he had.

The man stood there in the dark for what felt like ten minutes; then he backed away from the house, crept quietly around the side yard, and disappeared. Zephenaya didn't move for another ten minutes, until he was sure he was going to pee his pants. Then he got on his knees, peed into the tree as fast as he could, staring at the side of the house the whole time.

Back in his shed, Z found his blanket on the ground. Everything else looked the same. Shawna's letter was still inside the bag under a pot. His food and stuff was hidden because he'd worried about animals, so maybe it was okay.

To be extra safe, he opened up the narrow side cupboard where he'd removed the shelves and crawled inside to sleep. They'd called him a runt at school, but sometimes being small was a good thing.

Tucking his blanket around him, Zephenaya slid the cupboard door closed. Eyes shut, he tried to block out the creepy man as he fell asleep. His last prayer was the same as every night—that tomorrow he'd find Shawna.

# 11

Jamie dreamed about a ringing phone, saw it sink into a tub of water. She reached in, splashing. Beside the phone, her mother's face appeared. Her expression matched an old snapshot. Face underwater. Jamie stretched, fingers out, but couldn't reach her. Her mother sank farther, still smiling. Waved. Then she saw Marchek. His eyes were black in the water. He waved to her, wiggling his fingers. Put his face close to her mother's. Too close.

Jamie sat up. Awake. Thought of the dream, heard the phone. She blinked and looked at the clock: 8:15. It was morning again. Her notebook was open beneath Barney. She still wore yesterday's clothes. She exhaled and closed her eyes again.

The phone rang again.

Barney whined and stood up on the bed.

She rubbed her face, cleared her throat as she reached for the phone. "Vail."

"Jamie."

She blew out her breath. "Tim, I'm hanging up."

"You're my one call."

One call? "What?"

"I'm in jail."

She closed her eyes. "Jesus Christ."

"I didn't know who else to call."

She scanned the room for cigarettes.

"Natasha." His voice cracked. "I'm being charged with her murder."

"Where are you?"

"At the Hall. In a holding cell."

"You called an attorney?"

"Not yet."

"Don't talk to anyone. I'm on my way." She dropped the handset on the bed, unzipped yesterday's pants, let them fall. She considered not showering, but she had to. She would reek of cigarettes if she didn't. She soaped quickly, shampooed, brushed her teeth twice, rinsed, and emerged all in less than the time it took her to process what had happened. Tim was in jail. He'd come forward. She'd never expected them to book him, but she should have considered it. There was evidence—Devlin's blood, the argument at the banquet. Plus, the pressure to solve the case quickly would be overwhelming. But someone had to have seen Devlin with her real killer. Where had she gone after the banquet? And with whom?

Rubbing her face, Jamie wondered why the hell she was involved in this. It was not her job. She had no duty to Tim. But instead of stopping, she scrambled to find a shirt that looked relatively clean. Pulled it over her head. She fumbled with her pants, dragged a comb through her hair. She tried to tame the wildest strands. She brushed powder on her cheeks to even out the bags, pinched the skin to try to put some color in her cheeks. Then she gave up.

Questions tracked mud around her brain. Why had Tim come here the other night? To tell her he hadn't killed Devlin. Did he know he'd be charged? Could he be guilty?

Impossible. Not Tim. She ran down the stairs, let Barney out. Rushing, she filled his bowl with food, checked his water. She slipped her holster over her shoulders, lit a cigarette. Barney came back in, sniffed his food, looked up.

"No walk this morning, buddy."

He shrugged, dug into breakfast.

As she drove to the city, she left the driver's window down. She smoked one cigarette after another. The nicotine buzzed in her head as the same question swarmed like a pack of bees: Was Tim a killer? She'd once thought he'd never cheat. Told herself it wasn't the same. Was it?

She should have sent someone else. He needed an attorney, not her. She stabbed the cigarette out. Masochist. She wished she didn't care. It had been too long to care.

She dialed Ed Goldman, a defense attorney, and told his secretary who she was and what she needed.

"Goldman."

"It's Jamie Vail."

He clicked his tongue. "Inspector Vail. What an honor."

"I need an attorney at the jail."

He laughed. "You commit a murder?"

She swallowed the knot. "A friend is being charged."

She heard the rustle of paper, a pen click. His tone changed. "What are the charges?"

She drove, pressed the accelerator to the floor as she talked.

"I'll be there in an hour."

She hung up, considered going home. Instead, she kept driving.

By the time she pulled into the parking lot behind the jail at the Hall of Justice, her hair had blown into divided strands that felt like straw. She tried to run her fingers through it, but got stuck just a couple of inches into the snarled mess. She patted it down, tucked what she could behind her ears, and headed inside.

The jail was in the new section of the building, but the novelty had lasted only a week or two. Five years later, the yellow linoleum floors were scuffed and cracked. The smell of new metal and fresh paint had been replaced by some combination of cooked peas and the acrid stench of men's sweat. She hated the place, avoided it whenever she could.

She hated it now. She wanted to hate Tim, longed to hate him. Couldn't. Damn it.

She stopped at the front desk where a wiry woman sat on a stool, a foot dangling off each side. Jamie wondered how she could work with the smell. Probably she didn't notice it anymore, like people who lived near slaughterhouses. Jamie handed the woman her badge.

She recorded Jamie's badge number in the log. She wrote left-handed and at such a backwards slant, it looked like she was writing upside down. She returned the badge and nodded Jamie through.

As Jamie headed into the hall, the woman picked a romance novel up off the desk. Jamie wished she had some fantasy in her life.

Unfortunately, nothing short of the dismal reality captured her attention. For enjoyment, she read the crime sections of other major newspapers, mostly on-line, and she participated in a couple of cop chat groups. Solving crimes, especially when they weren't hers, was enjoyable. And it passed time when she couldn't sleep, which was often.

Inside the jail, Jamie passed through the metal detector, leaving her gun, her purse, and the lighter from her pocket.

"You want a room?" the officer asked her.

She shook her head. She didn't want Tim to be able to touch her. That was what she thought about—that and the fact that she probably had bad breath. "Phone's fine."

The officer shrugged and buzzed the door open. "Three," he said.

The heavy metal door closed behind her with a

deafening clank. She sat in the third cubicle, waited. She gripped her hands. The inner door banged shut and Tim shuffled in.

He wore prison orange. His hands cuffed together, they dangled at his waist as he walked. Another chain around his waist connected to the cuffs, kept his hands down. He stared at her. He looked terrified. She forced a smile to hide the fear tight in her chest.

The guard slid back the metal chair, motioned him to sit.

Tim held his hands out, shook the cuffs.

The guard shook his head.

Jamie picked up the phone on her side and rapped it on the glass.

Tim sank into the chair, took the receiver awkwardly between both hands.

"Have you talked to anyone?"

He shook his head.

"Ed Goldman will be here soon."

He frowned, distracted. He looked through the glass, behind her.

"He's an attorney. He's good."

He nodded.

"Tim, why do they think you killed her?"

His gaze shifted to hers, but he didn't answer. The rims that circled his eyes before were deeper and darker now. The bruise under his eye was gray-black, shadowed in the dim light of the jail.

She reminded herself that she'd had a similar set of rings after finding him and Devlin in bed together. What strange twist of fate had brought her to this point? She could have walked away. Tim Worley was not her problem. Only he was, because she couldn't let go. Had somehow refused.

"Tim," she repeated, knocking on the glass. "What happened?"

He glanced at the cuffs. "We had a fight."

"When?"

"The night before the banquet."

"Where?"

"In front of her house."

She watched him, shook her head.

"It was bad."

"Tim, you didn't—"

His gaze steadied, his eyes hard. "I didn't kill her."

She exhaled, sucked in a breath, nodded. "What was the fight about?"

"Her." He shook his head. "Us. About how she used me. She'd called me over, desperate. I gave up tickets to the Sharks game. When I got there, she said she had something more important to do. She had to leave." He paused, defeated. "I was furious." He dropped his gaze. "I slapped her."

Violence. Jamie felt her chest deflate. Tim had never touched her that way. She couldn't imagine what the hell had driven him to strike Devlin. "Did anyone see you?"

"The couple next door." He glanced up. "An older couple. The woman came out and asked Natasha if she wanted her to call the police."

Jamie sank deeper into the hard plastic chair. Bad. "What time was that?"

"Maybe nine or so."

"What then?"

"She got in her car and left."

"And you?"

"I went home."

"Tim?"

"Okay, I went and had a few drinks and went home."

"What about the next day?"

"She called—" He halted. "That day. I went to see her." He looked down.

"When?"

"Before the banquet. A couple of hours before."

"Where?"

"At her office. We were fine. It was like the fight had never happened."

Jamie frowned. "Then what was the deal at the banquet?"

He shook his head. "I don't know."

"There must have been something. What happened?"

"I don't know. She blew me off again. She does this from time to time—kind of freaks out and distances herself. But it got to me this time. I was furious."

"And you hadn't talked since you were in her office?"

"No."

She shook her head. It didn't make any sense. "So after the banquet you went back?"

"I went out to drinks with Marshall and Ramirez. Ramirez dropped me off. I saw her car in the lot, so I went up."

"And?"

"I called her name, but she didn't answer. I walked in. The office was dark and I saw her on the floor. I leaned down to check her and someone hit me."

"Did you see the attacker?"

He shook his head.

"Did you hear anything?"

He glanced up. "Yeah. He said something."

"What did he say?"

"He said, 'Stupid bastard.' " Tim's eyes widened. "I think he stuttered it, actually."

"Stuttered?"

Tim nodded.

"Did you tell all this to the police?"

"Yeah. I told them."

"So why do they think you did it?"

"They talked to her neighbor about the fight."

"Is that all?"

He didn't respond.

"Tim."

"I'd written her a note. I gave it to her when I was leaving her office that day—before the banquet."

The guard appeared behind Tim. He pointed to his watch.

Jamie put a finger up. "One minute." She looked back at Tim. "What kind of note?"

He didn't answer.

The guard stepped forward, took Tim's arm. Tim tried to pull free.

Jamie stood up and rapped on the window to get Tim's attention. "What did the note say?"

The guard yanked Tim to his feet. The phone clattered against the glass.

Jamie banged against the thick plastic window. "Answer me," she shouted.

Tim shook his head, kept silent.

"Christ, what did the note say?" she yelled.

He met her gaze. His words were barely a whisper. They struck her ears like thunder.

"That I couldn't live without her."

# 12

Hailey Wyatt parked the department's brown Taurus in a spot at the far end of Washington Square just below Russian Hill. The residential neighborhood was quiet at lunch time. Anywhere else, she would have flipped down the police lights on her sun visor and parked in the red. But when she was here, she didn't want to call attention to her car. Or herself. They always arrived separately. She always left first. Too much at stake professionally and privately to get caught.

She sat in the car, stared across toward Buck's building, wondering why she was there. There was plenty to keep her occupied with Natasha's murder. CSU and the lab were scrambling to solidify the evidence they had against Tim Worley. She and her team were interviewing everyone to identify any witnesses. Though they were trying to narrow the window, the time of death was currently estimated between eleven and two. Even at that hour, Hailey had to believe someone saw something. But despite the stresses of Devlin's murder, Hailey shouldn't have come here.

She pictured John kissing her good-bye that morning, saw the girls in their bath the night before. They'd had a good night. As near perfect as ever. So why did she do this? Why wasn't that life enough?

She imagined how she'd grown up—the coming and going of her mother's men. Men Hailey never knew, a long line of shadows whose faces never had the chance to imprint. She didn't blame her mother. That would be pointless. But she knew the answer lay in that past.

Giving in to her desire, Hailey stepped from the car and crossed through the park. The sun cut between two fat clouds that looked like unshorn sheep grazing in a blue pasture. A woman in sweatpants ate a McDonald's hamburger and fed bread to pigeons. She spoke to them in a low jabber that Hailey associated with mental illness. The pigeons didn't seem to mind.

The woman reeled her arm back over her head and threw bread to the far reaches of the flock like a fly fisherman casting a lure. She paid no attention to Hailey.

Head down, Hailey hiked the steep block of Union Street, then turned in to the familiar marble facade on August Aly. She stared at the bell, felt more guilt. Rang apartment number 10. The door buzzed and clicked open. Without a word, she climbed the two flights. The halls were empty. His door was cracked. The first time she'd done this with a nest of hatching rattlesnakes in her belly. Now, just the eager flutter of a dozen butterflies.

She let herself in, closed the door behind her, turned the lock, and made her way into the kitchen.

Buck drank ice water from a tall plastic cup, handed it to her. She took a thirsty gulp before he pulled it from her hands. He set it down with a splash and yanked her to him. She heard her breath seize as he took her mouth, pressed against her. Intense.

His mouth on hers, he backed her down the hallway toward the bedroom. Pulled her clothes off as they went. No words. Her jacket dropped to the floor. He unfastened her buttons, kissed her neck, the small of her throat. He hung her shirt off the bathroom doorknob. Sliding his hands under her bra, he cupped her breasts, groaned.

They fell onto the bed, the rest of their clothes soon a tangled mess on the floor.

"God, I missed you," he said when they were done. The first words they'd spoken.

She smiled, rolled over, and leaned her chin on his chest. "Me, too."

He tucked an arm under his head, wound a finger through her hair.

She pushed his hand away, the motion too much like John. They couldn't be the same. She forced the guilt out, closed her eyes. Tired.

Buck ran a finger down her spine. She felt the stretch of her muscles in the small of her back and legs. Sighed. "What's going on in IA?"

"You heard Scanlan's latest?"

"No. What'd he do?" Scott Scanlan was the deputy chief's son. Though she'd never met him, rumor said he was a kid who had a tendency to drink too much and act like a total asshole. He'd been kicked out of the Los Angeles Police Department after a drunken incident at the annual police ball, so he'd made his way home and hooked up with Daddy's department.

"Couple of investigators from General Works made some jokes. Scanlan got so upset, he took them on in the parking lot."

She winced. "He's only five seven or something."

"Yeah. And he was already on probation."

A few months back, Scanlan had been out drinking at Balboa Café, one of three bars that made up a hot spot called the Triangle in San Francisco's marina district. Drunk, Scanlan had demanded a college kid give up his burrito. The kid had refused and Scanlan had hit him. The kid hit back and although Scanlan had suffered most of the injuries, the kid had called the police.

The department had tried to sweep the incident under the rug. The attempt to conceal Scanlan's misadventure had led all the way to the chief of police.

But the media had gotten wind of the story and the attempted cover-up and hung the whole department out to dry over it.

"These are guys my age," he continued.

"Wow. Old, huh?"

He tickled her side.

She wiggled. "What did they say to him?"

"Burrito jokes."

"Oh God."

"I guess Scott took a swing at one of them."

"What'd they do?"

"They left him cuffed to the axle of his car."

She laughed. "That's terrible."

"Ah, he deserved it, the punk." He turned her over, kissed her again. They stopped talking for a few minutes. Then he sat up again, stared at her. "What's going on with Devlin?"

She put a leg over his, tucked herself against him. Put her head down. "You heard Tim Worley came forward? He was with her. Says she was already dead when he found her in the office."

Buck raised a brow.

"Claims he planned to take her to the hospital. He knelt down to check her pulse when he was hit in the head."

"Any evidence he was hit?"

She nodded. "He's got a goose egg. He claims he woke up a bit later and carried her out."

"Why carry her out if she was already dead?"

"Says he didn't realize she was dead until he was already moving her. Then he didn't want to leave her there."

"Is the story consistent?"

Hailey shrugged. "Hard to be sure. She was definitely killed in her office and definitely moved. That's about all I can say on it yet."

"You find a weapon?"

"No. And since he'd showered by the time he came

in, any trace evidence on him is down the drain. He was hit by something. CSU is working with photos and some molds of his injury to try to find out what it was."

"Where's he now?"

"In jail. We found clothes covered in Natasha's blood in his car."

He whistled.

"Did you see the blowup they had at the awards ceremony? Must've been three-dozen witnesses."

"Christ. Not good PR for the department."

" 'Cause he's a cop?"

He nodded. "How do you figure it happened?"

"Lovers' quarrel in her office. He came at her. She struck him in the head, and he slammed her against the desk or something to finish her off. Could've been an accident. We're still running some basic tests, but we've got two different semen samples. Our lab can't do anything with it, so the samples go to the outside lab. It could take months to get usable DNA results. And that's if we're lucky."

Buck frowned. "Shit."

"She got around. Once we match the other one, we'll need to talk to that guy, too."

"Well, it's good work. Lots of people watching that case. Better to have it wrapped up."

"It's not that simple. The evidence proves that Natasha had sex with someone else after Tim Worley."

"So you think Worley interrupted something and killed her?"

"If so, who's our other guy? Why didn't he come forward?"

"You printed her office?"

"This is where it gets bad."

Buck's eyes widened. "What? His?"

She shook her head. "The desk was cleaned off with some sort of bleach wipe. The door, too. No sign of any prints—not Natasha's or Worley's. None."

He frowned. "Can you link the chemical to a solution she had in the office?"

"Not yet. And we didn't find anything like it in Worley's stuff. The lab's still working on identifying it."

"That means somebody was prepared."

She smiled at the direction his logic took, that he thought just like she did. "That's the only hitch I see. A guy who has a big blowup with his girlfriend and follows her to her office isn't prepared to clean up after the kill unless it was premeditated. And from what I saw at the ceremony, Natasha was railing on Tim pretty hard. He sounded genuinely shocked at first. Then he got angry."

Buck was silent a minute. "Maybe he carried wipes in his car. Like a neat freak?"

She shook his head. "None."

"His desk?"

"Nope. And so far no trace of the chemical on his clothes or in his car, either."

"What about the murder?"

"Blunt-force trauma to the head. Coroner is trying to help us with the shape of the weapon."

"You know if Worley was hit with the same thing?"

"Not yet."

He kissed her neck.

Her stomach growled. "We going to eat?"

He pulled Hailey back on top of him, shifted under her. "You're not full yet?"

She balanced on him, felt his hips start to move beneath her. Smiled.

She sat up, kissed him. "Worley's the obvious because of timing, but the way I hear it, there was a long line of guys she'd dumped hard."

Something in his expression changed.

"What?"

"No, I just—"

Just then a cell phone rang. She sat up, looked at his sitting silently on the nightstand. "Mine."

She found it on the floor, glanced at the number. "Station?"

She nodded.

"Wyatt."

"Dispatch here. I've got a call from Jim Wyatt. Says it's urgent."

She pressed a fist to her gut. Her father-in-law. "Put it through."

She heard two clicks. "Jim?"

"Hailey."

"Jim, what's wrong? Is everyone okay?"

"Fine. I'm sorry to bother you. You're probably out at a scene . . ." He let the comment hang.

"It's fine, Jim. What's wrong?"

She met Buck's gaze. He nodded to the phone. She shrugged, had no idea what was going on. Her father-in-law rarely called her.

"I'm afraid I need a favor from you, Hailey."

She scowled, sat back in the bed. "A favor?"

Buck shook his head. He knew all about her senator father-in-law. He ran a finger across her thigh.

She pushed it away. "What is it?"

"There's been a murder. It happened this morning—here in San Francisco."

"Who's been killed?"

"Abby and Hank Dennig."

"Dennig?" She shook her head. "I don't know the names. It's not my case."

"Abby Dennig is Tom Rittenburg's daughter. Tom Rittenburg is—"

"The head of San Francisco's NRA. I met him at your fundraiser at the old Federal Reserve."

"Right," Jim said. "Good memory."

"How were they killed?"

"You haven't heard, then?"

"No. I've been out of the station for about an hour." She glanced at the clock. It had been more like two. She steadied her breath. "Do you want me to find out who's working it?"

"No. I already know that."

"What sort of favor do you need?"

Buck rubbed her shoulder. She shifted away from him, concentrating.

"I'd like you to take the case."

"I can't do that, Jim. We work in rotation."

"I've spoken to the mayor."

Just then, the call-waiting beeped. "Jim, hold on." She pressed the send button. "Wyatt."

"You're a popular girl."

Hailey frowned at David Marshall's voice. Her captain. "What are you talking about?"

"I just got a call from Deputy Chief Scanlan. He's been on the phone with the mayor."

"Shit."

"You've got a new case—It's Tom Rittenburg's daughter. He's—"

"I know who he is."

"The scene's already been processed, but the van they were killed in has been sent to the lab. You'll have full access to it whenever you're ready. The autopsy was done earlier. I'll get you the full report in the morning."

"Whose case was it?"

"Wade."

Rylan Wade. He'd been in Homicide longer than her and had a better solve record. "He's good, David. Why not let him have it?"

"Because the mayor asked for you."

"What about the Devlin case?" she asked.

"You've arrested a suspect, right?"

She stood. "I can't do both. If I take Dennigs, then put the other guy back on the Devlin case."

"What other guy?"

"Whomever you sent out to the scene that morning. The rookie cop saw him."

David snorted. "I don't know what you're talking about. There were easily a dozen cops in the vicinity that morning. If you haven't noticed, the building's full of them."

Hailey felt her voice rise. "David, I can't do both cases. There's too much media. They're going to want to know why the department isn't focused on finding—"

"Where are you now?"

She glanced at Buck, closed her eyes. Lied. "I'm talking to one of Devlin's neighbors, trying to get information on who else she might have been seeing." She felt her cheeks flush.

"Fine. Come in when you're back. We'll get you some support." With that, the line went dead.

She pushed send as Buck started to talk. She shook her head, pressed her finger to her lips.

"Jim?"

"I'm here."

"That was my captain. I got your message. I have to tell you that you've put me in an extremely awkward position. I wish you'd called me before you spoke to the mayor. Inspector Rylan Wade was working the Dennig case. He's got a higher solve rate than I do and he's been here longer."

"Rittenburg deserves to know what happened to his daughter. I know if it were mine, I'd push for the best, too."

"I don't know that you've gotten him the best."

"Why don't we talk later?"

She said good-bye, shut the phone with a clack. Her fingers trembled.

She dropped the phone onto the bed. Bent over for her pants. Pulled them on.

"I'm sorry," Buck said.

She nodded, too frustrated to respond.

"What'd you say about the Devlin scene?"

"Some other asshole was there first. David won't tell me who. They're all teaming up." She looked at him. "There's probably some club of men who screwed Natasha Devlin down at the station."

He didn't respond. She knew he wasn't used to seeing her all riled up.

She wasn't used to it either. "It just pisses me off."

He nodded. "So I can see."

She scooped her bra off the floor, snapped it on. Found her shirt in the hall, then her jacket. Went into the bathroom to wash up. When she was dressed, she came back. He was still propped in the bed, naked. "Don't you have to work?"

He patted the sheets.

She sat, tried to calm herself. "I can't have both cases."

"Talk to David. He's reasonable."

"The mayor called and asked Deputy Chief Scanlan for me specifically."

"Hey, if you close it, it'll probably mean a big raise."

She smiled, shook her head.

He pulled her back, kissed her hard. "Same time day after tomorrow?"

"You'd better feed me next time."

He grinned. "Promise."

With that, she slipped into her shoes, checked her rosy reflection in the hallway mirror, and headed back outside to an increasingly grim reality.

# 13

After lunch, Jamie called Captain Jules, requesting additional surveillance hours on Marchek. The activities they'd tracked weren't enough to get a child detention and she was nowhere on convicting him of rape. Her biggest fear was that another officer would be attacked. And it would happen if she didn't get him. It was inevitable.

Next she called over to Homicide and asked for Hailey Wyatt. She owed Hailey an apology. It wasn't Hailey's fault Jamie was being considered a potential suspect. It wasn't anyone's fault but Jamie's. Well, Tim's. Tim. His bail hearing was set for an hour from now. She'd spoken to his attorney that morning.

"I'm confident we'll get bail," Goldman had told her. But in his voice, Jamie heard a tiny catch she'd never noticed before. Insecurity? She didn't ask. She'd know soon enough.

"Hailey's over at building 606," the secretary told Jamie after she identified herself.

"On Devlin?"

"Nope. Dennig," she said with the cheery voice of someone talking about today's lunch specials.

"Dennig? Who's that?"

"New one. She'll be there awhile. You want to leave a message?"

Jamie declined. She preferred to see Hailey in person, owed her that much. She and Hailey *had* been something like friends when the rookie club began. Female bonding, someone termed it when the group grew to near ten. The word sounded weird: "bonding." Jamie had never bonded. Until that night, she'd never been outside a locker room or restroom with a group of only women. It had been a year and a half since she'd gone. Somehow female bonding had lost its appeal after she'd found Devlin in bed with Tim.

Halfway to Hunters Point, Jamie's phone rang. She recognized Chip Washington's extension.

"Hey, Chip. What's going on?"

"I heard about Worley."

Jamie frowned. She didn't want to be consoled about her ex-husband's arrest. "Are you handling the case?"

"No. Anderson's got it. I hear he came to your house from the scene, covered in blood. After their fight at the banquet, Christ—"

"I don't want to talk about it, Chip."

There was momentary silence. "I'm sorry, Jamie. I just wanted to make sure you were doing all right. Between Osbourne and Marchek that night and then this—well, I was just checking."

"I'm fine. I'll be fine," she said. "I'll talk to you later."

"Yeah, okay. Bye."

Jamie dropped the phone on the seat. She would be fine. This was about Tim Worley, not about her. Her case was catching Marchek. Devlin was someone else's problem. Somehow, though, it felt like she was about to get sucked into the cyclone.

It was almost one when Jamie arrived at the lab. Outside, they were having a rare cloudless November day and she was sweating under her blazer.

"You seen Hailey?" she asked at the lab.

"Down in the bay."

Jamie walked down the corridor that led into an

open warehouse the building's occupants called the
bay. Mostly, the bay housed patrol cars and the tank
that the Special Ops team used for heavy mob
situations.

Voices echoed from behind a partition wall. The
Special Ops task force often performed drills in the
bay. Today, a metallic green minivan sat on a sheet
of clear plastic half the size of a basketball court.

Hailey Wyatt stepped from the van. Her hair up in
a nurse's hairnet, she wore a clear plastic raincoat and
galoshes. The soles of the yellow galoshes were wet.
They slurped as she tracked dark prints across the
clear plastic. The stench confirmed the dark stuff
was blood.

Even in the getup, Hailey exuded sexuality. The
curves of her tiny waist and large breasts were visible
under the coat. Her wavy hair was tucked under the
pale green hairnet. Rosy cheeks and a sprinkling of
freckles seemed to only enhance her appeal.

Hailey had been one of those women Jamie had
avoided at first. Like Devlin, she'd looked too perfect
to be real and certainly too attractive to be someone
Jamie would want to be around. And yet, unlike Devlin, Hailey seemed unaware of her allure. She was
neither coy nor a flirt.

When a case had brought them together, Jamie
learned Hailey was grounded and confident and fair.
And she was kind. But whether she noticed it or not,
Jamie had seen the effect Hailey had on men. They
paid careful attention. Jamie had her share of attention but never like Hailey's. She wondered how Hailey
could possibly ignore it.

Jamie approached the minivan, nodded to a tech
who was working at a folding table covered in the
same plastic as the ground. He wore a lab coat stained
red. He gently rocked a sand sifter, searching for evidence the way pioneers had searched for nuggets of

gold. Beside him sat the small vacuum he'd used to collect evidence from the car. It was a red Dirt Devil.

Hailey turned to her, gave a little wave. "Hey." She seemed to hold no grudge.

Jamie apologized anyway. "I'm sorry about the other day. I was an ass."

Hailey shrugged. "Come take a look at my latest."

Jamie stepped to the edge of the plastic, careful to avoid the bloody footprints. The van was a new model with sliding doors on either side. Both were open, but there was no breeze to alleviate the smell. It was pungent, sour, and completely unmistakable.

"Who was it?" Jamie asked.

"Abby and Hank Dennig. It's her car."

Jamie shook her head. The names meant nothing.

"Mother of three. Drops the kids at their private school at eight thirty this morning, goes home, and parks in the basement of her building off of Broadway. Never makes it out of the garage."

"Leads?"

"From what I've found so far, I'm guessing they killed each other. She was beat pretty badly, but most of the blood is his. She had a letter opener."

"Odd thing to carry in the car."

"I thought so, too. But it seems it wasn't odd for her. It was engraved from Daddy, and she carried it so she could open mail when she was waiting for the kids at school or soccer practice."

"And to think I've been using my finger to open mail."

Hailey grinned, a spray of little lines around her eyes crinkling. "Hard on the manicure, though."

"She had the letter opener. Why didn't she just stab him?"

"There's a lot we don't know," Hailey admitted.

Jamie looked back at the bloody minivan, happy to have a momentary distraction from thoughts of Tim and Natasha Devlin. "Why did he even show up if she was taking the kids to school?"

Hailey followed Jamie's gaze. "They used to get coffee together some days."

"So if both are dead, it's a closed case. Why all the bother?"

"You heard of GGUNRA?"

"Anything ending NRA is familiar."

"San Francisco's chapter. Abby is the president's daughter."

Jamie shook her head. "Too bad Daddy didn't give her a nice little .22 instead. She might still be alive."

Another tech cut cloth off the center seat with a pair of heavy scissors. He dropped the fabric square into a brown paper bag, crumpled the top of the bag closed, and wrote on it with a black Sharpie marker.

"Looking for signs of a third party," Jamie said, thinking out loud.

"And you can imagine how many hair samples there are—we got kids, kids' friends, and all the junk they pick up. Plus, I think they had a couple of dogs."

Just then, a tech walked toward them. He held up a clear plastic Ziploc to Hailey.

Jamie watched the way he stared at Hailey while he spoke—another man infatuated. "Found this wedged down in the kid's car seat."

Hailey focused on what looked like a small button pin, never even glancing at the tech.

Jamie moved forward, read it over her shoulder. The pin was white with blue lettering. Around the outside it read, "Wage peace, not war." In the middle, inside a circle, were the letters "NRA" with a fat blue line through them.

"Probably not a gift from Grandpa," Jamie commented, stepping back.

Hailey's phone went off, and she looked down at her bloody attire. "Dang it." She snapped off her gloves, removed her raincoat and galoshes, and left them and the rest of the bloody clothes on a rubber mat. Last, she removed the hairnet and pushed a dark strand of hair off her face with the back of her hand. The tech watched her as if it were a striptease though she performed with utilitarian efficiency.

By then, her phone had stopped ringing. She dug it out of her pocket, put her finger up to Jamie, and hit a couple of buttons.

"This is Hailey Wyatt. I just got a call—"

There was a moment of silence as Hailey's gaze met Jamie's. "Perfect. I'm on my way now." With that, she snapped the phone shut and turned to the tech. "Bag that. We'll need to run it for prints."

He nodded.

"I'm going to the lab. Be back in ten." To Jamie she said, "Come with."

She started walking and Jamie caught up.

"Worley make bail?" Hailey asked.

"Hearing's probably over now. I haven't heard." She looked at the inspector. "What's at the lab?"

"Bunch of results came in earlier. I'm still waiting on Devlin's toxicology, but I thought you'd want to hear about the others."

"Any indications she was drugged?"

"None."

Jamie stopped. "Tim didn't kill her."

Hailey nodded, waved her on. "I'm not convinced he did. I sent a crime scene tech to the jail earlier so they could take some shots and a mold of his head wound. We also took a swab of the wound to search for foreign material. CSU's trying to work out what he was hit with, and we're looking for other suspects. The evidence isn't good for him, though. And we all saw the fight."

Jamie thought about how angry Tim had looked at the awards banquet, how pleased Devlin had seemed when she'd blown him off.

"You know anyone who stutters?" Hailey asked.

Jamie remembered Tim's comment about the words he'd heard just before he was struck. "I don't, but it's not particularly uncommon among criminals."

Hailey nodded. "Yeah. Violent offenders. I've read the same stats."

"You have a time of death?" Jamie asked.

"It happened between eleven and one. The coroner is trying to narrow it more. It helps that she kept the temperature in her office at exactly sixty-six degrees. The coroner's working with body temperature. Tim claims he arrived about twelve forty. She was on the ground. He was leaning over her when someone struck him."

"I know."

Hailey glanced at her.

"He came to my house afterwards. He was freaked out."

Hailey frowned.

"He swore he'd come forward immediately. I didn't want to tell you yesterday morning because I knew it would look better if he did it himself." She paused. "And I knew he would."

"And if he hadn't?"

"I'd have told you before the end of the day."

Hailey didn't respond.

"Also, I can provide an alibi for the whole night if you need it. I didn't help Tim. I just told him to turn his ass in."

Hailey opened the hall door and let Jamie pass in front of her. "You were with someone?"

"I was on the computer, on the Web."

The door clicked shut behind them. Their shoes ticked against the linoleum floor.

"Doing what?" Hailey asked.

"I belong to a group."

"Like a chat group?"

She nodded. "For cases—other cops."

"What time were you online?"

"Off and on between quarter to two when I got home and around four o'clock. I tried to go to sleep earlier, but Tim showed up around two fifteen and I couldn't sleep after that. There will be records of the dialogue. We're working a nasty rape/murder in Chicago. There are three or four other officers who can confirm my presence, if you need them to."

They turned left into the lab corridor. Jamie considered the evidence Hailey had, wasn't sure she wanted to be surprised by it.

Hailey paused at the lab door, her hand on the knob. "You ready?"

Jamie nodded, not so sure.

Inside, the head of CSU, Sydney, walked along the edge of a huge cut of red-stained carpet. The piece, spread out on the lab floor, was maybe nine feet by twelve. Her straight strawberry-blond ponytail swung as she moved. She wore khakis and a white lab coat. Freckles dappled her cheeks, giving her skin a glow despite a lack of makeup. Sydney circled the rug, holding a black Sharpie. Every few steps, she'd stop, lean over, and circle a spot of red.

"I'm here for the Devlin update," Hailey said.

Sydney turned, blinked hard. "Mike, will you get Tasha's file for me?"

Hailey met Jamie's gaze. Neither spoke. Jamie knew Sydney and Natasha Devlin had been close. The few times she'd seen Devlin at rookie club dinners, she'd always sat beside Sydney. Jamie felt the gap between herself and the other officers who had once been her comrades widen. Natasha Devlin would haunt her forever—dead or alive. Unless the truth shed a symphony of light on her death, people would rarely think of her murder without hearing notes of Jamie Vail somewhere in the background.

Sydney swiped at her face with the back of one hand, still focused on the rug. "I'm almost done with this."

"Take your time," Hailey told her, leading Jamie to a small table to one side.

Hailey sat and Jamie forced herself to join though she would have preferred to stand.

Sydney circled another three spots on the carpet and then stood, removed the medical gloves, dropped them in the biohazard trash bin, and tossed the contaminated pen into the trash. She brought a file to the table and sat. She wiped her eyes with her palms, shook her head. "I keep losing it. They should have someone else doing her work, you know. Damn unthinking bureaucracy."

Jamie struggled to find something to say, something that would alleviate any doubt. Instead, she shook her head. "I'm very sorry, Sydney."

Sydney glanced at her, nodded. "She wasn't the best with men, but she was a wonderful person."

Jamie nodded. "She didn't deserve to die. I hope you believe me."

Sydney blinked again, shook her head, and sniffed to clear her nose. "Okay, let's see what we got. From the car, we found dozens of smudged partials but only nine full prints—three inside the car, six outside. Six we've matched to officers, the other three no match yet. And we still haven't finished her office."

Hailey drew out her notebook. "Start with the inside."

"Your rookie on the neck. Devlin's prints and another one." She scanned the pages, flipped.

"Worley?" Hailey asked.

Sydney shook her head. "Scott Scanlan."

Jamie watched Hailey's face. She had not expected that news. "Scanlan?"

Jamie knew Scanlan by reputation. From what she'd heard, he was not a likely target for a Devlin conquest. He seemed young, even for her, and not all that bright. Of course, he was the deputy chief's son. She could see that appealing to Natasha.

Sydney nodded, lowered her voice. "He's been dating someone in here—our new tech, Stephanie Rusch. He's actually been sweet to her—taking her out, flowers, the whole bit. I know his reputation, but he's young, you know. I don't think he belongs on the force, but for the most part, he's just a confused kid, trying to fill Daddy's shoes."

Hailey nodded. "My husband's sometimes guilty of the same. Does Stephanie know?"

"About the prints, you mean?" Sydney nodded. "She got the match and I had to pull her. Have them double-checked. I've got her on an outside case now. The whole thing is conflict of interest."

"Christ, what a nightmare."

Hailey nodded. "I'm sorry too, Sydney."

Jamie started to stand. "I shouldn't be here. I'm making it harder, I'm sure."

Sydney shook her head. "Don't go. It's fine. I'll get through it." She touched Jamie's arm. "Stay."

Hailey nodded.

Jamie sat.

Sydney straightened. "We found dozens of partials, but Scanlan's was clean—on the dash above the glove—so it's recent—at least relatively."

"And outside?" Hailey prompted.

"Outside we've got Wallace again—"

"The rookie," Hailey said.

Sydney nodded, still reading. "Devlin, Worley, two unknowns, and an officer named Daniels. Know him?"

Hailey's expression narrowed, her brow furrowed. "Daniels?"

Jamie nodded. "I heard he was there. I figured it was because she was a cop, but I wouldn't have expected him to touch the car. Kind of a rookie mistake for IA."

Hailey turned to Jamie, shook her head. "Daniels was at the scene?"

"Yeah. You're surprised."

Anger flashed across Hailey's expression. "I was told no one was there before me."

Jamie looked back at Hailey. "You okay?"

Hailey nodded stiffly. "Just sick of bureaucratic BS."

Jamie watched her, wondering what she wasn't saying.

"What else?" Hailey asked.

"The sex kit. We've got positive tests for saliva, semen, and we've got a half-dozen hairs."

Jamie felt her mouth drop. "She was raped?"

Sydney paused. "No signs of trauma, but she'd had intercourse."

Jamie stared. "With—" Then suddenly she didn't want to know. The band around her ribs tightened and she couldn't seem to draw a breath. "It's okay. I don't need—"

Hailey touched her arm. "Tim told us, Jamie."

Her stomach contracted like she'd been hit. She didn't know they'd slept together that day. Tim said he'd arrived and they'd had a fight. She shook her head, felt sick. He'd lied. Stupid. Of course he'd lied.

"Jamie, are you—"

Just then, a pager began to beep. Both inspectors grabbed their belts.

"It's me," Jamie said, thankful for the interruption. She stood and excused herself, read the number off the pager as she pulled out her cell phone and stumbled into the hall.

Hailey said something, but Jamie kept moving.

She had been so focused on clearing Tim, so concerned that they would do everything to frame Tim in an effort to solve the case quickly. The more pressure there was to solve it, the easier it would be to let Worley hang in the noose. Maybe, though, the noose was exactly where he belonged. Damn him.

Trembling, Jamie punched the number into her cell phone, hit send.

"Dispatch," came the response.

"This is Jamie Vail. I just got paged to this number."

"We received a call from the Marin County sheriff's department. A neighbor called on a break-in at 129 Payne Road. I'll patch you through to the responding officer now."

Shit. That was her house.

"Officer Arguello here."

"This is Inspector Vail. I'm the owner of 129 Payne. You have an intruder there?"

"Guy broke a window over the kitchen sink to get in. Dog went crazy, so the neighbor called us. We caught your perp. He's wasted drunk and swears he knows you."

Could Tim have made it from the courthouse that quickly? Why go to her house? "I don't think so."

The officer laughed. "Yeah, they all say they know you when they get busted."

"You have an ID on him?"

"Yeah." He paused. "Name is Tony Galen."

Jamie clamped her eyes shut.

"You know him, Inspector?"

"Yeah, I know him."

"We've got him at the station. You want to come pick him up?"

"I'll be there in an hour."

"We'll try to get some coffee in him."

Jamie hung up the phone and headed for the door. Tony Galen. Jesus Christ. Tony and she had grown up together. Their fathers had been best friends, partners on the job, and shared a duplex. When their wives died, they were widowers together. Tony was the closest thing she had to a brother.

She hit end and looked down to see she had a voice mail.

"It's Ben," her captain's voice said. "I'll give you another twenty-four hours surveillance. Let's hope we get something."

She sighed. As she erased the message, the phone began to vibrate in her hand.

"Vail."

"It's Ed Goldman." His voice was quiet and she heard the disappointment in his voice. It wasn't good news. "What happened?"

"Tim didn't make bail."

Jamie rushed out the front door, felt the sun bright in her eyes. "What do you do now?"

"We appeal. In the meantime, the police have warrants for his house and car."

She didn't speak.

"I'll call you later."

For a moment, she just stood there, let the sun warm her face.

What else could go wrong?

# 14

Tony Galen pressed his forehead against the scarred table in the interview room. The plastic surface was cool, and he let his eyes fall closed again, trying to shut out the pain in his head and throat.

The room reeked of bad coffee and stale cigarettes, and under that he smelled the sharp odor of liquor oozing out of pores—his. It had been whiskey going in, but he thought it all smelled like gin coming out. Like rotting limes. He opened his lips, tried not to swallow. He held an arm against the rumbling in his stomach, fought the urge to throw up.

They'd tried to get him to eat something, but he couldn't. The room had been spinning when he'd first come in, and now that it had stopped, he wished it would start again. At least then his head hadn't been pounding.

He drank five—or was it six—cups of burned coffee in the hopes that it would start to mix with the alcohol in his blood and bring him down enough to stop the nausea. Again, no luck. That was the story of his life—no fucking luck.

He turned his head sideways and felt the burn of the wound on his neck. The lacerations had scabbed over and healed, but with each turn of his head, he felt little stings in the old wounds. The collar of his shirt was carefully closed over his scar. He had enough to answer for. He didn't need to go into that. It was bad enough to have to explain what had happened to his hand. He kept it carefully hidden under the table now.

He had spent four months locked up for that. He didn't need to pay any more for his mistakes.

Before that, he'd been in twelve states in the eight months since Deborah had kicked him out. He hadn't known anyone along the way. He'd worked his way from state to state, if you could call it working. He'd bummed rides and cigarettes and worked a day here and a day there. Over three fucking years since Mick had died. No. Since he'd killed Mick.

Almost that long since his father had died of a broken heart. "I can't believe my Mick's gone," he'd said, sitting in that sterile room, looking like warm death. The room was pungent with the smells of bleach and urine. Mixed in was the chalky scent of Maalox.

His dad had died a week and a half later, before Tony had made it back to see him again.

He heard the door open and assumed it was another cop with more coffee. It was because of Jamie. He knew if Jamie weren't on her way right now, he'd be behind bars and no one would give a shit that his head was ready to explode. There would be no coffee, no niceties. That's what knowing a local cop did for you.

"You want to tell me what the fuck I'm doing here?"

Tony raised his head and looked at Jamie Vail. He blinked, which felt like hammering his head with his fist. Bluish circles shadowed her eyes. Tired. How long since he'd seen her? They'd been like siblings growing up—Jamie, Tony, his brother, Mick. Now, Jamie was all the family he had left.

"You hear about Mick?"

She nodded.

"And Dad?"

She nodded again. "I'm sorry."

"Shit happens," he said.

"Is that your excuse for my window?"

Their eyes met and she shook her head. Her shoulders dropped. "I didn't mean it like that. The window doesn't matter. Shit, none of it matters."

He lifted himself up. "I knew what you meant."

She looked around, seemed anxious to be released from the discussion of the dead people in their lives.

"You got your hair cut. It was longer before."

She looked back and touched her hair. "I haven't seen you in nearly a decade. It's about the same. I haven't had it done in forever."

"If it was recent, I was going to suggest you ask for a refund."

"Asshole," she said, a smile tugging at her lips. It looked foreign on her face.

More awkward silence followed.

She glanced around the room, pulled out a chair, and sat. "Why did I come here again?"

"To pick me up?"

"You ever think of calling first?"

"Breaking the window was so much easier. Plus, I didn't think you had a phone."

She stood, motioned to him. "Let's go."

He followed. Jamie was the closest thing he had to family now. The rest of them were gone. Thanks to Tony.

Without speaking, Jamie filled out the paperwork, retrieved what was left of his worldly possessions from the police and handed the manila envelope to him, raising an eyebrow at the scar on his hand. Still, she never asked. That was Jamie. Don't ask, don't tell. It was the way they were raised.

When they got to the car, she unlocked it and they both got in. "Where to?"

He leaned back. "Home?"

"And where is that?"

"I thought you'd know how to get there. The cops

drove me here and I was kind of drunk when the cabbie dropped me off."

Jamie pulled a cigarette out and lit it. He took one, too. They smoked in silence, the car unmoving until she finally said, "What are you doing here?"

It was the question that burned in his mind, too. Why had he come? Because there was no one else. Because he needed a job, a life, and he could no longer have one in New York.

Just then, her phone rang. "Vail."

On the other end of the phone, he heard a male voice. It sounded like cartoon talk. Jamie nodded and smoked. She glanced over at him and he knew exactly what was going on—she was checking on him, his past. When she hung up, she turned to him.

"America's KESWICK?" she asked.

He looked out the window, blew smoke and watched it curl up against the glass and roll back at him like a gray wave. Instead of talking, she ran records. How the hell had they gotten so fucked up?

"It's a residential addiction recovery center in Whiting, New Jersey."

She nodded. "Yeah, I got the little commercial on KESWICK. One hundred and twenty days for men eighteen and older. Also a Christian conference and retreat center."

"I didn't find Christ, if that's what you're asking."

"No, Tony. I want to know why you're drinking again."

Shit, he wanted to know why, too. And not just to that. Why was Mick dead? Why was he alive? Why had he come? Why had he lost his job in the first place? Why had he failed to quit the bottle? Why wasn't he the one to take the South Tower? Why, why, why. He blew out his breath. "I don't know."

"So you came here? I'm the backup to KES-WICK?" She shook her head. "I don't think that's a good plan."

"I need a place to stay for a while."

She reached over and touched his collar.

He grabbed her hand.

"I want to see."

"No."

"Let me see."

He finished his cigarette and looked over at her. Their eyes never quite met. There was too much to say if they finally had to confess it all. Tony unbuttoned his top button. His hands shook. He needed a drink. The spinning and pounding had finally stopped and now he was shaking. Shit, he'd liked the spinning better.

He pulled the collar open and let her look.

She leaned forward but didn't touch. They never touched, never had, like it might be contagious. And no one needed to catch what he had.

"What happened?"

He said nothing, feeling the warmth of their bodies and the cigarettes fill the car. He touched the back of his hand to the window, wishing he were out there instead.

"You can't do that in my house," she said. "I'll take you there if you promise."

Promise. How many promises had he made and broken?

He nodded.

"No. Look at me and swear it. Swear on something that matters. Swear on Lana's grave."

Lana. Beautiful Lana. Why did the one person who had mattered most leave first? He'd never even known his mother. Not as a person, not really. She'd been like a beautiful spirit. He could remember her laugh and the smell of her hair. He remembered the Irish prayer she used to say before putting him to bed. He could still hear her whispery voice.

*May the raindrops fall lightly on your brow*
*May the soft winds freshen your spirit*

*May the sunshine brighten your heart*
*May the burdens of the day rest lightly upon you*
*And may God enfold you in the mantle of His love.*

Jesus, may the burdens of the day rest lightly. May they rest lightly. They'd stopped resting lightly after Lana. Or maybe they never had. And there'd been no mantle of love for Tony. God had taken Lana and forgotten the rest of them.

He told himself that she was watching. All these years, watching. What did she think of him now? She must have been so ashamed.

"Swear."

He pulled his collar from Jamie's grip. "I swear on Lana's grave. And on Mick's. And Dad's. Your mom's." He looked over at her. "I miss anyone?"

"Shit." Jamie stubbed out her cigarette.

"Can we go now?"

"Why did you do it?"

"Why does anyone do it?"

"How did you stop it?"

He ran a finger over the scar on his hand, took the last drag of his cigarette, and then put it out in the overflowing ashtray. He couldn't do anything right. That was the real reason—not school, not be a kid, a son, a brother, fireman, husband—not even at the end.

Jamie gave up on an answer and started the car, revved the engine, and drove out of the police station lot.

He'd had the rope, the stool, but he'd had to hold that knife just in case. He'd been almost gone. The pressure in his eyes had been so strong, he couldn't see. But the rope hadn't been quite strong enough. And he'd been weak.

And at the last moment, he'd chickened out and cut it. The rope had split and the knife had sliced right into his hand.

There it was. He couldn't even kill himself right.

# 15

Jamie had barely pulled into her garage when her cell phone rang. "Vail."

"I've got something you'll want to see."

It took her a minute to place the caller. She finally recognized the crime tech's voice. "Roger?"

"Yeah, it's me. Can you come into the lab?"

She glanced at Tony. "Uh—"

"It's big."

"Can you tell me?"

"You've got to see it."

"Okay. I'll be there in an hour." She shut her phone and looked at Tony. Then, without hesitating, she backed the car out of the driveway.

"Where are we going?"

"Station. Something's come up."

"Can't I stay here? I need some aspirin."

"They'll have some there."

"You don't trust me long enough to go to work and back? I'm not a puppy you can just drag along."

Jamie measured her breath. "You came to me, Tony. Not the other way around. My turf, my rules."

They spoke little on the way to the station. Jamie turned the music up to fill the space though it shouldn't have bothered her. In the Brooklyn duplex where they'd grown up, long silences were as common as honking horns on the streets below.

At Hunters Point, she went straight to the lab. Tony shuffled behind. When she walked in, though, Roger wasn't there.

"He left you that," Sydney said, pointing to a microscope.

She crossed to it and setting her bag down, peered in. She had seen enough to identify the sample. It was semen without DNA. "I already saw this."

Sydney shook her head. "No. We just finished this one."

"It's not Osbourne?"

"No. Devlin."

Jamie felt her mouth drop. "Devlin? I thought she had sex with Tim." As soon as the words were out, she felt Tony's stare. Her cheeks flushed. She ignored it.

Sydney nodded. "She did. First Worley and then another guy."

Jamie whistled. "A guy with no swimmers?"

"Right."

"Just like my serial." Jamie was tracking a serial rapist with no sperm in his semen. She didn't like the coincidence.

"Maybe, but we're just doing an initial workup. We don't have the technology to do much with it."

Jamie frowned. "Because there were two samples, you mean?"

"Right. We're not even sure if the samples can be individually identified. This is just something Roger tried."

Jamie felt her pulse run a little quicker. "Has anyone talked to Hailey Wyatt?" She glanced around. "And where's Roger?"

"He went back to the evidence storage locker for something else."

Just then, the door opened and Roger entered carrying a cardboard file box. He set it down on the table and began rummaging through it.

Jamie waited, trusting he'd tell her what was going

on when he found what he needed. In her opinion, Roger Sampers should have been the head of CSU. His reports were as meticulous as any she'd ever seen. He was the one people turned to for help in solving particularly complex evidence dilemmas. She was sure that the reason he wasn't in charge had to do with his appearance.

Roger had alopecia universalis, which left him completely hairless. Not just bald, but without hair on his arms or legs or face. No eyebrows, no eyelashes. She had always wondered if that was why he'd decided on CSU. He was a model employee—one who never left a trace of hair behind at a scene. But because he had no eyelashes, he blinked three or four times as often as someone with them. Some people found it distracting to talk to him.

Just then, he pulled a manila folder out of the box. "Got it."

Jamie stepped forward. "What have you got?"

Roger pulled on gloves and emptied a series of clear plastic cards onto the table. They were fingerprint cards. Each one had a black smudged print in the center of the plastic, one that had been lifted from the scene. "These are the prints from Devlin's office that we haven't run yet." He glanced up, blinked twice. "We had nearly a hundred and it's a time-consuming process." He paused, looked over at the microscope. "You heard about the semen sample?"

"Just like Osbourne."

"Well, not exactly. Since there were two samples, it's going to take us longer to be sure we've got them separate. In the end, we may not be able to. But I ran some initial tests and it looks like one of the samples may not have any DNA. I'm not anywhere near certain, but when I saw that, I went back and looked at the scene a little more closely."

He flipped through a few cards until he found what he wanted. "I was in charge of processing the evidence

from the department and Devlin's office. We focused
on running the prints inside her office, but there was
one on the outside that struck me." He shook the
plastic card in his hand. "Let's check it out."

He crossed the room to a table with a gray computer and sat down in front of it. He slid the clear
card into a reader slot. He typed a few commands and
then the computer began running the print for a
match. Roger drummed his fingers on the table as he
waited. "Could take a few minutes."

"Where did this print come from, Roger?"

He nodded and stood. "I'll show you." He returned
to the file box and pulled a stack of eight-by-ten photos from a manila folder. He flipped through ten or
twelve and then slid one out of the stack.

Jamie stared at a photo of the sign outside the
Crimes Against Persons Department where Devlin
was an inspector. The Crimes Against Persons Unit,
or CAP, used to be called General Works. CAP acted
as a catch-all for crimes that couldn't be divided into
the other personal crimes units like Homicide, Rob-
bery and Sexual Assault. It also helped with other
departments' overflow, of which there was always
plenty.

The department's sign was a generic, black plastic
plate base with individual nameplates glued on top of
it. The plate was worn and scratched and dried glue
was evident where names had been removed or
replaced.

The first plate read the captain's name, Morris
Travis. Below his, each inspector had his or her own
plate. They were listed alphabetically. Devlin's name
came first. Roger flipped to another photo. This one
showed a closeup of Devlin's plate. It was taken at
an angle and the flash had caught a smudge between
"Natasha" and "Devlin."

"See that?"

Jamie nodded. "It's a print."

Roger smiled. "A perfect right index."

Just then, the machine beeped.

"Let's see whose it is."

Jamie followed, Roger's enthusiasm rubbing off on her. Even Tony came along.

Roger dropped into the chair and typed quickly. When he hit enter, a new screen appeared.

"Holy shit, yeah?" Roger said.

"Yeah," Jamie agreed. Holy fucking shit.

At the very top, in bold yellow letters on a black background was the name Michael A. Marchek.

# 16

Jamie arrived at Michael Marchek's apartment with Roger and his team. Tony had opted to wait in the car. The idea of searching a rapist's house hadn't appealed. Jamie didn't blame him. She remembered hangovers like the one Tony had now.

Hailey arrived a few minutes behind them. She'd stopped off at the courthouse for the signed warrant. Marchek lived in a garage that had been converted into an apartment in the area of San Francisco where the Mission and Potrero districts met. The only window in the apartment was a rectangle seven feet off the ground. Twelve square feet of sunlight that faced Highway 101 just a half block over. At least the freeway managed to drown out some of the drunken neighbors.

Despite the unfortunate apartment, Marchek maintained the epitome of a pristine home. Jamie had been here once before, but Hailey led the pack this time. According to surveillance, Marchek was at work. Even so, a patrol officer rang the bell and when there was no answer, he used a crowbar to break the lock. The wood buckled against the steel and the door tumbled open. Two officers went in first and declared it clear before anyone else entered.

Roger walked through first. Leaving his bag at the door, he surveyed each room, ceiling to floor. He made notes on a clipboard and then stepped outside to address the two techs who had come with him.

"We'll run the light first." He pulled out a small black satchel with the words "Mini CrimeScope" printed in bright green along the side. The tech shut off the overhead lights while Roger donned a pair of red plastic glasses and lifted the small black box from the bag. The other tech handed Jamie and Hailey each booties to cover their shoes and a pair of red shades. Roger flipped on the machine, which purred softly, as he directed the beam across the floor and up the walls. Fingerprints glowed blue against white paint that now looked pink through her glasses. Each time some evidence was located, the tech marked it with a numbered yellow sticker. The process took forty minutes. Fingerprints were all they found.

When he was done, they split up. Roger directed his first tech to run the vacuum. "Pick up anything he's left. Judging from the light source, there's not much. Alex, you take the bathroom and closets." He paused. "Take your time with those. If we're going to find something, it'll be there. Martin." He pointed to a shallow rubber tray at the door. "Drain the bleach solution in that bin and let's take it with us. We might get some hair or something out of there. I'll collect the prints.

"Once we're done, we'll tackle the clothes. Specifically, we're looking for a shirt that might match the button we found in Devlin's office. Watch where you're walking until the floors are clear." Roger turned to Hailey and Jamie. "Have at it, ladies."

Jamie pulled a pair of rubber gloves from her coat pocket. Snapping them on, she started through Marchek's house, praying they'd nail this slippery son of a bitch.

The apartment was a studio. A thin off-white cotton curtain separated the sleeping area from a small living space. Hailey passed through to Marchek's bed, so

Jamie tackled the living room. One wall was covered with built-in bookshelves. They looked recently painted, but there wasn't a single book. Instead, model airplanes lined each shelf.

Each depicted a different model of plane though they all looked circa World War II. Each plane was painted with precision and Jamie thought Marchek must have a steady hand. She moved slowly along the wall as she studied the models. She lifted up several and turned them in her hands. There were a few new ones, but she thought most were the same as they'd been before. She did notice, though, that Marchek dusted them. There were no cobwebs between their wings, no dust on their noses.

She scanned the rest of the bookshelves, walked her fingers along the trim in search of anything hidden. Found nothing. Turning to his hobby table, Jamie sat in the small plastic-backed chair and surveyed the newest model. The plane was half built, unpainted. The rounded body sat on a small wood block that was carved out in the middle to hold the plane upright. The tools were put away. The table had been cleaned off. Jamie dropped to her knees and peered up at the underside of the table. Nothing.

Next she opened Marchek's tool chest. She removed the top tray and set it in her lap. Slowly, she lifted each tool, studied it, and set it on the table. She knew Marchek would be furious that someone had pawed through his precisely organized tools. The image offered a moment of satisfaction.

She lifted a tool that looked like it belonged to a dentist. It was the width and length of a pencil with a sharp, curved hook on one end. She suspected it was for carving out tiny grooves. Jamie imagined the mark on Emily Osbourne's thigh and thought it was the perfect size for that, too. She pulled an evidence bag from her pocket and dropped the tool inside.

"Found something," one of the techs called out.

Jamie set the tools down and walked into the bathroom.

Hailey stood at the door. "What is it?"

The tech grinned. "This bathroom outlet is loose." He drew out a master lock key. "Found this inside."

"Good work," Hailey said.

Jamie nodded. "Now we just need to find out what it fits to."

"Some storage facility, maybe," Roger suggested.

"Is there anything in the building?" Hailey asked.

Jamie spoke up. "No storage here, but we can do a search of sites in the area. He doesn't have a car that we know of, so he can't be going far."

"It's a step in the right direction. Thanks, Alex."

Alex blushed at Hailey's attention and Jamie returned to the tool kit. Nothing else stood out. She went through the chest twice before moving on.

Hailey had continued to the closet, so Jamie took Marchek's kitchenette. The room was spotless. The floor was cracked linoleum with a couple of mismatched pieces, but it gleamed of a recent waxing. She studied the mismatched linoleum. Thinking she might find something, she tried unsuccessfully to pry them loose.

Next she turned to the cabinets. The first two cupboards she opened were empty. The third contained perfectly stacked cans of corn, black and kidney beans, chilis and soups—mostly chicken noodle. His refrigerator held an almost full gallon of one percent milk and three nonalcoholic beers. He had three glasses, three plates, two bowls, and one set of silverware. It was all clean and stacked beside the cans. A roll of paper towels was the only thing out on the counter. The freezer was empty. Not even ice.

Under the sink, Jamie found a scrub brush, a small container of Dove dishwashing soap, and a single pot with no lid. It was almost as though Marchek kept a full residence somewhere else and the thought was terrifying.

Jamie dragged the chair from Marchek's modeling table into the kitchen. Standing on it, she searched the empty cabinets. She had reached the last one when Hailey walked in.

"Any luck?"

"Nothing. You?"

"No. This place is amazing. There are no papers, no checkbooks, nothing." She looked around. "How does this guy live?"

"Like a criminal."

"Does he have a bank account?"

"He does. We checked it. Nothing unusual. Wells Fargo, few hundred dollars in it. Deposits his paycheck, all withdrawals are in cash. No credit cards. Pays rent in cash. Buys his models and very little else."

Hailey glanced into the cabinets. "I see that. What about utilities?"

"He's got a deal with the manager. They're included in the rent."

"So if he's got a rental space, it's going to be hard to trace."

"Damn near impossible." Jamie stepped down from the chair, grabbing the edge of the sink as she did. The faux panel on the front of the sink seemed to shift as she came down. She stared at it. A small hole where a knob had been was empty. Her sink was the same way. It was just a panel made to look like a drawer. No drawer could fit there because of the sink. Still, she ran her hand across it, frowned. Using her fingernails, she pried the side. It didn't budge.

She dropped to her knees and stuck her head under the sink. Glancing up, she could see a small cupboard.

"What is it?"

"I think this thing opens." Using Marchek's knife,

Jamie pried at the edge until a small triangular-shaped drawer fell open.

Inside were several pieces of paper and a small digital camera.

Hailey lifted the camera. "Nice work, Vail."

Jamie picked up the papers by a corner. One was Marchek's birth certificate and the other was a list of model airplanes with little check marks next to the first twenty or so. "Nothing here. What've you got?"

"Holy shit."

Jamie looked over as Hailey stared at a small screen on the back of the camera. The screen was small and dark and Jamie squinted at the image of a woman getting out of a dark car. Behind her, there might have been another person, but Jamie couldn't tell. She could see that something hung from the rearview mirror. The light from the car shined through it, creating little rainbows in the photo.

Jamie focused back on the woman until the image cleared in her mind. "Shit. That's—"

"Devlin," Hailey said.

Both women fell silent.

# 17

Hailey had spent the afternoon in the lab with Roger. There was only one photograph of Natasha on Marchek's camera, and they'd worked for two hours to try to clarify the image. They had confirmed the photo was of Natasha, but Hailey had known that immediately. In her hand, Natasha held the small, engraved trophy that she had received for her training efforts. The presence of the plaque confirmed that the photo was taken the night of the awards banquet—the same night Natasha was killed.

The car and the man in the background were still unidentifiable. Hailey had even called in the rookie Mackenzie Wallace in hopes she might have recognized the car from that morning. But no luck. Hailey's captain had denied her request to bring Marchek in again. Taking a photograph of someone was not illegal. Until they had some evidence, he stayed a free man. Roger was turning his attention to the mold he'd made of Tim Worley's head injury with the hopes that it might lead them somewhere.

Hailey and Jamie Vail had also drafted a memo to go out to the division captains in an attempt to compile a list of men Natasha was recently involved with. She knew it was going to be hard for everyone. The case demanded truthful disclosure, but some of those men were married. They weren't going to want to come forward and admit to infidelity much less infidelity with a woman who had been murdered. And more public embarrassment was the last thing the department needed. Plus, from what she knew of Natasha, it was going to be a lengthy list.

Exhausted from the day, Hailey had almost considered skipping the rookie club dinner tonight. But she'd convinced Jamie to go and she wasn't going to give her an excuse to miss another one. Hailey was clearing the piles from her desk in preparation for leaving when Buck walked into the department. He'd never done that before, and seeing him gave her an uncomfortable start.

"I'd like to discuss the Devlin case with you if you've got a minute." He nodded to the small, windowless conference room in the corner of the department.

She considered denying him but decided against it. Refusing IA was on level with refusing a captain. It would garner suspicion. Bruce knew that and she was certain he'd used it to his advantage. "Unfortunately, I've got only a couple of minutes. Let me get the file."

He waited while she found the binder she'd started on Natasha's murder and followed him into the conference room.

He let her pass and shut the door behind her, leaned against it. "You've been ignoring me."

She crossed her arms. "You were there that morning—at her murder scene. I found out from Jamie Vail. You said you didn't know anything about it. Why didn't you tell me?" She put her hand up, lowered her voice to a whisper. "I don't even care now. I don't want to talk about this now. I'm on my way out."

"Going home?"

She shook her head. "Rookie club dinner."

"Can we have a drink after?"

She closed her eyes, shook her head. "I don't think so." She walked to the door.

He took her arm, pulled her close.

She let him hold her for a moment, then pulled gently back. "I can't have you lie to me, Bruce. There's too much at stake. I won't let you ruin my career."

"You think that's what I was doing?"

She shrugged. "It doesn't matter if that was the intention. It can't happen again."

With that, she pulled the door open and walked back into the department.

Jamie Vail stood propped against Hailey's desk. She eyed Hailey, then Bruce.

Hailey forced a smile. "You ready?"

"Ready but not excited."

Hailey nodded. She knew Jamie hadn't been to a rookie club dinner since Natasha and Tim.

"Thanks for the update," Bruce said.

Hailey waved as he left, her chest tight with Jamie's eye on them. "No problem. I'll follow up tomorrow."

Jamie said nothing while Hailey packed up her stuff and locked her desk.

"Everything okay?" Jamie asked when they were in the hall.

She didn't trust herself to meet Jamie's gaze. "Same old bullshit."

Jamie nodded, said nothing else. Hailey noticed she wore makeup now. The dark circles under her eyes looked lighter than they had only a few hours earlier at Marchek's. A dusting of blush added depth to her cheeks and a subtle shimmer shone on her lips. When she glanced up, Hailey saw even her eyes seemed brighter.

Outside, the rain was more like heavy mist. Hailey pulled on her trench coat, tied the belt. She wished she'd brought a hat. The wave in her hair went nuts with moisture. "You hear anything from the DA on Marchek?" She still held out that they would find a way to put him behind bars, despite how little evidence they had.

Jamie shook her head. "Captain told me he didn't think it was enough. Circumstantial at best. Doesn't prove Marchek was with Devlin at the time of death. Doesn't prove he'd ever even interacted with her."

"I got the same from Marshall."

She glanced over. "We can't find a speck of evidence that Marchek was in her office. His print on the department sign isn't enough without something linking him to the crimes. And we have nothing on Osbourne, either. He's immaculate, but he's got to have his stuff somewhere."

Hailey nodded. "I put a call in to get a list of the local storage units so we can disseminate a photo."

Jamie didn't respond.

Hailey thought justice sometimes moved way too slow for her liking.

"You still meet at Tommy's?" Jamie asked, pulling up the hood on her windbreaker.

"Yep."

"Still drink well margaritas?"

Hailey smiled. "Not much has changed."

"Everything has changed," Jamie said, sounding almost breathless.

Hailey nodded. "That, too."

The ride was quiet. Hailey always looked forward to this night, to the combination of these women. Most were intensely passionate thinkers, and the dinners reminded her how the police department's struggle against crime brought out the strongest will in people.

But it wasn't an especially happy bunch, either. Most of them had dealt with great trauma in their lives—personal as well as professional. Divorce, alcoholism, and suicide were rampant among police officers, and the women were not immune.

Hailey acknowledged that she was among the luckiest of them for the stability of her home life. And for the fact that she had an existence completely separate from police work. Many officers married other officers, which compounded the difficulties of the job. Escaping work became almost impossible. But she knew the communal spirit of two people in the same business. With Bruce and John, she had both. It was perfect. She thought about Bruce, wondered what she'd do, knew she'd try to make it work. She wasn't ready to let go. She wished she were.

These women should have been enough. The rookie club served the same purpose as a professional organization. There were other professions where like-minded people sought out the company of those in their same situation—doctors, lawyers, artists, writers. Those situations didn't match theirs.

Maybe the doctors were closest. They, too, faced issues surrounding the delicacy with which questions of life and death were handled. With cops, it was the most extreme stresses that came out of nowhere, where split-second decisions had to be made and carried out and then defended in months upon months of follow-up investigation. Some lasted years. Cases and cop decisions, especially bad ones, were discussed for decades.

And somehow, it always felt like it was the women against them—the brass, the chief's office, the men. It was easier to divide into groups and sort each other out, trust only who you had to, speak freely only in that company because you really never knew who would be called to speak against you until it happened. In those situations where things went sour, cops were frequently called to testify against their own partners—the very people to whom they'd entrusted their lives. When it happened, neither officer had any choice in the matter.

For Hailey, the rookie club had always been the obvious group from which to choose the most trustworthy candidates. And the chances were always good that, because there were so few women and so many men, those who were called against her would be male. Therefore, the ones to confide in should be female.

The rookie club had been in existence for several years before Hailey joined the force. She'd been somewhat surprised that it was still around. Things like that had a tendency to lose steam after a while. But somehow the word about a woman band of law enforcement officers kept a steady stream of new members.

Her first rookie club dinner, Hailey had come with Shelby Tate, now an assistant medical examiner. Hailey had been a rookie with her first DB, a hell of a floater case. Shelby had been brand-new in the medical examiner's office. Neither had fared all that well that day. When the autopsy was over, they'd agreed to shower twice and get a drink. They'd ended up at the rookie club dinner. Tonight Hailey had invited the rookie, Mackenzie Wallace, to join them.

Hailey parked a block from the restaurant, half in the red and put the visor down. She and Jamie ran into Mackenzie halfway down the block.

Mackenzie turned to Jamie. "How's Emily Osbourne doing?"

"She'll live."

Hailey watched Mackenzie bristle at Jamie's tone. It was the kind of response she should probably get used to in this business. Still, Hailey wished Jamie had softened it a little.

There was a silence amongst the three, some sort of quiet moment for those who wouldn't survive and for the survivors who would never be the same. She knew why Jamie didn't say, "She's okay." She wasn't.

Chances were, even when the physical wounds were long healed, the emotional ones would remain. Their job was to help the victims survive the physical wounds long enough to get a chance to try to heal the emotional ones. She knew there were casualties in that process like anywhere else.

"You think Marchek is responsible?" Mackenzie asked.

Jamie's eyes hardened. "I do."

"You think we'll get him?"

"He'll make a mistake eventually. They always do." The words came out like a pep talk and Hailey felt certain Jamie aimed it at herself. The belief that the system worked, that the perpetrators would be punished for their crimes, was the only thing that kept them in this job. Otherwise, the fight wasn't nearly worth the tremendous effort, the low pay, the long hours, and the constant evidence of human cruelty that were their daily existence.

After seeing the photograph of Natasha at Marchek's house, though, Hailey wondered if there would be a higher toll before Marchek was stopped. She tried to set the thought aside as she walked through the doors of Tommy's. The restaurant was already packed as they weaved through the throng of Friday-night bar goers.

Mackenzie, who had the advantage of six extra inches, pointed to a spot by the far window. "They're over there."

Mackenzie and Hailey arrived at a table where five women were already seated. It was a table of very powerful women. Most were nearly forty, a few older. They'd been on the force long enough to be jaded, but they were still there, braving the fight. As Hailey looked around the table, she saw the marks of battle in their lined faces. Cameron Cruz had a greenish bruise on one side of her neck that Hailey suspected was probably from some drill involving the large guns she wielded in her job as a sharpshooter.

Her arms raised as though she were aiming a rifle, she told the story. Shelby Tate and Linda James were attentive as Cameron recounted some small victory.

Sydney Blanchard sat next to Jess Campbell from INS. Jess looked heavier than the last time Hailey saw her. Her eyes red. She clasped an empty beer glass in two hands.

Hailey introduced Mackenzie just as the waitress came by for drink orders. Mackenzie ordered a Rolling Rock and Jess ordered another draft, sliding her empty pint glass toward the waitress.

"Margarita," Hailey said.

Sydney pushed an empty glass toward her, pointing to the half-full pitcher on the table.

Over the years, Hailey had seen the rookie club change and grow, shrink and almost fall apart. A few times there were only three or four of them. It had been six months or so since she'd seen Jess Campbell, and Jess looked worse for the wear. Her shuttered gaze also suggested she might be on more than her second beer.

Jamie appeared with a glass of what looked like Coke in one hand. She raised her hand and said hello. She looked back over her shoulder, brow furrowed.

Hailey leaned in. "Everything okay?"

Jamie glanced at her, then back into the crowd. "I thought I saw someone."

Hailey narrowed her gaze. "Who?"

"I'm sure it's nothing," Jamie said, shrugging her shoulders in a way that looked more like a shudder than a casual motion.

When the waitress had delivered new drinks, Jamie was the first to raise her glass. "To Natasha Devlin."

All eyes were on her.

"She didn't deserve that kind of an ending."

Glasses raised, clinked.

"First one down," Jess said.

Hailey nodded. Christ. A dead cop.

A crowd in the far corner roared, their laughs like distant applause erupting. The women officers were silent.

"I always thought if we lost one, it would be in uniform, you know," Jess said. She shook her head, took a big swallow of beer.

Hailey searched for a way to break the silence, to give Natasha the kind of send-off she would have appreciated. Or at least to ease the tension.

Cameron Cruz spoke up first. "Did you guys hear about the case where Devlin went undercover?"

"As a prostitute, right?" Linda James asked.

Cameron nodded. "Man, she had ten cops drooling all over her. And the perp didn't even put up a fight. He would've followed her all the way into a jail cell."

They laughed.

"She actually got a date that night, right?"

"No way. With a john?"

Cameron laughed. "No, another cop."

Linda nodded. "Right. It was—"

"Steve Stilwell," Jess chimed in.

Linda shook her head. "Right. God, he was in love with her. Used to show up at roll call with a different-colored rose each day."

"The guys called him Lovewell."

"That lasted—what—a week?"

Cameron nodded. "Three days, I think. Then she was on to Charlie Parker."

Linda nodded. "She collected phone numbers like lint."

"She loved the attention," Cameron agreed. "She never settled down."

Linda shook her head. "Ten years and I swear she had a new guy every time I saw her. She broke more hearts than Elvis."

"Good thing it's a big department," Cameron added. "I wonder why she never settled down. Seems like she could have picked her man."

Hailey glanced at Jamie. She was looking over her shoulder again. Hailey cast a glance into the crowd. No one stood out. Faces swam together. How many men in that room had raped a girl? More than two, she'd bet. Killed? One, maybe. Impossible to say. It would certainly make the job easier if they were branded like cattle.

Hailey thought about the comment Jamie had made about Emily Osbourne. She would live. Being okay was a totally different hurdle.

Hailey considered her own mother, those relationships that lasted only a week, sometimes just one night. What had made her mother run through men like that? Was that why Hailey couldn't love only one man? She sipped her margarita, let the salt burn her lips. God, it was complicated.

"Did you have to do the next-of-kin notification?" Mackenzie asked, her beer half drained.

Hailey nodded. "I met her parents. And a brother."

"God, I would hate that part of the job," the rookie said.

She thought of Camilla and Ali, prayed she never had to hear that news. That they never had to hear it.

"Man, I hope it was a stranger killing," Jess said.

Jamie shook her head. "It wasn't."

Hailey watched her, waited.

Jamie shrugged, ran her finger through the perspiration on her glass. "This person had unforced sex with her before she was killed. Not a stranger crime."

Hailey nodded. "It was someone she knew."

"Shit," Jess said.

"You think it was an officer?" Linda asked.

Hailey shrugged. "It doesn't seem smart to have sex with a woman and then kill her. The timing suggests that's how it went down."

"A crime of passion," Cameron said.

Hailey nodded. "And from what we know, he used something from the scene to kill her."

Jamie smiled from one corner of her mouth. "Yeah. From experience, I'd say it's much easier just to pull a gun and start shooting."

The table erupted in laughter.

Jamie shook her head. "Sorry. Couldn't resist."

Cameron turned to Hailey. "You caught it, though, eh?"

She nodded. "Lucky me."

Jess shuddered. "Damn, I hope you close it soon. Murdering a cop takes a shitload of balls."

Mackenzie jumped up, the metal chair scraping across the floor. "Holy crap."

Hailey turned to see her staring out the window, her expression frozen.

"What?"

Mackenzie pointed out into the rain.

Hailey followed her gaze, looked back. It wouldn't be the first time dinner had been interrupted by a crime in progress.

Jamie stared, too.

Then the whole table turned.

"It's Stephanie," Linda James said.

"And Scott Scanlan," someone added.

"They're dating."

A dark car was parked on the curb, the door open. Stephanie had one foot out. Scanlan could barely be seen in the shadow of the car.

Hailey saw his face appear as he leaned over to kiss Stephanie. As she moved, Hailey caught sight of something dangling between them.

Mackenzie slammed the beer bottle down with a loud thunk. The neck filled with white foam. The rookie bolted for the door, darting between tables.

"Jesus Christ," Jamie exclaimed, sliding off her chair to follow. "I see it."

"See what?" Adrenaline streamed in Hailey's belly. She jumped up to follow, the others behind her.

She reached the door, saw Scott Scanlan step out of the far side of the car. He came around and opened the door for Stephanie.

Stephanie stepped out.

Jamie turned to Mackenzie. "Can you see it?"

Mackenzie shook her head. "He's in the way."

"Scanlan," Jamie shouted. "Step to the curb."

Scanlan didn't hear, or didn't look up.

Hailey stopped beside her.

Jamie called to him again.

A group of people had spilled from the restaurant to watch.

Hailey turned to Mackenzie. The rookie stared into the car. Was there someone else? She whispered to Jamie. "Think first, okay?"

Mackenzie grabbed her arm. "Who is he?"

"The deputy chief's son."

"Damn," Mackenzie whispered.

Stephanie stepped forward, tried to interject, but Hailey cut her off with a sharp stare. "Stay out of this."

Stephanie retreated, but the crowd continued to surge like a swelling storm. This was getting out of hand.

Scanlan turned toward them.

He stared at Jamie, his face set in the grimace of a scared teenager.

"Step away from the car," Jamie repeated.

"What is this about?"

"Please."

"Who are you?" Scanlan called.

Jamie didn't seem to care. She flashed her badge. "Inspector Jamie Vail."

He didn't budge. "What do you want?"

"Please step away from the car," Jamie repeated.

He didn't move, scanned the group of women

watching him. Color rose in his cheeks and his eyes narrowed in anger. "What are you guys? Fucking Charlie's Angels?"

Hailey stayed quiet, no idea what was transpiring.

Jamie didn't smile. "Yeah, we're Charlie's Angels. Now, please come over here before I pull out my gun and shoot you."

Scanlan looked momentarily stunned as he stepped away from the car. At least no one had drawn a gun yet. Scanlan was in trouble over the burrito thing, but this wasn't going to shine well on them, either. In general, it was best not to embarrass a cop in public and this was getting to be pretty damn public.

Jamie glanced back. "Hailey, look at it."

Confused, Hailey glanced at the dark car. She felt the jolt in her gut. "It's—"

Jamie nodded. "Look at the crystal hanging from the rearview mirror."

Hailey pictured Marchek's photograph in her mind—imagined the tiny rainbows. The unidentifiable man with Natasha Devlin in the photograph—the last man with Natasha Devlin—had been the deputy chief of police's son.

"Damn."

# 18

Emily Osbourne sat awkwardly in the car as her boy-friend drove toward the city. She'd spent the past three days with her parents in New Haven and Paul had picked her up at the airport in her car. He always drove no matter whose car it was. She didn't know why that seemed weird now. Maybe because it was the first time she'd been in her car since it happened. Or maybe it was because Paul had picked her up out-side instead of coming in to baggage claim. And be-cause he'd said almost nothing so far.

When she'd gotten into the car, it had smelled like lavender. She'd almost been sick. She'd pulled the small sachet she'd gotten from their trip to the Ritz out of the glove compartment and thrown it in the trash before they'd left the airport. Still, the smell haunted her, seemed to ruin the memory of their night away.

Now she remembered the hospital room, the inter-view. Jamie Vail had worn lavender perfume. Paul had watched the whole thing in silence. He didn't want to know why she didn't like the lavender smell. He didn't want to know because he knew what it was about. It related to her— She stopped, couldn't think it.

She ran a finger across the stitches above her eye. She had a few fading bruises under her clothes, but the stitches and her black eye were the only visible signs of what had happened.

Paul turned left onto Greenwich from Franklin and found a parking space a block from her house. He parked, pulled the keys from the ignition, and handed them to her.

"How are you going to get back to work?"

He palmed his cell phone. "I'll grab a cab. I've got my car parked downtown."

She nodded, fiddling with her little silver heart keychain.

When they reached her apartment, he lifted the suitcase up the stairs.

She unlocked the door and stepped inside, Paul behind her. She gathered her mail and Paul followed her down the short hallway.

She had barely gotten the door to the apartment open when he set her bag down and stepped away. "I'll talk to you later."

"Are we ever going to talk about it?" she asked without looking up at him.

"About what?"

"About what happened."

"You are—" He stopped himself. "I don't know." He looked away. "I don't know if I can handle it."

She stepped back into the hall. Her hands trembled with anger. "If you can handle what?" Her voice echoed in the small space.

He didn't answer, but he wasn't getting off that easy. Furious, she stepped forward again. "Handle what, Paul?" she repeated, seeing the spark of fear in his eyes—or maybe it was shame.

He shook his head.

"If you can handle what happened to *me*?" She poked her chest with her index finger, her heart pounding as she waited for his response.

"I don't know how to act around you now. I don't know if you're going to fall apart on me, you know."

"No. I don't know. I might. I might cry, Paul. I might have a nightmare. I was raped, for God's sake."

He scanned the stairs above them and then glanced over his shoulder to the street.

"Did someone hear me? Are you worried what your friends will think?"

He glanced at her before his gaze skidded away again. He pulled his phone open and then closed it again. "I—"

"That's it, isn't it? It's not me. It's you. You don't want to be with me now. Is that it?"

He flipped his phone open and shut, open and shut. She reached over and grabbed it from his hand.

He frowned. "Give it to me."

"Answer the question."

"I don't know."

"You don't know if you want to be with me?"

Paul looked down at his feet, nodded.

"Say it."

He looked over his shoulder.

"Say it," she repeated.

"I don't know if I want to be with you."

"Because I was raped."

"Maybe. Maybe because of other stuff."

"Bullshit," she shouted. "We were at the fucking Ritz three weeks ago and you were talking about marriage. Now you're not sure you want to be with me? Because someone attacked me? What—you think it was my fault?"

He didn't answer. He just kept his hand extended for the phone.

"Fuck you, Paul. Fuck. You."

"Can I have my phone?"

"Sure. Here's your damn phone." She turned and pitched it as far as she could. She heard it land—crunch, crack, skid as the pieces shattered against the wall of mailboxes.

Then she turned around and marched to the door

of her apartment. Her hand shook as she pushed the door open, reached back to grab her suitcase. Paul was already out the door.

All she saw was his back, his hands pressed into his pockets as he made his way down the stairs and out onto the street.

Furious, she pulled her bag inside, slammed the door. She thought of how far she'd thrown that phone. Her father would have been proud.

She tried to smile, looked around at the empty apartment.

Then, buckling to her knees, she sobbed.

# 19

Jamie hadn't even gotten Scanlan into an interview room before Internal Affairs stepped in. It was like the asshole had some homing device that alerted Daddy and his cronies whenever he was in trouble. Jamie had insisted she be part of the interview, but they'd denied her.

So she'd done the only thing she could. She'd called Captain Jules, roused him from bed, and been told to cool her heels. Then she and Mackenzie and Hailey had sat outside for more than an hour, waiting. They'd taken turns getting coffee, talking, and half dozing in their chairs, none of them willing to leave until the interview was over.

Something had to come of this. She was pissed off that someone showed up to ride that asshole Scanlan into the sunset. She'd like to hang him from his damn toenails instead.

Jamie listened to the messages on her voice mail—both were from Tim. Though he was still in prison and mentioned his concern about whether he'd get bail in the appeal, his calls were all about Devlin's murder. She had called Goldman to tell him about the photograph found at Marchek's home. Nothing unexpected had turned up from the search of Tim's house and car. They'd found some clothes with Devlin's blood on them, but Tim had already explained that he had carried her out of the building after she was murdered.

Goldman had assured Jamie that they had enough reasonable doubt to get Tim released from prison. The appeal wouldn't fail again, especially with the other suspects that were emerging. Though skeptical, Jamie hoped Goldman could make it happen.

When Scanlan finally emerged from the interview room flanked by the two Internal Affairs investigators, he looked relieved, which was not how Jamie wanted him to look.

All three women stood.

Bruce Daniels waved them into the conference room. "Let's talk in here."

Jamie eyed Scanlan.

"Wait for us out here, Scott."

"Sure," he said.

Jamie followed Bruce into the conference room, stood against the wall.

Daniels motioned to a chair.

Hailey and Mackenzie sat. Jamie stood.

The other IA sat, too.

Daniels looked at Jamie. "You don't have enough on him."

"I've got a photograph. What were you hoping for? A confession?"

He shook his head. "You've got a picture that shows Scanlan dropping her off at the station. That's it."

Jamie clenched her jaw. "We need a blood test for DNA comparison to the scene. He could make this easier and just submit to the tests."

He shook his head. "I don't think he will."

"You're protecting him," Hailey said.

"I'm doing my job," he responded. He sat back in his chair. "We'll continue the investigation from our department," he added, sounding like the perfect bureaucrat.

"Christ," Hailey said. "You're going to take over the murder case?"

Bruce frowned. "No. Just this aspect of the questioning."

"This aspect is the suspect—it's the whole case," Jamie countered.

Hailey launched herself out of her chair. "You're giving him special treatment because he's the deputy chief's son. That's bullshit, Bruce."

"No, we're not," Daniels responded, his voice even. "We said we'll pursue it tomorrow. He said he went straight home. And he's got an alibi. We'll check it out."

"What's the alibi?" Jamie demanded.

Daniels spoke first. "He stayed at his parents."

"Mommy?" Jamie was outraged. "Mommy is his fucking alibi?"

Daniels frowned. "Understand our position. We have to offer him the benefit of the doubt. He's a police officer."

"So was Tim Worley when he was arrested for murder and denied bail."

Daniels frowned.

"We've got his print in the car," Hailey added. "You can't just let him walk because of who his father is."

"We'll check it out."

"You'd better bet we will," Jamie said, but the threat felt empty.

Hailey stood, crossed her arms, stared down at Bruce. "I would've expected more from you."

"Sorry to disappoint." He didn't look sorry.

But Hailey shook her head at Jamie as though to say it wasn't worth the fight. Then, without another word, she turned and left the room.

Jamie looked back at Daniels and wondered what had passed between them. Was there another time when he'd offered more? Or maybe something else.

Without a word, Mackenzie got up, too, and left.

Jamie walked from the room, passing by Daniels and the other IA officer who remained seated.

When she walked out, Scanlan stood against the far wall. He held his fingers up like they were a gun and shot at her. Then he blew the smoke off like an old gangster movie. The gesture made him seem more like a surly teenager than any kind of real threat.

"Watch it, asshole," she warned him. "And don't go anywhere. We're not anywhere close to finished."

"I can't wait," he said, blowing her a kiss. With that, she left Scanlan alone. She hurried to the lot, hoping to catch Hailey and get her take on it.

But Hailey was gone.

Her cell phone rang as she turned back toward the building. "Vail."

"Jamie. It's Chip Washington. I got a call that you found a photo of Devlin at Marchek's. Does it link him to her murder?"

"News travels fast."

"I talked to Evidence, but they couldn't say who was in the picture. Can you tell who it is?"

"We can tell all right."

"Who?" He sounded breathless.

"Are you running?"

"Sorry. Just walking up stairs. Who is it? The picture, I mean."

"Scott Scanlan." Jamie described the photo Marchek had taken. "He must have seen them arrive at the station."

"Christ. And there was only that one photo?"

"Yeah. Unfortunately, just one."

"Damn."

"Thanks for getting the warrant."

"Yeah. Don't worry. I just wish it had helped more."

"We'll nail him," Jamie said. "I'm going home for some sleep."

"Okay. Have a good night and keep me posted."

"Will do." Jamie ended the call, went back inside, and signed out a department car. Revving the engine, she lit a cigarette as she headed for home. She had a momentary thought about settling in for a quiet night of rest.

Then she wondered where Tony had been all day, why he hadn't answered her calls. An image of him hanging in a closet made her shudder. He'd promised on Lana's grave that he wouldn't do it again. Not here, not in her house. Christ, not Tony.

She sucked hard on the cigarette, drove too fast, and prayed he had kept his promise.

# 20

Hailey was three blocks from the police station when her cell phone rang. She knew who it was without reading the familiar number.

"Wyatt."

"I'm on my way home. Can you please come for one drink?"

"I should get home, Bruce."

"Twenty minutes. I want to talk about this. I want to explain."

She hesitated.

"It's Friday night. I won't get to talk to you again until Monday. Please."

She glanced down at the clock. It was only nine. "Okay, but just a drink. Just talk." The weekend belonged to her family. It felt like Buck owned her during the week, so she was adamant about weekends. And the firmly drawn lines helped her keep the worlds separate. Somehow, the rules also kept her from feeling too much guilt.

"I promise. I just want to talk. Thank you."

She hung up, changed lanes, and waited at the turn signal. Behind her, the driver of a Camaro revved his engine. Friday nights brought out the worst. More of every crime happened on Friday night. Payday, the end of the work week, it was a heyday of lawlessness.

Hailey just hoped there were no murders tonight, though she knew it would be someone else's turn.

She arrived at Bruce's apartment at 9:25, parked just up the street from the entrance to the building. It was too close and she considered moving, but couldn't rouse the energy. After this week—Natasha, the Dennigs, Scanlan—she was ready to put the job aside. Ready to watch Camilla and Ali argue over whose turn it was with the Barbie car. Ready to spend some time on the couch with John, to watch a movie about horses or baseball, anything but murder.

Hailey stared at the facade of Bruce's building. It wasn't too late to go straight home. She'd promised him twenty minutes. She was angry, but didn't want the relationship to end, especially not like this. She locked her gun in the glove box, stood from the car, and set the alarm with the key fob. She put her purse over one shoulder and across her chest and walked to the apartment door.

It was dark and the single old light over the doorway gave off a pale amber glow. She thought momentarily that it wasn't a very safe entryway. She pressed the buzzer for his apartment and heard the click of the door unlock. She stepped inside and felt her purse catch on something. She reached back, turned, and someone bulldozed her into the dark apartment stairwell.

Before she could scream, a man was on her back. He shoved her face to the floor. She called out as he coiled the purse strap around her neck, tightened it on her throat. She tasted the dust of the old rug, saw white blotches as the strap cut off her air. She dug her fingers into her neck, struggled to pry the strap loose. She sucked a breath, tried to roll to one side.

He pinned her down with his hips, held the strap like reins. Bruce, she thought. Where was Bruce?

The strap tightened. Breath caught in her throat.

Her eyes bulged in their sockets. She reached down and clawed at his ankle, felt her nails dig into his skin.

The pressure loosened momentarily. She struggled left, then right.

He struck her.

Her face slammed into the ground. She tasted blood.

The strap crushed her throat again. Her vision blanked. She choked, struggled to scream. She blinked, saw black as she started to lose consciousness. Blood surged in her face like a pounding drum. Black. It was all black.

She heard a click above her.

"Hailey?"

She screamed. The sound caught in her throat, faded out.

She heard Bruce again.

*I'm here. I'm right here. Help me.*

Black swam across her vision. Then bright white lights. She heard footsteps and tried to yell.

Louder. Someone was coming.

The strap went slack. She sucked in air, panted. Tried to move. Couldn't.

More running.

A sound like a hand hitting glass. The door clicked opened, slammed closed.

Bruce's voice. "Christ. Christ."

His touch was cool. His hand tingled against her skin.

She looked at him. Spots in her vision blocked his face. She tried to smile.

Then everything went black.

# 21

When Jamie woke on Saturday morning, Tony was
still asleep. He'd been asleep when she'd gotten home
the night before, too. At ten thirty, she went out on
errands, leaving a menu to a local pizza place and a
check with a note. When she returned home at four
thirty, Tony was gone—no note, no message. The
check sat untouched on the counter.

She spent a quiet evening alone, ate a Lean Cuisine
chicken teriyaki, washed it down with Coke. It was a
typical Saturday night, but somehow worrying about
Tony left her feeling more hollow than usual.

When the phone rang at nine, she snatched it up,
hoping to hear Tony's voice. Even drunk, it would
have been a relief.

"It's Tim."

"You're out?"

"Yeah. I got released this morning."

She didn't respond, couldn't think of anything to
say.

"I wanted to thank you for the help with Ed Goldman and everything."

"You're welcome."

There was a pause. "J, can I see you when this
is over?"

She shook her head, cleared her throat. "I don't
think so, Tim."

"How about the phone? Can I call you?"

It was a bad idea.

"Please. Just once in a while?"

"I guess."

"Thanks."

There was a pause. "You're welcome" didn't sound right.

"I'll talk to you soon, then."

"Bye, Tim."

"Bye, J."

As she hung up, nostalgia caught in her throat.

She stood and found her cigarettes, lit one. Smoking, she felt no better. Trying to distract herself, she logged on to the computer to catch up with the cases the chat group was working. A few others were online, and the group spent an hour corresponding about the case in Chicago. When they'd gotten as far as they could, Mary Dodgson, a forensic psychology Professor, asked about Devlin.

*JVail   How'd you hear about that one?*

The screen remained blank for thirty seconds and for a moment, Jamie assumed Mary must have gotten up from the computer.

*MDod   We got the update from you this morning.*

Frowning, Jamie stared at Mary's words.

*JVail   You mean yesterday? I wasn't on this morning.*

Jamie watched the cursor blink on the screen. Waited for a response. Nothing came. She heard the ping of a new e-mail and changed screens. When she saw Mary's e-mail address, she opened the letter.

The e-mail simply listed a Chicago phone number.

Her pulse humming, Jamie dialed the number on her cell phone.

"Jamie?" Mary asked.

"Yeah. It's me."

"We were on for more than hour this morning. Are you okay?"

"It wasn't me, Mary. I've been out."

Mary paused. "Someone have access to your computer?"

Jamie thought about Tony. It didn't make sense. He didn't even know anything about Devlin. "What time?"

"About ten a.m. Chicago."

That was eight o'clock in California. It couldn't have been Tony. At eight o'clock, they were both still asleep.

"What's your password?"

Jamie frowned.

"I mean, is it easy to guess?"

"Shit. It's my birthday." Fear danced up her spine.

"Birthdays are easy to get."

"Christ."

"It makes sense now," Mary commented.

"What does?"

"You—or whoever was pretending to be you—asked some pretty basic MO questions. I wondered if you were just trying to get a fresh perspective. I think I even commented on it, and you responded that you'd had a long night."

Jamie considered that. "But whoever used my ID has to be on the list, right?"

"Not necessarily."

"How else would someone know about it?"

"That's the scary part."

Jamie's throat tightened. "What do you mean?"

"You ever Googled yourself?"

Jamie frowned. "What?"

"Are you online right now?"

"Yeah."

"Go to Google.com."

Jamie launched her Web browser and typed in www.google.com. "Okay."

"Now type in your name."

Jamie typed in her name and hit enter. "I get about forty-seven thousand responses."

"Sorry. Put quotes around it."

Jamie did it. "Forty-nine." She scanned the first one. "San Francisco Sex Crimes Inspector Jamie Vail." She clicked on the link. The San Francisco Chronicle Web site came up and she read a brief article about the hearing on one of her more recent cases.

"You there?"

"Yeah. I found me. It's an article on a case."

"Keep scrolling."

"What am I looking for?" She scanned the next few entries—all newspaper articles—then clicked to the next page.

"You'll find it, but basically, the bulletin board we use is public. That means anyone can apply to join us. They have to come through the moderator to get in. That's how we keep out the unwanted element, limit it to police officers and forensic folks."

Jamie listened, still scanning the list. So far only one link didn't refer to her.

"But the main page lists who's online at any one time. So if you signed up with your name, anyone who Googles you will find it there."

Just then Jamie saw her full name next to the screen ID "JVail." She hit the link, watched as the log-in page for their chat group came up. "It takes them right to the chat group's log-in screen."

"Right. It gives them your ID and if they've got the password, they're in."

A dead weight sank in her gut. "I made it too easy." Thoughts trampled across her mind. "Mary, you were probably talking to her killer."

The line was silent for a moment. When Mary spoke, her voice was nearly a whisper. "I thought about that. It's why I had you call."

He'd been there. There had to be something she could use. "Is there an abstract for the session?"

"No. I'm the one who usually logs the sessions, but I didn't. The conversation was sort of roundabout and off topic. I'll e-mail the others and ask if anyone else logged it."

Christ, had Devlin's killer been online using Jamie's ID? She tightened a fist. But why her—why not Hailey? Maybe they had searched Hailey Wyatt, too. Maybe the chat group was the opening they found. "Did anything stand out?"

Mary paused. "I was trying to think. A lot of it was what we'd read. He did mention she was promiscuous. Oh, jeez—how could I forget?"

Jamie felt herself tense. "What?"

"He said that she'd slept with your husband."

Jamie didn't respond.

"I'm sorry."

She started to say that it was okay, but couldn't bring herself to do it. "He's my ex now."

Mary gave her a moment, then said, "You should consider that, Jamie. Who knew about that incident? Sounds like someone within the department."

Jamie nodded, dread pooling in her limbs. "I was thinking the same thing."

"Have you brought in a suspect? I thought he mentioned that you'd been looking at a cop."

She thought about Scott Scanlan. He was someone to consider. "What did he say about that?"

"Just that you'd pulled in one suspect who didn't look good for it." She stopped. "You thinking it might be him?"

"I don't think so." Tim wouldn't have access from the city jail.

Mary seemed to consider this. "He didn't let on any

real emotion about the suspect. That's why I didn't
really consider it out of character for you except for
the questions about who I would look at based on
the scene."

Jamie considered Marchek. Tim's arrest had made
the news, but would he have access to the fact that
Devlin had slept with Tim? It seemed far-fetched.

Mary interrupted her thoughts. "I've got to go, but
I'll dig up what I can remember and e-mail it to you."

"Thanks, Mary."

"And change that password."

"I'm doing it now."

After hanging up, Jamie changed her passwords on
the chat group and her personal e-mail. She had no
way of knowing if someone was in her e-mail and the
realization was terrifying. She left a message for
Hailey and lit a cigarette. She was tired, but she
couldn't imagine going to bed. Couldn't fall asleep
now. Not with the notion that someone was in her
personal information. What else did he have? Did he
know where she lived? Just how close was the killer?

Jamie shivered and stubbed out her cigarette. Forcing herself up, she checked the doors and windows.

As she mounted the stairs toward her bedroom,
Jamie had the haunting sense that someone was
watching. And more than ever, she wished Tony
would come home.

# 22

Jamie had drifted into sleep when something woke her. Startled, she sat up in bed. Her heart clashed in her chest. Her head pounded. She crept to the window and looked out, saw nothing. She turned her ear to the door. Was it inside?

She glanced back outside as a shadow crossed the grass. Adrenaline burned in her gut. Tony?

Tightening the tie on her white terry-cloth robe over the T-shirt and sweats she slept in, Jamie stepped into a pair of suede moccasins, pulled her holster off the back of the bedroom door, and started downstairs. She caught her reflection in the hallway mirror. She looked like a cross between Martha Stewart and Annie Oakley.

She drew her gun, flicked the safety off. Gripping it in her right hand, she held it barrel down, her finger off the trigger. At the bottom of the stairs, she turned off the inside lights and stared out the dining room window into the backyard. The shadow was gone. She flicked on the outside lights, wishing she'd spent the money to have them upgraded to motion sensing. With a quick breath, she opened the back door, her gun in front of her.

She heard Barney's claws click on the stairs and soon he was beside her. "Nice of you to wake up."

He growled into the dark.

"Be my guest."

Barney didn't move.

Jamie stepped out onto the small back deck and surveyed the yard. She was almost never out there. What little grass there was had been displaced by the weeds. Like the tougher gang marking its territory, the weeds had won out here. A lone tree stood in one corner—a maple, she guessed, though she'd never been good at that kind of thing. Bushes dotted the yard like green islands about to be washed over by a sea of brown weeds.

Nothing flowered. Even with all the rain, the green was limited to a few bushes and the tree. It was a sad yard. She turned back inside and saw the same thing. Weeds outside and inside a sea of brown boxes littered the rooms. Jesus, how pathetic. Barney moaned as though understanding, and she patted his head.

She locked the back door when she heard the sharp ping of glass breaking on the front porch. A man howled.

Through the small window beside the front door, she saw Tony on his knees. He lifted a piece of crooked glass toward his lips.

Jamie holstered her gun and yanked the door open. "What the hell are you doing?"

His tongue out, he poured brown liquid into his mouth.

She grabbed the piece from his hand, skimming it across the insides of her knuckles. She dropped the glass as blood pooled in her hand. "Shit."

Tony reached for another piece, but Jamie grabbed his arm, smearing his skin with her blood.

The smell of whiskey was overwhelming, and she was both nauseated and desperate at once.

Tony twisted his arm away, but she tugged back harder. "Stop it. Jesus Christ, Tony. Fucking stop it!"

He looked up at her, green eyes bloodshot. Dark circles cast shadows under his lids. She clutched his arm, dragged him toward her. Blood dripped down her white robe. She ignored it, held Tony. His arm felt spindly in her grasp. As he turned to look back at the broken glass, she noticed the way the light cast shadows in his cheekbones. Jesus, he was thin.

"Where have you been?"

He didn't answer. He glanced down at the broken bottle with longing.

She kicked the glass off the porch.

Tony stood motionless, watching the last bits of Jack Daniel's spill onto the dirt.

Shaking, Jamie went inside, leaving the door open. Tears burned her eyes. Damn it. At the sink, she ran her hands under the water, waiting for her pulse to slow. The water stung the wound.

Tony wasn't her child. She'd never played the parent role—that had been Tony's older brother Mick's job. As kids, they had spent nearly every evening together. Their dads mostly worked opposite shifts, so one could be in charge of the kids. Although even then, Mick was the one who helped with homework and made sure Tony and Jamie were in bed on time. Pat and her father made the meals. That was a rule—no cooking without one of them around. Fire safety, of course. If both men were going to be out, Mick made cold sandwiches for dinner.

Jamie looked down at her bloody hand. She washed the wound out with soap, wincing at the sting. She wrapped a paper towel around her knuckles, pinching it closed with her fingertips.

Where had they all gone so wrong? Besides a few rules, her father mostly ignored her as she developed into a woman. From time to time, the women her father or Pat dated tried to help. When it came to Jamie, though, her father just smiled and shook his head, casting one of his wide blue-eyed winks. "My Jamie can take care of herself," he'd say, the Irish brogue always thicker around the ladies.

For a while, Jamie assumed the distance her father kept was because she was a girl. And maybe that was part of it. But Tony and Mick's father Pat ignored them much the same way. Maybe it was the loss of their wives. Maybe the reminder in their little faces was too much to bear.

Sometime in high school Jamie also realized that growing up in America was completely different from what her father, and Pat for that matter, had experienced in Ireland. Being an immigrant, they had no idea what to expect for their children here.

Whatever the reason, Jamie's father didn't ask and she didn't tell. That rule became the basis of their entire relationship. And it had spilled over to the relationship between her and Tony and Mick, too. Despite all the death and tragedy, no one ever talked. Christ, look at them now.

As she shut the water off, she stared down at the stains on her robe. Most were still bright red, but she caught sight of a tiny patch of brown. The water had stopped, but she heard it rushing in her ears as she lifted the robe and smelled the stain. She closed her eyes and drew in the unmistakable scent of whiskey. She touched the liquid with her finger and brought it to her mouth. Her tongue reached out for it and the two almost met. But Barney nudged her leg, nosing her.

She looked down at him, the liquid still moist on her skin. She closed her eyes and steeled herself. Before she could think more about it, she turned the water on high and washed the whiskey from her finger.

She slid the holster off her shoulders and hung it on a cabinet knob. She shook the robe off. Bunching it into a ball, she threw it in the sink and let the water drench it.

Barney walked to the back door and whined. She let him out, stared at the dark yard. She shut the door and turned.

She saw Tony standing in the doorway, swaying as though to a slow tune only he heard.

"I have to work tomorrow," she said, though it was the weekend.

He didn't answer.

Blinking, she swiped tears off her cheeks and turned for the back door to get Barney. She couldn't bear to discuss it now—not the alcohol and definitely not everything else.

As she touched the doorknob, Tony spoke. "I killed him."

In his voice, she heard the slightest tint of her father. A bit of brogue that came out only when he and Mick drank. She thought momentarily of her father—where he was, when they'd last spoken, what he thought of her, what he'd ever thought of her. She closed her eyes and leaned against the wall.

"I can't get it out of my head."

She stared into the dark, wishing she could go, escape. Instead, she turned around slowly, dragging out the time before she met his gaze.

When she did, it was like a physical blow.

His shoulders hunched, he gripped his hands together. A smear of blood—hers, she assumed—made a hash mark down his cheek, tears just beginning to blur it.

"Those were dad's last words to me."

She moved toward him, and it was like walking through moving water, the sense of being dragged back by so many forces. "You didn't kill him."

Tony sank onto the couch, then slid onto the floor. "He said, 'I never thought it would be Mick. He was always the quick one, the bright one.' "

Jamie perched on the edge of the couch. "You didn't kill him."

"My own father," he said. The words were slurred in drunken anguish.

Jamie pressed her hand to her chest, searching for something to say. Christ, why was it so hard?

"He wanted it to be me."

"No, he didn't."

"The hell he didn't. He told me. 'It should've been you, Tony. Mick was too good.' "

She turned back, anger rising. "Fuck him, then."

"Ha!" he shouted. "That's what I told him, the bastard. I said to hell with him."

"Good for you."

"Yeah, good for fucking me. He died, you know. He died the next week. I never talked to him after that. My last words to my own father were 'Go to hell.' " He choked back a sob.

Jamie sank to the floor beside him, rubbed her eyes. "He was wrong, Tony."

Tony shook his head, dropped it to his knees.

"He was wrong to say that. He didn't mean it. He was angry. Shit, we all say things we don't mean when we're angry."

"He meant it. He was calm when he said it, not angry. He was just disgusted that I was the one he was left with. So disgusted that he went and fucking died."

Jamie pressed her hand to the back of his neck, felt the moisture of his sweat. She laid her hand flat, felt his pulse, the rough edge of the wounds under her fingers. How long had it been since she'd touched another person? The tears fell harder. "They never got over Lana and Mom, you know. Neither of them ever did. They had a raw deal, those two—one shitty thing after another. We were just reminders of the women they'd lost."

"Like we had it so fucking easy."

Jamie thought back on her childhood. It hadn't been that bad. There were moments when it had seemed pretty great. She put her head on his shoulder, listened to the rhythm of his breath. The constant beating, the promise that things would continue. She savored it.

He sat up, leaned his head into hers. "God, haven't you got anything to drink?"

"I quit."

"That was a stupid idea."

"I was about to lose my job. It's no good, you know. We can't handle the booze. Dad and Pat never could either. It's lousy Irish luck." She lifted her head, looked at him. "You've got to quit it, Tony. You can't do it anymore. Trust me. It'll get easier."

He pulled away. "You're as self-righteous as the rest of them."

She frowned. "Damn it, Tony. I want to help, but you can't drink here. I can't do it—I'm not strong enough to hold us both up."

Tony stood unevenly. "Who asked you for help?"

Jamie didn't move, felt the anger burn her skin. "Isn't that why you're here? Because if you're not here for help, what *do* you want, Tony?"

"Nothing. Shit, I don't want anything. God forbid I ask you for anything."

Jamie stood and moved around the table until she was standing inches from Tony's chest. "I'm trying." She shoved him back down. "It's not my fault things ended up the way they have. Mick's not my fault— your dad, our mothers, the past—none of it. I'm sorry life's been so fucking hard on you, Tony.

"It's been pretty shitty here, too. I'm sorry you lost your job, but did you ever stop to think that losing your job saved your damn life? You'd be dead now if you hadn't gotten drunk and kicked out of the department."

Tony turned from her. "Maybe I want to be dead."

"Fine," she roared, striking her finger out at him like a sword. "Then go kill yourself, but don't come to my house to do it. Don't go asking for my help. You want to do that, then you do it somewhere fucking else." Her throat went hoarse. She coughed.

"Jesus, you're a hard bitch."

"Yeah, well, life's made me hard."

He turned then, marched for the front door. He hadn't quite reached it when the doorbell rang.

As Tony pulled the door open, Jamie wondered what neighbors they'd awakened. Why wouldn't everyone just leave her the hell alone?

"Oh, Christ. Jamie, quick!"

Jamie came around the corner as Tony stood up and turned back to her. He stared at his hands. They were streaked in red—blood.

Jamie ran. He'd cut himself, but she couldn't see how. "What the hell happened?"

"He's hurt."

"Who?"

She passed Tony. Barney lay on his side on the doormat. She lifted his paw and saw his heaving chest. Blood caked one ear.

"Barney!" Jamie touched his matted coat, the blood dark against his brown fur. "Oh Christ. He's been cut. He's bleeding."

"He must've cut himself on the glass," Tony said.

Jamie shook her head, heart pounding. "Then who the hell rang the doorbell?"

# 23

Mackenzie and Alan spent Saturday night together. Alan had come back from a bike ride, fixed gin and tonics, and they sat out on the small stoop overlooking the park. The lime fizz reminded her of Montana summer nights, sitting on the back deck. For the first time in months, she wasn't overcome by homesickness at the image.

She'd told Alan about the rookie club dinner, about the buzz of identifying Scott Scanlan's car. He'd listened, fixated, while she talked.

"Mackey, that's big-city stuff. Weren't you terrified?"

She leaned in to him, taking in the smell of sweat and cologne mixed with limes. "Of course. God, I was a wreck."

"But you liked it."

"Yeah, I did."

His face sobered. "I wasn't sure if you were happy here."

She looked at him, shook her head. "I wasn't. I wanted to go home so bad."

He kissed her cheek. "And now?"

She stopped. "I'm not sure. I miss Montana. I miss the space and the dogs. I miss our friends."

He nodded. "Me, too. Especially the space. That apartment is ridiculous."

"It's the size of our garage back home."

"Are you kidding?" He hitched his finger toward the building. "Our garage was twice that size."

She laughed, felt the warm buzz of alcohol.

He kissed her ear. "It's good to hear you laugh."

They sat in silence, listened to the cars hum past.

"You want to go out for dinner?" she asked.

"I'd rather eat in."

She turned around, caught his mouth with hers.

He rubbed her shoulders through her shirt. "You want me to go grab some sushi takeout?"

She closed her eyes and let her head loll forward, a little moan bubbling in her throat.

"We can chill that bottle of wine, just relax."

She didn't need to be in until tomorrow evening. "Do you have to get up early?"

He laughed softly, pulled her close, his chest firm against her back. "I think I could miss one morning."

"I thought they ran that place like an army."

He spun her around and tucked his nose to her neck. "I might be convinced to go AWOL for a few hours."

She found his lips with hers and took them, feeling an almost immediate release of the built-up pressure. "You really want food?"

He raised a brow. "I'm going to need something for energy."

She laughed and kissed him again. "Let's go order. I'll pick it up while you shower."

"Really? I can go. Or we can walk together."

She shook her head. "I can use the air." She kissed him. "And you definitely need a shower."

"Deal."

She ordered their favorites and left the apartment as Alan was getting into the shower. She thought about the charge Jamie had exuded when she'd ordered Scanlan from the car. Jamie loved what she did.

She was passionate about it. That's how Mackenzie wanted to feel. For the first time, she thought maybe she could. Watching Jamie, Mackenzie had felt inspired.

For herself, Mackenzie wasn't certain if Homicide or Sex Crimes or something like Burglary would ever do it for her like that. But maybe. For the first time she thought maybe.

The air outside was cool and damp. It wasn't raining, but it felt like she was walking through a mister. She blew out her breath, but still no smoke. She wondered if it ever got cold enough here to see her breath. Maybe in January.

Mackenzie crossed Funston at Irving and headed east toward 9th. Ebisu was the first San Francisco restaurant she and Alan had discovered. They'd come for a weekend to check out places to live and someone had recommended it.

In the end, it had also been part of the reason they'd chosen to live on this side of town. The rents were cheaper than the Marina and Cow Hollow or Russian Hill. Even the places South of Market had become trendy and outrageous. But in addition to the lower rents, having Ebisu close was a definite plus. Extra rent money generally went to sushi. It was one thing San Francisco definitely had over Montana.

Traffic was light on Judah. She reached 9th and turned south, thinking how nice it would be to have a night with Alan.

She tucked her head down into the neck of her fleece, suddenly wishing she'd brought a heavier jacket. The moisture was chilling. She continued down the quiet street, passed an alley less than two blocks from the restaurant.

A car backfired in the distance. Dress shoes shuffled on a sidewalk behind her. She started to turn when someone jumped her.

He swung her into the alley and she pitched forward onto all fours, landing with a grunt. Her pulse raced. Her belly burned with adrenaline. Get up.

He flattened his chest to her back, the weight bearing down on her.

She threw her head back. Hoped to connect with his nose. She missed.

Her body sank under his weight. Her arms trembled. "No! Someone—"

He cut her off, swinging his right hand under her. His forearm connected with her arms. Her elbows collapsed. Her face smacked the pavement. The air rushed from her lungs. She struggled for a breath. Push up. Fight, she thought.

"Don't."

She opened her mouth to scream. He pressed something hard to her head. She pictured the shape of the barrel, the hard edges of the gun. Felt the divot where the bullet would come out—out into her head.

Her eyes brimmed with tears. "Please."

"Don't say a word."

She closed her eyes, her breath catching. She trembled. Be strong. Someone would come, she told herself. Someone would be there. Please.

"You're going to deliver a message."

She released her breath. Just a message. She would live. She inhaled, fought to slow her racing pulse. She considered Scanlan. It wasn't him. Not the right tone, older. More wicked, the voice lower.

"A message," he repeated.

She nodded. Be agreeable, get him to talk. Anything to buy some time. Someone would come. New tears pricked at her eyes. She blinked hard. It was okay. Stay calm.

The gun shifted. She lifted her head, turned it.

He rammed the piece into her skull.

The bone above her left eye cracked against the concrete. Her bottom lip exploded in a bright red flash of pain. Her head throbbed. She squeezed her eyes to block out the pain.

"Don't move."

Blood ran thick from her nose.

"This is a message to the inspector."

She drew a shallow breath. "What inspector?"

"The one screwing with my stuff."

She shook her head. "I don't know what—"

"Shut up," he snapped, pressing the gun to her aching skull.

She moaned, tried to focus. She forced her eyes open, tried to see him in her peripheral vision. She wanted to be able to ID him.

"The inspector," he repeated.

Don't make him mad. She nodded. The throbbing in her head crescendoed like a symphony's finale. She closed her eyes, fought for breath under his weight.

"Tell her not to play games with me."

She thought about Jamie, about the rapist. It was him. It had to be. "Will she know what you mean?"

He lowered his face to hers, pressed his lips in her ear. "Tell her one of her own is a killer."

Shivering, she fought the urge to struggle against him. She pinched her eyes closed, forced them open. He's not hurting you, she reminded herself. Don't move.

Out of the corner of her eye, she saw dark curls against her cheek. Felt them, moist on her skin. She shuddered.

"She better listen this time. It's one of you," he hissed. He pressed his lips to her face and slid his hand over her clothes.

His right palm closed over her breast. He palmed her nipple, then pinched and twisted. She gasped. He knocked the gun against her head. He was left-handed, she thought, struggling to be analytical, not to think of his hand groping her.

She closed her eyes, battled the images. Tears heated her cheeks. Sobs rose in her chest.

"Tell her to leave me alone or next time it'll be worse." His fingers clenched tighter, pinching her. "It'll be like the inspector that asshole killed. Next time I might be forced to kill someone."

Natasha, she thought. Oh God.

He pinched harder.

She cried out.

He laughed, snaking his hand lower.

Sobs burst from her lips.

"You hear me?"

She nodded. "Yes."

Just then she heard a car accelerate toward them. Headlights skimmed over her head and shined on the brick of the alley behind them. They were hidden behind a row of parked cars. The car couldn't see them unless she moved. Someone would come. Alan would miss her. He would come. She lifted her head a few inches, tried to look around.

He grabbed her hair and shoved her face into the pavement.

She halted. It was almost over. He'd paused. Maybe he was done or maybe he was just starting. She shuddered as panic clamped down on her lungs.

He grunted as he struck her again with the gun. Then he slammed her to the ground. He pulled her hips up and tore at the buttons of her jeans.

"No," she moaned. Panicked, she flattened her hips to the ground, grinding his hand into the pavement.

He wrenched it free and sat up. She felt the air on her back and started to twist from his weight. He wasn't going to shoot her. Not with people so close by. She couldn't sit there. She wouldn't let him rape her.

She rolled onto one side. His fist pounded the small of her back. She doubled over, gripped her knees. Sobs burst from her lungs. "Help me!" she screamed.

She saw his fist dart at her. She ducked her head to her knees. His knuckles caught the side of her head with a crack. Her skull thundered. White flashes smeared her vision. She struggled to focus on him, couldn't.

He stood. She couldn't see his face—just a dark shadow.

She didn't move. Set her throbbing head down. Blinked at the darkness. Slowly, the forms returned. She closed her eyes, the pain too much.

She prayed it was over just as his shoe smashed against her ribs. She heard the sickening crack of bone. The pain crashed down on her in unrelenting waves. Hot chills flooded her. She turned her head, threw up. Couldn't move. The cement was cold on her cheek.

She didn't see the next blow coming. It struck her head. White stars flickered in the dark.

Then suddenly there was only black.

# 24

Jamie woke up to a phone ringing. She bolted upright. Tony. No, Tony was here.

"Hello," she gasped.

The voice was breathless on the other end. "Wallace has been attacked."

"Wha—who?" She blinked, wiped her mouth with the back of her hand. Who the hell was Wallace?

"It's me, Hailey. Mackenzie Wallace was attacked. I just found out from Linda James."

"Attacked. When?"

"Around eight last night. Near Irving and 10th."

There was a pause and Jamie felt her pulse still.

"He was brutal," Hailey added.

Jamie pressed her fist to the hollow pit in her gut.

"But she's conscious now."

This was her fault. Jesus Christ. First the dog and then a rookie cop. She glanced at the bedside clock. Eight a.m. Sunday morning. She'd gotten to bed sometime after three. Barney was still at the vet hospital. Already there had been another attack.

She threw the covers back, stood. "Where is she now?"

"She's at General. I'm going there. But, Jamie, I have to tell you something."

"What?"

Hailey didn't speak.

Jamie heard a door close with a click. "Hello."

"I'm here. I had to go into another room." Her voice was a whisper.

"What happened?"

"I was attacked."

Dread splashed hot in her gut. "What? When?"

"On Friday night," she whispered.

"Where? At home?"

Silence.

Jamie frowned. "Hailey, what the hell happened?"

Hailey sighed. "After we left the station, I was headed home. But I got a call."

"From—"

"A friend. He invited me over." She hesitated. "I went to his apartment."

Jamie nodded, thought about that night. "Daniels." It wasn't a question.

Hailey didn't respond.

Jamie knew she was right. "What time did you get there?"

"About nine fifteen. Listen, Jamie, this could ruin so much for both of us."

"I don't care about the affair, Hailey."

She heard Hailey's breath release in a long hiss. "I hate that word."

"Call it what you want." Tim. Devlin. Now Hailey. Christ, the world was full of cheaters. She forced it aside. "Tell me exactly what happened."

Hailey told Jamie about the attack. How she'd gotten out of her car, locked her gun in the glove box, put her purse strap across her chest, and walked up to the apartment. She hadn't noticed anyone. The street was quiet. It was always quiet, she said.

Jamie closed her eyes, pressed her fingers to her temple. The purse strap across Hailey's chest had been the big mistake. Cops were supposed to know better. Straps, long ponytails, and hoods all made good things for an attacker to grab on to. Hailey described how he'd had her facedown, how he'd knocked her head into the floor, tightened the strap on her neck. She'd passed out once, maybe twice. Then she'd heard a voice above. Someone coming down the stairs. The attacker ran.

"Did you go after him?"

"I was half conscious."

"Did anyone else?"

"No. He—he was worried about me."

Jamie closed her eyes, searched for another clue. "Did the attacker speak? Say anything?"

"Nothing. I didn't get a look at him, and he didn't say a word. I don't even remember him breathing. I was alone and then he was there, strangling me."

Her voice caught. "It was clean, Jamie. I didn't get anything."

"Prints? I don't suppose you—"

"I didn't. I let the scene go."

"Shit."

A moment of silence passed before Hailey spoke. "I assumed it was random, but now, after Mackenzie, I don't think so."

Jamie thought about that night. They'd confronted Scanlan. He could have pulled something like that. But Hailey wasn't at the forefront of that—Mackenzie and Jamie were. Then there was Marchek. Had she really seen him at Tommy's? Could he have followed Hailey to Daniels' apartment?

Mackenzie was badly beaten. That sounded like Marchek's work. Christ. She ran her hand through her hair. She'd never forgive herself if Mackenzie had been killed.

"I blame myself, Jamie. I should've spoken up."

"Don't."

Hailey stopped.

Jamie shook her head. "I thought I saw Marchek when we were at Tommy's. I'm not sure. It was a flash of something familiar, a sense."

"Oh God."

"I'm to blame as much as you." She paused. "More."

"We could do this all day. It won't help Mackenzie."

Jamie nodded. "Has she been unconscious?"

"In and out through the night, according to Linda James."

"Has anyone talked to her about what she saw?"

"Not yet."

Jamie heard someone in the background.

"I need to go, but I'm heading to the hospital soon. Will you come?"

"Yeah. I'll be there as soon as I can. It'll probably take me an hour."

"Thanks. And, Jamie, if you could—"

"I won't say a word about it unless my only other choice is to let Marchek go."

"Thank you."

Jamie thought about Mackenzie as she hung up. Goddamn it. The rookie had to be okay. The fact that Marchek was out there, following them away from the station, was terrifying. It was no longer just a case. Marchek was hunting them. She had to stop him before he killed someone else.

Before he killed her.

She wondered how close he'd come.

# 25

Hailey held her breath as she walked through the automatic doors of San Francisco General. The smell of it—ammonia and lemon cleaning fluid and the faint odor of feet almost stopped her. She hated hospitals, would much rather spend time in the morgue. It was this halfway house—not dead but not well—that made her feel like she needed to rush home and shower, put herself on antibiotics. At least she didn't worry what she would catch from the dead. It didn't help that today guilt ate at her from the inside out. She was partially to blame for Mackenzie's attack.

She thought again of the rookie, of the stressed phone call she'd gotten from Mackenzie's captain, Linda James. Hailey had a duty to let someone know about her attack. She and Bruce had even discussed the possibility that the attack was part of a series of events. They had dismissed it. She knew in her gut that they hadn't taken the threat seriously enough. They had chosen to protect their own hides instead.

Now Mackenzie was in the hospital. Hailey turned her gaze to the ceiling and swore to God that she'd never see Bruce again if the rookie came out okay. That night, after the attack, she'd considered the symbolism of it. She'd been attacked on the way into her lover's home. What sign could be clearer?

Jolted from her reverie, Hailey saw she'd stopped in the middle of the hallway. In the lobby, people milled around her—nurses and doctors with cups of coffee, patients in wheelchairs with oxygen or IV's hanging. Pregnant women walked in slow circles to induce labor, nervous husbands beside them.

She felt herself turn back toward the door, couldn't. Instead, she marched to the desk and looked down at a young Asian man. She dropped her badge on the counter in front of him. "I'm trying to locate a patient who was brought in last night. Her name is Mackenzie Wallace."

He nodded without a word. His shoulders hunched as he focused on the computer screen, his fingers clicking across the keyboard. When he looked up, he said, "Orthopedic ward. Third floor. Elevators are there." He pointed across the lobby.

She thanked him and thought the orthopedic unit was a good sign. She knew Mackenzie had broken her arm—had to have a screw put in. It was the emergency department or intensive care that Hailey dreaded. The ICU was where her mother had been right before her liver had failed. No, this was better. Wallace wasn't going to die. *Please don't die, Wallace. Just don't die.*

Hailey rode the elevator alone, thankful for a moment of reprieve from the sick. When the doors slid open, she followed signs to the orthopedic unit and stopped at a nurses' station. It was unmanned. She spotted a nurse coming down the hall.

"I'm looking for Mackenzie Wallace."

The nurse glanced at a large whiteboard that was divided into a chart with black tape. Hailey saw a row of patient names, followed by room numbers and a second set of names she assumed were the doctors' because the same ones appeared multiple times.

She spotted Wallace on the fifth line.

"She's in room 1027, but it's early for visitors."

Hailey brought her badge out again and flipped it open, swallowing down her rising stomach. "Is she going to be okay?"

The nurse nodded. "Concussion. She had a bad break in her elbow. She'll be in a cast for a while."

"Can I see her?"

The nurse frowned at the clock. "She's been out of the OR for only two hours."

"I'd really like to see her."

"I'll get her doctor and ask, but I don't think the patient's going to be up to talking."

Hailey put her hand on the nurse's arm as she turned. "I'm just a friend. I don't need her to talk. I'd just like to see her—please."

The nurse hesitated, looked back at the board. A phone rang and then something else buzzed. "It's around the corner," the nurse said, pointing left as she grabbed for the phone. "Make it short."

Hailey took two steps when she heard her name. She turned back and saw Jamie Vail half running down the hall, a man trailing behind.

Hailey stopped and waited. The man with Jamie was average height—maybe five ten and medium build. He'd been strong once, she could tell, but he looked thin and out of shape. He had wavy, dark brown hair cut close to his head and soft green eyes. His brow was tight with concern, and Hailey assumed it was for Mackenzie, too, though Hailey didn't recognize him. Perhaps whatever worried Jamie had spilled over on to him. She wished John reacted that way. Instead, he'd seemed put off that she'd had to come back to the city on a Sunday.

Though Hailey didn't recognize him, the man could have been a cop. Seeing Jamie with someone made Hailey realize how little of herself Jamie revealed. She wondered where he had been on the night of Natasha's murder.

"Have you seen her yet?" Jamie asked.

Hailey shook her head. "Just going now. Nurse said she might not be able to talk."

"But she's conscious?"

"Yes."

Jamie blew out her breath and opened her coat to take it off. She looked worried, too. Hailey knew she probably blamed herself as well.

Hailey had started to turn when she spotted the dark stains on Jamie's shoes. She'd seen enough dried blood to recognize it. "What's that from?"

"Someone attacked Barney last night."

She glanced at the man. "Who?"

Jamie shook her head. "Barney's the dog—my dog. Someone cut him up, then rang my doorbell at about one in the morning."

Jamie turned back to her friend. "This is Tony. He's—" Jamie stopped.

"I'm just visiting." He stepped back, pointed to a chair. "I'll wait here."

Leaving Tony, the two women walked down the corridor in silence. Hailey was thinking about the dog attack. First Hailey, then Mackenzie, then Jamie's dog.

"It could be the same guy," Hailey said.

Jamie nodded. "I should've warned you guys when I thought I saw Marchek."

"You didn't know."

"I should've known. I sure as hell know what he's capable of."

Had he been going for both of them in one night? Or all three? "You think it's him?"

Jamie hesitated. "Maybe. After we were in his house, he'd be angry. I can see him coming after us."

Hailey repressed the shudder that built in her spine.

The two of them stopped in front of room 1027. Hailey knocked. No one answered. Jamie nodded, then slowly pushed the door open.

Before she could enter, the beep and whoosh of noises assaulted her. Too many machines. She wanted to leave, to run. She imagined her dying mother. Sucked in a breath, forced a step into the room.

Mackenzie lay on the narrow bed, covered by a thin white cotton blanket. One slender arm rested at her side, pale against the ugly green hospital gown. The other was bent and covered in a thick, white cast. The head of the bed was tilted up six or eight inches and Mackenzie faced the window. From Hailey's angle, Mackenzie looked too thin and too young to be a cop. Christ, how had they let this happen to a rookie?

Mackenzie turned toward them. As her face came into view, the air swept from the room. Hailey had to steal herself from stepping away. She blinked hard, fighting back emotion as she moved closer to the beautiful woman she'd met only two days before.

Tears streaked Mackenzie's cheeks. Her left eye was swollen purple and black. It looked like a rotting plum crushed on her face. Lacerations covered both cheeks, and her top lip was swollen and cut. White butterfly sutures crisscrossed her scabbed cheeks. Black stitches laced her lower lip.

Mackenzie let out a guttural noise like hello, but her lips didn't move.

"Oh, Christ," Jamie said, moving to the far side of the bed. She took the rookie's hand and perched on the bed. "Jesus Christ, Wallace."

Hailey moved closer, too, but Mackenzie faced Jamie.

Jamie was crying. Tears falling down her cheeks, she made no move to stop them. "I'm so sorry. Jesus, I'm so fucking sorry."

Mackenzie's one eye blinked and her tongue came out to catch a stray tear. She shook her head. Her words were slow but discernable as she said, "Not. Your. Fault."

Jamie glanced at Hailey and they shared a brief moment of relief. Hailey recognized them. She was speaking. It was good news. She would recover.

But when Jamie turned back, her frown deepened. "Like hell it's not. It's completely my fault." She stopped talking, but Hailey could tell the retribution continued in her head.

Jamie caught her eye, stared up at the ceiling, and inhaled deeply as though trying to bottle back some of the emotion that had come uncorked. Then she focused back on Mackenzie and looked her over. "Did you get a look at this guy last night? At all?"

"A flash of dark hair," she said, licking her lips. "Curly." Mackenzie hesitated. "Left-handed," she added, then motioned for her water.

"Sounds like Marchek." Hailey lifted the cup and put the straw to Mackenzie's lips.

"Was it him? Would you recognize him?" Jamie pressed.

Mackenzie shrugged.

"It wasn't random," Hailey said. "I can't stomach a coincidence this big."

Jamie brought the focus to the attack. "Are you up to talking about it?"

Mackenzie nodded.

Jamie watched her. "You're sure?"

"Positive."

"Okay. Walk us through it. When did you first realize he was there? How did he sneak up on you?"

Mackenzie told the story, stopping every few minutes for water. Hailey held the straw to her lips. Jamie never let go of her hand, urging her to go slow, to take a breath.

Hailey had never seen Jamie like this. At first, she'd thought the patience was all about her own guilt. But as she continued, Hailey realized Jamie knew what it was to be a victim. Or else she was incredibly good at sympathy.

Mackenzie blinked, a new herd of tears crisscrossing her cheeks. "Warning," she whispered.

"What?" Jamie asked.

"It was a warning."

"A warning. What kind of warning?"

Hailey and Jamie stood on either side of the bed as Mackenzie recounted what her attacker had said about Natasha's killer. A cop. They were looking for a cop. Christ, maybe it was Scanlan.

Hailey suppressed shivers.

"He said, 'It'll be like the inspector that asshole killed. Next time, I might be forced to kill someone.' "

Jamie remained silent. When she finally spoke, her voice seemed to catch in her throat. "He saw something that night—the night she was killed. More than just her getting out of the car. He knows. That bastard knows."

"Or he's bullshitting us," Hailey suggested.

Jamie stared at her hands, shook her head. "No. He likes to brag. He has power now. He has something we want, something he knows we need desperately."

No one spoke for a minute.

"Shit," Hailey finally whispered.

"But a cop?" Mackenzie croaked.

Jamie and Hailey exchanged glances. Neither spoke. Hailey wanted to believe Marchek was just screwing with them. The confirmation that a cop had killed Natasha was unsettling. "How did he find Mackenzie? Why her?" she finally asked.

Jamie paused, glanced at Mackenzie without answering.

"Jamie?" Mackenzie pressed.

"Yeah," Hailey continued. "I'm the name on the case. You, I understand. But why Mackenzie?"

Mackenzie furrowed at Hailey. "He attacked you, too?"

Jamie glanced at Hailey. Turned to Mackenzie. "There have been other incidents. We appear to be the focus for him—whoever he is."

"Maybe he picked her out at Tommy's." Hailey considered where else Marchek might have seen Mackenzie. She shook her head. "But there were eight of us there. Why her?"

"I can only think he watched the thing with Scanlan. Mackenzie was front and center." Jamie glanced over at Hailey. "He probably found that exciting."

Mackenzie shifted against the sheets.

"If a cop killed Natasha, how was Marchek there that night? Coincidence?"

Jamie shook her head. "I'd bet he followed her. He hoped to catch her alone, but she never was."

Hailey considered that Natasha might have been raped that night if someone hadn't killed her. Christ. "The photograph," she whispered. "Marchek took a picture of Natasha with Scott Scanlan. Maybe he just assumed Scanlan was her killer."

Jamie shook her head. "I thought about that. It doesn't work. He knows the identity of who killed her."

Hailey frowned. "How do you know?"

"Because Marchek followed them to her office. He left a perfect fingerprint on the sign with her name." She looked up at Hailey. "That was his way of taunting us. He has something we want and he's not going to give it up."

No one spoke for a minute.

Hailey broke the silence. "How do we work it from here?"

"I don't know," Jamie confessed. "But if it was a cop who killed Natasha—Scanlan or someone else—then we have no idea who we can talk to because the killer most likely has access to the case."

Hailey considered that. "There's you and me."

Mackenzie made a sound. She raised the hand that wasn't in a cast and pointed to herself. "Me," she said.

"No way," Jamie said.

Mackenzie let go of Jamie's hand and struggled to push herself up in the bed. She had to stop once and catch her breath.

Hailey found the remote and pushed the up button until the head of the bed had risen another six inches.

Mackenzie nodded thanks and focused on Jamie. "Please."

"You're going to be out of commission for a while, Wallace," Jamie told her.

"After."

Jamie focused on Mackenzie, but Hailey saw her raise a brow.

"I could use the help," Hailey said.

Jamie met her gaze, nodded. Hailey knew they were both thinking Mackenzie might be safer if she weren't on patrol for a while.

Jamie nodded. "She could help."

"I'll talk to Captain James about getting you a temporary stint in Homicide." Hailey turned to Jamie. "That okay?"

"Perfect," Jamie said.

"But nothing goes outside us. Not until we know who we're homing in on," Hailey said, directing the comment to Mackenzie.

"Or until we can nail Marchek on the rapes and force him to tell us who he saw," Jamie agreed.

"Like a rookie club investigation," Hailey said, offering a smile to Mackenzie.

The rookie let out a little laugh, then coughed. "Charlie's Angels."

Jamie nodded and Hailey remembered Scanlan's comment.

"We'll nail him," Jamie said. "Whoever he is."

Just then the door burst open and a frazzled-looking man in a T-shirt and jeans came in carrying a cup of coffee. He halted at the sight of Hailey and Jamie, then pushed through to the bed. "What's going on?"

"Alan," Mackenzie whispered. She waved her hand to indicate the others.

Hailey introduced herself and Jamie to Mackenzie's husband. "We were just checking on her," she added.

"We're leaving now," Jamie said.

Alan came straight to Mackenzie and set his coffee on the table beside her head. "You okay, Mac?"

She nodded. "Much. Better."

His shoulders slumped in relief as the women started for the door.

"I'll check in later today," Hailey promised and Mackenzie nodded.

In the hall, they paused.

"You think it's smart to involve her?" Hailey asked.

"She's one hell of a tough lady," Jamie answered.

Hailey just nodded.

"Rookie club investigation," Jamie said, shaking her head. "I like Charlie's Angels better."

They shared a superficial laugh, neither feeling any humor as they walked toward the elevators.

Hailey thought about what Mackenzie had been through. Jesus Christ.

But Jamie was right about something else, too—they were going to nail this bastard. She just prayed they could do it before someone else ended up in this place.

Or worse—down in the basement where they stored the cold bodies.

# 26

Jamie didn't leave the house Sunday afternoon. She
made calls to every member of the rookie club who
had been at the dinner the other night, including the
late arrival, Stephanie Rusch. She gave each a modi-
fied version of the truth, which included Mackenzie's
attack and Barney's and warned them each to be especially careful. She left messages for the ones who
weren't home. The few she spoke to hadn't taken her
warning as seriously as she would have liked. How
could they?

If a cop worried about every threat, she would never
leave the house. A cop's job was to put herself in
constant danger. The fact that Jamie thought the risk
was higher today than usual didn't mean she was right.

She also convinced Captain Jules to sign off on another eighteen hours of surveillance on Marchek to
cover through tomorrow. A meeting was called for
first thing in the morning to discuss how to proceed
both with him and Devlin's murder. In the meantime,
Jamie just prayed the tail on Marchek was enough to
prevent another rape. God, she wanted this case to
be over.

And seeing Mackenzie this morning had only made
things worse. Damn it if she didn't look like shit. At
least the doctor thought they'd release her in the

morning. They wanted to keep her another night because of the head injury.

All of Jamie's victims were recovering. According to one of the local trauma psychologists, Emily Osbourne had come in for counseling. The subject matter was protected by patient confidentiality, but Jamie was always relieved to hear that victims were seeking out help. Emily's father left Jamie a message at least once a day. Her mother had called the rape crisis center for resources on therapy. Jamie had also followed up on all the call-in tips the department had gotten. She had nothing to show for the effort.

She thought about Marchek as she watched Barney circle the floor until he found a comfortable spot to lie down. He appeared to be favoring his right leg, but the vet was confident he'd recover. Barney had been the lucky one.

At half past four, Tony entered the living room juggling her car keys. "I thought I'd pick up some fixings for chicken parmesan."

She sat up. "I'll come."

"Don't. I can do it. I know where the store is."

Jamie closed her eyes. She didn't want to go, yet she felt responsible for him. What would he do if she didn't come? Get drunk again? Total her car with him in it?

"You need some smokes?" he asked.

She shook her head. Stopped. "Okay, just a couple Marlboro Lights—hard packs. And get something sweet—some of that Chubby Hubby or something."

He frowned. "Chubby Hubby?"

"You know, ice cream."

Tony shrugged. "Never heard of it, but I'll find it."

The door clicked closed and she sat up, suddenly anxious. She ran to the door, pulled it open. "Tony."

He looked back, a half smile on his face. It was the expression of a kid about to be let out on his own.

Don't call him back. Don't do it. "Please be careful, okay?"

"I won't scratch the car, I promise."

Jamie shook her head. "I don't give a rat's ass about the car."

He smiled, turned with energy in his step.

She stepped back into the house, watched him go, knowing it was the right thing to do. At the computer, she signed into the chat room and exchanged a few brief messages about the case in Chicago. It felt weird to be there—exposed—and she signed off after a few minutes.

When the doorbell rang a few minutes later, Jamie assumed it was Tony.

She pulled the door open and said, "You have a key—" She halted midsentence.

Tim stood on her doorstep.

"Sorry. I thought you were—" She shook her head.

"Can I come in?"

Jamie hesitated. Looking at Tim, she didn't feel angry. She realized it was the first time since she'd found him with Natasha. "Okay. For a few minutes."

"Thanks." Tim followed her to the kitchen. She could feel his gaze stop on Tony's shoes, which sat just inside the back door.

"You want some coffee?"

He nodded. "That would be great." He sat down and traced the wood grain on the table. Watching him, she had a vision of them lying in bed together, Tim reenacting a car chase with his fingers on the pillowcase. She searched her mind for the moment when things had gone wrong. She couldn't find it. Never could. Just one day it was bad.

"How are you?"

"I'm not back to work yet. I went by and there's a bunch of picketers in front."

"Picketers?"

"Protesting my release."

Jamie poured two cups and sat down. "I'm sorry."
He shook his head. "It's my own fault."

Jamie thought about the question that had bothered
her from the start. "Why did you move her?"

He met her gaze, shook his head. "She looked
asleep—a little pale, maybe, but not dead." He turned
the coffee cup, stared down at it. "I'd been hit in the
head and I came to a little dizzy. When I saw her, I
just picked her up instinctively. I knew she was hurt.
I didn't get far before I realized . . ." He stopped,
blinked.

She could see the emotion in his eyes and had to
look away. She took a drink of coffee, felt the liquid
burn her tongue.

"Maybe I knew she was dead and didn't want to
accept it." Maybe she should have asked more questions, but she couldn't. She already knew Tim had
slept with Natasha before she died. That was enough.
Plus, the murder wasn't her case.

Jamie didn't know what to say, couldn't find the
words.

They sat in silence for a few minutes before Tim
stood up. "Thanks for letting me talk, Jamie."

She started to stand, but he stopped her. "I'll let
myself out." Then, before she could stop him, he
leaned down and kissed her on the cheek and was
gone.

Jamie dumped the coffees in the sink and stared
out the window, trying to discern exactly how she felt.
The very absence of anger felt so foreign. She wasn't
even sure she could say it felt good. The anger was
easy. This—forgiveness maybe—this was hard.

Upstairs, she showered, lingering under the scalding
water. She tried not to think about Tim. Or even
about Marchek or Scanlan or Tony.

Out of the shower, she dumped dirty clothes off the
chair in her bedroom, dragged it to the window. Sitting in the light, she brushed her hair with the wood-

handled brush she'd had for a decade. She fought with the gnarled bits. Eventually, she won and the knots came loose. She turned her head over and brushed the underneath and then flipped it back up. It was cool on her neck. She passed the brush through the smooth strands, daring it to catch.

She held the brush in her hands, ran her fingers across the smooth wood. For some reason, brushing her hair reminded her of the first female friend she'd had. Marisa Caltabiano was Italian, her father a police officer in the Bronx. She and her family—parents and two younger brothers—had moved in down the street from Tony and Jamie. They hadn't come from far, just from somewhere else in the Bronx. As a kid, though, a couple of blocks seemed like across the world. Marisa had lived near them for four years, beginning when Tony and Jamie were nine or maybe ten. No, it would have been nine.

She had moved away when they were thirteen—after the attack. Her father had been the one to find them. It had been his call. Jamie pushed those memories aside and thought about the early days.

Tony had discovered Marisa playing jacks down the street and had brought her home like a stray puppy. Jamie had disliked her immediately. She had thick curls and olive skin and perfectly almond-shaped eyes. She was nice, not sweet, and held her own from the start. Tony and Mick were so taken with her that Jamie's Irish temper had been thrown into overdrive.

Jamie had been so protective of them, especially Tony. She wasn't used to sharing him. Marisa was the first time it had ever come up. Marisa and Tony had dated a bit; she was his first girlfriend. All of it before the attack, the rape. Before everything had changed.

Jamie glanced at the clock. Forty-seven minutes had passed since Tony left—not nearly enough time to get groceries and get back, especially on a Sunday.

Her throat closed. She ignored it, found the pack

of cigarettes on the floor by her bed. As she walked across the room, she shook one out. She opened the window and lit the cigarette, curling back into the chair. It was cool outside and she grabbed a sweatshirt off the floor and pulled it on over her head. She inhaled with a hissing Darth Vader sound, exhaled.

The muscles in her neck loosened and she focused on a spot up the road. Cars passed in the distance, too far to hear. The room was quiet except for the whine of the wind through the open window.

Barney let out a moan on the bed, went back to sleep.

Her mind settled on her family—on Tony, Mick, on Pat Galen, and her father. And on their mothers. She couldn't remember her own—the memory was always still, an image from a photograph. But Lana—she could remember Lana with her light hair and eyes. Jamie pictured her bright eyes, wide and open and smiling, her contagious laugh. When she let it loose, it was untamed and free, like she couldn't control it. It used to make the kids smile just hearing her.

But in the end, the pain had stolen her laugh. Even her eyes had lost their humor. That Lana tried to mask it from all of them was her way, but it was there just below the surface. In the last weeks of her life, she'd let the kids into her room for only a few minutes at a time. Then she'd ushered them out so she could rest. And as soon as their backs were turned, her face would grow rigid in agony. Sometimes, when Jamie would look back, she'd see it.

Mick had been a fireball just like Lana. Always the first out of the station house, he was a born leader. Tony had been quieter, shy, more like Pat.

Tony had said they'd had it hard growing up, but Jamie disagreed. They'd had two parents—three for the years with Lana. Their fathers had taken them to the firehouse every few weeks so they could climb on the truck and slide down the pole. The men had taken the kids bowling, had thrown the ball with them. Pat had taught them to play gin rummy for pretzels.

And then somewhere, it had fallen apart. It hadn't been as far back as the rape, although she was confident it had started there. Marisa left, but they remained in the same house with the memory of it all around them. Each of them shared the guilt—the dads, but also each of the kids for not having been there or not being able to stop it.

Mick turned fifteen and started to hang with a pack of older boys. Tony and Jamie were thirteen and had started high school. They were sucked into the mainstream. Four years later, Jamie left. That was it. She'd come to California for college and the boys—Tony, Mick, Pat and her father—had stayed in New York. Most right until the end.

She heard the garage door open, felt relief. She walked down the stairs, Barney trailing slowly behind. She opened the door. "Can I help?"

Tony nodded. "Sure. Grab a bag."

They unloaded the groceries into the kitchen and Jamie slowly pulled things out—cheese, lunch meats, chips, chicken breasts, ice cream. "You got a lot of stuff."

He looked at her for a moment. "I thought we could use some food around here."

She nodded, felt relieved. Suicidal men didn't buy food.

"I found these, too. Remember them?" He passed her a pack of baseball cards like the ones they had collected as kids.

She smiled.

"You used to sell me and Mick your cards and you'd hide the gum in your drawer with the money."

She frowned. "I don't remember that."

He smiled. "You did. I was collecting Willie Mays cards. Must've been seventy-four because he was back in New York a couple years then, and I didn't have any money. Dad wouldn't give me any and Mick would just buy the damn cards and keep them for himself.

"I was desperate for more cards and you gave me a bunch of money. It felt like a thousand dollars to me. You must've pulled ten dollars out of your sock drawer one day. And you gave it all to me."

She smiled at the memory, tried to picture Tony's excited face. She was sure it had been worth every cent. "I hope you still have those cards."

"Ah, shit. Deborah probably has them now."

The moment burst like a bubble. She turned to put the groceries away, wondered where Tony got the money to pay for them. It had been a long time since he'd worked. "You okay for cash?"

His eyes hit the ground. He turned his back, whispered, "From Mick. From nine eleven. I was next of kin. Well, Dad, then me."

Jamie watched his back, searching for the right thing to say. She walked to the kitchen sink, struggling. Damn it. Why did it have to be so hard? She took a breath. "I'm glad you're here, T."

He looked up slowly. His wide eyes were glassy.

She blinked hard. *Come on, Tony.* She glanced at the ceiling and back, felt her own eyes fill. She stepped out, sucked a deep breath. "Shit," she said finally.

Then she crossed to him. She pulled a box of crackers from his hand, set it down. She wrapped her arms around his back, pulled him against her.

She heard the quick intake of his breath and felt his sobs as they let loose.

"Jamie," he croaked, and she held tighter as if she could squeeze the pain right out of him.

"I'm here, Tony."

"You're it, Jamie. You're all I've got."

"I'm not going anywhere, T. You've got me."

He gasped and sobbed harder, and she closed her eyes, the tears flushing down her cheeks. They stood

184        *Danielle Girard*

there for a long time. She thought about their families
and about Tim, about Emily Osbourne and Hailey and
Mackenzie and even about Natasha Devlin. About all
that life had handed her and all she knew was yet to
come—the never-ending cycle of hardships. And the
moments of relief. The tiny grains of joy. They were
there, too.

As she loosened her grip, swiped the tears from her
face, she wondered what obstacle would come next—
a new rape victim, another attack?

Surely, things never settled for long.

Then she considered that maybe she'd had enough.
Maybe this time would be different.

Maybe.

# 27

Monday morning traffic was bumper to bumper on 101 heading south toward the bridge, which had seemed empty over the last few months. Everyone said that there were fewer people on the roads because of all the layoffs. Well, if everyone was unemployed, there must have been some sort of mass interview happening that morning.

Jamie arrived at the station house late and already sweating underneath a navy wool blazer.

As she rushed through the department door, Dorothy, the Sex Crimes secretary, snarled, "You're late."

Jamie bit her tongue and passed the woman without a comment. "Hag," she whispered loud enough for a few others to hear as she knocked on the conference room door.

"Come in."

She recognized her captain's voice and opened the door. The small room was full, and it took a few seconds to absorb all the faces that surrounded the pitted old table. To her left, at the head of the table, was Captain Jules. Next to him, Linda James and then Mackenzie.

Jamie stopped on her. "You're out. You okay?"

She nodded without speaking. Her face looked worse today—the bruising deeper, the swelling worse. One eye was completely closed. At least she was there. She could think and walk. Speak. She would survive.

Chip Washington sat beside Mackenzie, and beyond him was a man she didn't recognize. She finally made it around the table and found Hailey Wyatt on her left.

"Sit down, Vail," Ben Jules said, pounding on the table in an unfamiliar gesture of impatience.

Jamie took the chair directly in front of her.

"You know everyone?"

She looked around and nodded. The man at the other head didn't stand and didn't offer a hand. "Captain David Marshall, Homicide."

Jamie nodded and looked over at Hailey, who raised an eyebrow just slightly. Marshall was an asshole, the look said. So far Jamie agreed.

As soon as she was seated, Captain Jules turned to Mackenzie. "Your statement said you're sure Officer Scanlan wasn't your attacker."

Mackenzie nodded.

"You still sure?" he asked.

"Positive."

Jamie sat forward. "It's all related, somehow, Captain—Devlin, the rapes, Mackenzie's attack."

Jules nodded. She'd already told him her theory when they'd spoken yesterday. He looked up at Captain Marshall. "They want to work it as one case, share information. I don't have a problem with that. Do you?"

Marshall steepled his hands. "Wyatt's got two high-profile homicide cases going. I can't have her pulled off of them on any tangents related to rape or any other crime. I need some arrests made on these murders."

Jules frowned and opened his mouth to speak, but Linda interjected. "Officer Wallace would like to help. She's sharp and will be good for legwork and that sort of thing—phone calls, follow-ups. Plus, she won't be doing her beat for a while—not until we catch this guy."

Marshall frowned and started to shake his head.

"Chief Jackson agrees they should work it together," Jules added.

Jamie watched Jules, wondered if he was lying. It seemed odd that he would have talked to the chief of police on Devlin's murder, especially since it was Marshall's case, not his, that was so high profile. Maybe it had to do with Scanlan.

Marshall didn't test him. Instead, he looked at her with narrowed eyes. "Fine. Get to it, ladies. But don't let this conspiracy theory trip you up. I think you discovered some coincidences—nothing more."

Captain Jules began to address Marshall on a few logistics.

Mackenzie turned to Jamie and whispered, "Where do we start?"

"I'm going to drag Marchek in, see if you can ID him in a lineup."

Mackenzie nodded and Jamie could see her throat tighten with anxiety.

Jamie kept her voice low. "If we trust the message we got, I guess the best place to start the murder investigation is with men Natasha was involved with inside the department."

Linda James nodded. "If this guy's a cop and he killed Natasha, that seems like as good a place as any."

"That's going to be a long list," Jamie said. To Hailey, she whispered, "Maybe there will be a stutterer on it."

Hailey nodded, eyes narrowed.

Jamie watched her. "You have an idea."

"I think maybe I know who to ask first."

From the corner of her eye, Jamie saw Linda and Mackenzie exchange a questioning glance.

But when Hailey's gaze met hers, Jamie knew exactly whom she meant. If Bruce Daniels was having an affair with Hailey, why not Devlin, too?

Hell, everyone else had.

"People. People," Marshall called, returning the focus to the meeting at hand. "Is Daniels coming in with Officer Scanlan or are we done? I've got a briefing in twenty minutes."

Jules glanced at Jamie.

"I'm ready," she said.

Chip Washington opened the door and waved them in. Scanlan came in behind Daniels. He took the seat beside Jamie.

Jules spoke first. "Okay, we're all here to talk about the incident on Geary on Friday night. Officer Scanlan has agreed not to press any charges of misconduct by his fellow officers. So we can avoid an investigation on that."

Jamie sent a glare at Scanlan and turned to Captain Jules. "That's a load of crap."

He raised a hand. "Let me finish."

She crossed her arms and tilted her chair back.

Scanlan put his foot under the leg of the chair and pushed her back.

She lost her balance and the chair toppled backwards. Hailey grabbed hold of the chair in an attempt to stop her from falling on the floor. The chair hit the wall, preventing Jamie from landing on her ass. She rocked it back onto all four legs and was out of the seat in two seconds. She bent over Scanlan, fist raised. "Listen, asshole. You touch me again and I'll shoot your fat ass."

Jules was up, too. He took her arm and pulled her back.

Hailey stood beside her. "He knocked her back, Captain. He was out of line, not her."

"Enough," Bruce Daniels said. "If we can't act like adults, then we'll have to put someone else on this case."

"Fine by me," Jamie said. "You want to take it?"

Daniels' face reddened.

Captain Jules led Jamie to the other end of the room, away from Scanlan, and motioned for her to sit in his chair. "He's got something to help, Jamie," he said, motioning to Scanlan. "Let him get it out and then we can get rid of him."

She nodded.

He wiped his brow and turned back. "Officer Scanlan, watch yourself. Your father doesn't run Sex Crimes. I do. You understand me?"

Scanlan dropped his head. "Yes, sir."

"Okay, Daniels. Let's hear what your boy has to say. Then I want all of you out of here."

Daniels didn't look happy, but he nodded at Scanlan. Scott leaned forward in his chair, rested his elbows on his knees. Jamie glanced around the room, settling on Mackenzie. Mackenzie gave her a quick look and Jamie thought she saw a smile behind the remains of a very swollen lip.

"I drove Natasha—uh, Inspector Devlin—back from the awards banquet that night."

"And you had sex with her?" Jamie interrupted.

Daniels glared at her.

Scanlan shook his head. "No." He kept his head down.

Jamie felt a shift in the room. She looked at Jules, who looked perplexed. He didn't know, but Daniels looked distinctly uncomfortable. Marshall looked awkward and annoyed, and Washington didn't meet her gaze. No one spoke. What the hell was going on?

"Someone had sex with her in that office just before she was killed," Jamie said. "And you brought her here."

"I didn't have sex with her."

Jamie watched Scanlan. His face was ruddy, sweat beading on his lip. He looked like a schoolkid in the principal's office. "You're lying."

"Enough," Daniels snapped.

Jamie stared at Bruce Daniels. He looked away. They were lying—both of them. She glanced at Washington, who studied his hands. What were they hiding? Jamie opened her notebook to the pages where she'd noted Roger's findings. She skimmed the words. Devlin had two samples of semen inside her—one six or so hours old, one within a half hour of her death. The most recent sample contained no sperm.

According to Roger, there was no way to tell why the sample was aspermatic. It could have been a genetic anomaly or the man had undergone a vasectomy. Pure odds favored the vasectomy. She looked at Scanlan, frowning. He was young. He'd never had children. Why would he have a vasectomy?

She looked up at him, glanced at Daniels. "Did you bring Devlin back to meet someone else?"

Scanlan's eyes widened.

Daniels spoke up. "I think it's enough that Officer Scanlan has told us that he wasn't with Devlin that night."

"It's not enough, Officer Daniels. Because whoever *was* with Devlin that night is a key suspect in her murder."

"I have to agree with Inspector Vail," Jules piped in.

Daniels looked at Scanlan, who seemed to plead with his eyes.

And suddenly it made sense. Scanlan's discomfort, the other men's awkwardness, the vasectomy. "It was your father, wasn't it? He was the last person to have sex with Devlin?"

Scanlan dropped his head into his hands.

Daniels sank back into his chair, let his head fall back.

Washington shrank down in his chair.

Someone else uttered a curse under his breath.

The room silenced.

Jamie glanced at Hailey. She shook her head. Deputy Chief Scanlan was the last person to have sex with the murdered inspector.

Their case had just gotten a hell of a lot more complicated.

# 28

Mackenzie had been sent home after the meeting. They'd all insisted she go—Linda, Hailey, Jamie. She'd wanted to protest, to tell them that she was ready to start on the case right then, but she wasn't. Everything ached, and sitting upright, even for fifty minutes, had been torture.

The vertebrae in the small of her back felt like they'd been crushed, and her cracked ribs howled with the slightest breath. Even the thick white tape the nurse had wrapped around her middle offered no support. And the drugs made her feel worse—out of control and fuzzy.

Only while lying completely horizontal did she feel any physical relief. But that was when her mind spun a web around every creak in the house. Was he back? The fear remained lodged in her chest, and sleep came with a backlash of violent dreams.

She was terrified. She struggled to be analytical about the attack, to search her memory for exactly when he'd made his approach, which direction he'd come from. Had he been with her right from her house? Had he watched her with Alan on the front stoop? She tried to find him in her subconscious, to recall every word he'd spoken for the next time she'd see his face, hear his voice. But mostly she felt bombarded by a thousand moments of terror and anxiety at remembering the event. A creak, a door somewhere in the building, almost anything could set her off.

For a few hours the night before, her brain had released the images, dove into some other place. And for those hours, she had really rested. When she arrived home from the station, Alan had the house armed and ready. He'd bought an electronic alarm that hung on the back of the door for the times when he was out. In the bedroom, he had littered the bedside table with her favorite foods and plenty of water and juice. She sank into bed, glanced at the magazines, then chose to stare at the ceiling instead.

Her parents phoned every few hours; her brother, Jake, had called to hear the story. When she was done, all he could say was, "Why didn't you just shoot his ass?"

She hung up on him.

The phone continued to ring. She didn't want to answer the same questions again. Yes, she was fine. No, he hadn't been caught. No, she wasn't moving back to Montana tomorrow. Yes, she was still a cop. She didn't consider if the answers were honest. They were knee-jerk reactions.

It was nearly four o'clock when the Caller ID showed a number from the station.

She shifted up in bed, felt a stabbing pain. When she answered, she sounded like she'd been running. "Hello."

"It's Jamie. You okay?"

"Fine."

"You sound like shit, you know. Why are you answering the phone?"

Mackenzie laughed and pain stabbed her side. "Ow."

"See, you can't even laugh. I'll call you later."

"No, no. I'm just lying here bored. Please at least tell me why you called."

Jamie paused.

"Hello?"

"Okay, we brought Marchek in for a lineup."

Mackenzie resisted the urge to push herself up. Felt breathless. Anxiety stabbed her chest.

"You there?"

"I'm here. He confess?"

"No. Not Marchek."

"I want to do it."

"We'll do a video lineup. You can see it later."

"No, I want to see him." She hesitated. Did she really want to see the man who'd attacked her? This wasn't like the bear that had attacked the tents in Yellowstone. She'd insisted on seeing him before they put him down. He was just an animal trying to survive. This was a man. A rapist. A sexual sadist. Maybe even a killer. But the answer was still yes. A resounding yes. She needed to see him. She forced herself up, swallowed the howling pain.

"Mackenzie?"

"That's why you called, right? To do the lineup."

"To check on you." Jamie hesitated. "And yes, about the lineup. But you don't need to come in here."

"Yes, I do. I need to see him. I want to. And to hear his voice."

"You can do that from a tape."

"It's not the same."

There was a pause. "I don't know—"

"I can take a cab. I can be there in an hour."

Jamie's voice dropped. "Are you sure?"

She was upright now, taking short, painful breaths. "Positive," she lied.

"Okay. Give me your address. I'll pick you up."

Mackenzie dictated her address and cross streets.

"Is a half hour enough time?"

"Do I need to be in uniform?"

"Hell, no. I just meant to get some pants on."

Mackenzie held back a painful laugh. "I'm wearing pants already."

"Perfect. Then half hour should be plenty. See you then."

Mackenzie made it downstairs in twenty-five minutes and Jamie was already at the curb. She stepped out of a dark brown department Taurus and came around to open the passenger door for Mackenzie. Jamie helped her ease into the seat and then closed the door.

Mackenzie expected the car to smell like a diesel truck the way Jamie smoked. Instead, the car's scent was thick with lavender and behind it, a hint of mint.

Jamie maintained an even speed on the trip to the station, doing her best to avoid stopping and starting. Mackenzie appreciated the effort. The image of the seat belt snapping against her chest made her nauseous.

As they drove, Jamie explained the lineup. "There will be five men. All will have dark, curly hair because it's the identifier you mentioned. If I put only one dark curly-haired guy in there, his lawyer would claim he was framed and he'd get off on a technicality."

Mackenzie nodded as Jamie continued. "I'm not going to go into the room with you. Same reason. I'm biased. I've asked Officer Ann Dye to go. You know her?"

Mackenzie shook her head. She knew only a handful of cops, but she was relieved that the cop was female.

"Ann is in Burglary and is looking to move. She's spending some time in Sex Crimes. Won't end up there, though."

"Why not?"

Jamie frowned, focusing on the road. "Couldn't stand it, I don't think. Not many women can. I'm the only one who's been there any length of time. It's just ugly."

Mackenzie watched Jamie, the lines that were like exclamations around wide brown eyes. "Why do you do it?"

Jamie shook her head, eyes narrowing as she smiled. "Glutton for punishment." She sobered a moment. "I have to believe I'm doing some good."

Mackenzie nodded.

The rest of the ride was quiet, and Mackenzie closed her eyes for a moment, thinking a rest would be good. But with nothing else to focus on, her pain intensified. She must have flinched because Jamie said, "You okay?"

She swallowed her nausea, nodded.

Jamie parked in a handicapped zone, threw her inspector's parking pass on the dash. Then she came around the car to open Mackenzie's door.

Mackenzie ignored the nerves that drummed against her belly.

Jamie took her arm. "You sure you're okay?"

She nodded. "Little dizzy."

"There's a chair in there so you'll be able to sit."

Mackenzie pressed the back of her hand to her forehead, cool sweat beading there.

A woman met them in the hallway and Jamie introduced her as Ann Dye. Officer Dye was tall—five ten or so, and mid to late forties. She was trim, with short highlighted hair and big blue eyes. She looked like she could have been a waitress in Mel's Diner back in the day.

"Ann, this is Mackenzie Wallace. Mackenzie, Ann Dye."

Mackenzie nodded.

"I'll take her, Jamie. We'll ring when we're ready."

Jamie looked at Mackenzie as though she was going to issue some last bit of advice, then decided against it. She turned without a word and disappeared.

Ann took Mackenzie's arm and held on. "Jamie said

this guy got you, but she didn't say how bad. You should be in bed."

They took a few steps down the hall and Ann opened a door, held it for Mackenzie. Mackenzie shuffled awkwardly into a room not much larger than Alan's writing closet. She hesitated on the perimeter, panicked. God, she couldn't do this. With a quick breath, she forced herself inside.

On her right, a series of old metal shelves stood against the wall. Rows of black plastic videotape cases lined the shelves. Along the side of each tape was a ten-digit code Mackenzie assumed was a case number. At the far end of the room stood a rolling cart with a smallish Panasonic TV on one shelf and a VCR on the other.

On her left was a darkened window with a shade pulled over it.

Ann helped Mackenzie into the chair. She gave Mackenzie a minute to adjust and handed her a bottle of water.

Ann motioned to the window then. "You know how this works?"

Mackenzie nodded. She knew they wouldn't be able to see her and still the drumming in her gut intensified.

"Jamie will give them the signals to step forward and turn. She'll also ask them to talk. There's a number on the wall behind each suspect. The lines are to help with height.

"After that, you can tell me if you want another look, to hear them again, anything like that."

A small red light on the wall above the window went on. "They're ready when you are."

Mackenzie took a breath, nodded.

Ann gave the shade a tug and released it. It disappeared into the roll at the top of the window with a snap. Mackenzie stared into a dark room.

"Ready," Ann said into a black box beside the window.

The light flicked on. Mackenzie blinked and glanced at the line of men. All five stood along the wall, facing forward. Gripping the water bottle, Mackenzie studied the room first. Eggshell paint, the lined wall, dirty linoleum. Slowly, she made her way to the men. She saw the row of pants—three in jeans, two in slacks. She scanned their shirts—button-downs, a gray T-shirt, a yellow sweatshirt.

Finally, her nerve up, she stared at their faces. One was shaven, one unshaven; she saw beady eyes, large ones, almond, blue. She saw a high forehead, angular cheeks on one, jowls on another.

She homed in on one with longer curly hair and a beard. His eyes were narrow and dark. Was that him? She scanned his eyes for some sign—some viciousness or conceit. But saw nothing.

It was like the bear they'd caught. She had expected the bear to be hostile and angry. Caught, he had acted just like every other bear she'd ever seen up close—scared and a little caged in, like he hadn't known why he was there.

"Let me know when you want them to turn."

"Not yet." Mackenzie sucked in a breath, choked on the searing pain as her lungs pressed against a cracked rib. Her eyes teared and she closed them for a long moment. Forcing them open, she examined their faces. She searched for the man she'd envisioned, but suddenly she couldn't picture him.

She scanned each set of eyes—light, dark, tired, alert, shifty. Each looked guilty of something, but none looked familiar. She hadn't seen his eyes, she told herself. Suddenly she realized that she didn't know which one he was.

"Give yourself time," Ann said, placing a hand on her shoulder. "It might be a side shot that does it, or the voice. You didn't see him head-on, did you?"

Mackenzie nodded, sucked a shallow breath. "Can you have them turn to the side?"

"Side view," Ann called into the speaker.

Jamie gave the direction and all five shuffled sideways. Mackenzie studied their motions. The one with the long hair moved succinctly like he was doing an army drill. The most clean-shaven of them moved like he was in water. One sort of stumbled like he'd caught his toe on something she couldn't see. A couple studied the mirror as they turned, their eyes scanning the surface as though seeking her out behind the glass.

She shivered. The water bottle slipped from her grasp and landed on the floor. She ignored it, commanding herself to calm down. She was a cop. She could do this.

Ann picked up the bottle. "Anything?"

Mackenzie didn't answer, didn't want to admit she had failed. She struggled to remember something about the man who'd tried to kill her. Jesus Christ, why couldn't she pick him out? Was he even there? Maybe it would be his voice. Calm down and just work through it. Four of the five were over six foot, so she discounted the one who was only five nine or ten. Her attacker was taller than she, wasn't he? "Other side," she said.

The men turned again. She watched them spin, heard one of them say something to another.

"No talking," Jamie thundered.

She stared. Still nothing.

"Anything?"

She looked at Ann, shook her head.

"Voices?"

Mackenzie nodded, blinking back tears.

"Lines."

"Starting on the far end, then. Number five, give us your line."

Number five stepped forward. He was the shortest

of them, the one Mackenzie had discounted. "You're going to deliver a message," he said.

The words made her shudder. My God, was that him? "Again," she said, her throat catching.

"Repeat number five."

"You're going to deliver a message," number five repeated, getting into his lines.

He furrowed his brow, bunched his fists. He looked angry. Then, as soon as the words were out, his shoulders dropped. Acting. She shook her head. Not him. "Next."

Each spoke. Several performed the lines with no feeling. Number two nearly shouted it. Number five's performance had been the most real, but none was the voice she remembered.

Mackenzie asked for a couple more repeats and then took a last look at the line. "Damn it."

"No luck?"

She shook her head.

"You want them to turn again? More lines?"

She turned toward Ann, refusing to look at the men. One of them had most likely attacked her. He'd been on top of her, groped her. She'd heard his voice. Yet she couldn't identify him. "I can't."

Ann nodded, pressed the button. "Done."

The men filed out of the room. Mackenzie studied them as they went.

Jamie opened the door, stepped inside, and closed it behind her. Her eyes were wide and excited, but her expression flattened when she saw Ann. She glanced at Mackenzie. "No?"

Mackenzie shook her head. "No."

Jamie bunched a fist. "Damn it."

"Which one was Marchek?"

She shook her head, gave Mackenzie a little smile that didn't even begin to cover her disappointment. "Doesn't matter. We'll get him."

Mackenzie stared back at the empty room, her mind

running over the five faces. She hadn't even considered that she wouldn't know him, that she wouldn't be able to pick him out of a lineup.

"Let me get rid of these guys and I'll take you home. Ann, can you stay for a minute?"

"No problem."

Jamie left the room quickly and Mackenzie heard her voice in the hallway as she released the lineup.

Mackenzie studied her hands, turned them slowly and watched the lines grow deeper as she created a fist. She spotted a scrape on her left hand where he'd knocked her into the pavement. She ran her fingers across her swollen lip, felt the hard plastic of the stitches. She wondered when the lip would stop feeling strangely disconnected to the rest of her face. She started to cry, blinked the tears back.

She pushed herself up from the chair slowly and turned toward the door.

"You've got a few minutes."

Mackenzie shook her head. "I'm going outside. Tell Jamie I'll wait by the car." She opened the door, hoping to catch something in the hall, some glimpse of which man had been the one Jamie had hoped to arrest. The hallway was empty.

She wondered where Marchek was, whether he might wait for her. She told herself he wouldn't attack her here, not in the middle of the day. She'd take the elevator anyway.

Mackenzie shuffled awkwardly toward the elevator, wishing more than anything that she could release her emotional energy somehow. There would be no running today, no running for a long while. No, she'd be back in bed within the hour.

Her back ached. She should have taken a pill before she left. Now pain overwhelmed her. But worse than the sharp agony in her ribs or the dull ache in her back was the knowledge that the man who'd attacked her had just walked away again.

She fought back a rush of tears that swelled in her
eyes, streamed down her cheeks.

Her attacker was back on the street.

And she'd let him go.

# 29

Tony waited a half hour after Jamie left. He stared at the clock, not allowing himself to go near the garage, not until thirty minutes had passed. The last five minutes were the longest. Then it was finally over. It wasn't even nine o'clock in the morning. He didn't care.

He half ran to the garage and pulled out the fifth of Jim Beam he'd hidden under an unopened bag of potting soil. He stared at the bottle, shook his head. Goddamn it. He couldn't help himself. He twisted the black cap in his fist, felt it pop off in his hand.

He closed his eyes, searching for the strength to resist. In the end, desire won out. He tipped the bottle to his lips, savored the harshness of the whiskey, the way his throat automatically closed on the liquor. He coughed, cupped his hand over his lips to catch the bit he spit. Then he licked it off his fingers like a kid with a melted ice cream cone.

The burn in his throat was the best part—that and the numbness. He needed the numbness today, just for a while. He hadn't expected to find liquor in a grocery store. In New York, you couldn't buy it there. But in California, it was right alongside the wines and beers.

He'd spent the weekend thinking about the first drink he'd take once she was gone. Just enough to survive the day. Maybe Jamie knew, but she didn't let on. She didn't want to know about his problems. Maybe she had once. Maybe a long time ago. He tried to remember life back then, but it was gone. Any tangible memories had grown into a handful of snapshots of grinning kids in goofy outfits.

He walked back into the house, cradling the bottle like a child. He sank onto the couch, rested his eyes. The bee buzzed in his brain. Thank God for the bottle. He glanced around at Jamie's house, at the unpacked boxes, the uncovered windows.

She was as fucked up as he was—maybe more so because she wouldn't admit how bad off she was. He was relieved that she was gone today. The constant weight of her stare had grown too heavy. Deborah had become the same way, especially at the end. It felt as though she was just waiting for him to fuck up—to go get drunk, to lose the latest no-end job, to come home a failure again. And it was that stare that ultimately led him to do just that—all in one fucking day.

"You're going to be late for work, Tony. You can't be late. We need this job. We have to pay the mortgage. I can't do it alone." It was like a tape on repeat, and the words bounced off his skull until it was too much.

And then there was the day he just didn't want to go. It was a worthless job at a stupid factory in Jersey. It wasn't even a job he would have taken if not for her. He would have just collected unemployment and waited for a chance to get back into the department. He was a firefighter—that was his calling. He'd been a firefighter in New York's Battalion 1, Civic Center, for eleven years. And she wanted him to go to work in a fucking factory. Christ, even a lame security position was a step in the right direction compared to that.

So then he woke up on a Tuesday—a Tuesday so much like the one when Mick had died—a beautiful crisp Tuesday in the fall. Blue skies and clear. Clear enough to fly a goddamn plane right into downtown Manhattan.

Shit, he just didn't want to go to work, couldn't handle it.

"I'm not going in today," he'd said. That should have been okay. She should have known that he just needed to blow off some steam. It was understandable. It was almost exactly a year after that day. Shit, September 11th. On that September Tuesday, he'd been out of the department for two months. And he'd been sober.

Thank God he'd been sober that day. Not that it mattered, not that sobriety had kept him from fighting with Mick, from sending his brother off to the South Tower to die. He replayed it in his head three or four times a day until he had every possible scenario down pat.

Maybe if he'd been drunk, Mick would still be alive. Mick might have gotten Tony tossed out of there altogether. Tony might have stumbled home, away from the towers before either had fallen. And Mick might have gone up the North Tower instead of the South Tower. Or maybe Mick would have been the one to drag Tony away. Maybe taking care of his little brother would have saved his life.

If Tony hadn't been there, Mick might have gotten out. Tony took another drag on the bottle. He closed his eyes and pictured that day—the cloudless sky, a perfect fall day in New York.

Two months earlier he'd been canned. After eleven years, three months, and twelve days on the force, Tony had been fired for showing up drunk. It had been a four-alarm fire at the Millennium Hilton on Church Street. They'd called him in and he'd come. It was his day off, but they needed the manpower. He shouldn't have gone.

Deborah had tried to stop him, but he didn't listen.

He got in his car and drove there, stinking drunk. Mick sent him home immediately, but he didn't listen. Mick had pleaded and fought, dragged him away from the burning building. Mick had tried to save Tony— his life, his job. And in return, Tony had gotten Mick killed—gotten him killed with his own stubborn stupidity. Tony thought he could handle it. Tony always thought he could handle it.

He knew better now. His battalion commander had come to see what was going on, why Mick wasn't up in the building, why they were wasting time fighting each other instead of the angry blazes. Tony had tried to push by. He'd fought with his commander, told him off, and was fired. That was July 9th.

Two months, two days later, he was working security in 5 World Trade Center. He'd been on at seven a.m., was in the lobby of his building, watching people in fancy suits come and go when they'd heard that first explosion. He'd looked at his watch exactly one minute before—eight forty-five. He had a break at nine. He never took it.

When Tony woke, he felt like he was sucking on cotton. He sat up, blinked hard, and stood. The room turned on its side and he grabbed the couch for support. He looked down at the bottle, two-thirds gone, and gave his head a light shake. It pounded. He staggered to the kitchen and turned the faucet on, let the water run over his hands. He splashed his face, then drank thirstily, using his hand as a cup. The clock on the stove said 7:50. It was dark outside. He hadn't eaten all day.

He shut the water off, leaned against the cool tile of the countertop. When he opened his eyes, he stared out the window. Clouds filled the gray sky, the sight of it almost soothing. He blinked hard and wondered if Jamie had any aspirin in the place. He opened a cupboard, then another one, before turning toward the

bathroom. Jamie would be home soon. He was surprised she wasn't already. He had to get his shit
together.

He passed through the back hall when he heard a
scream. He stopped, stunned, and listened. The wind
whined against the window. He heard something slap
the side of the house like a gate slamming closed.

He opened the back door. Behind him, Barney's
claws ticked against the wood stairs. He heard only
the wind.

He started to close the door when Barney barked.
He glanced at the dog, stepped outside. The wind
cooled his face. He heard a sound from the far side
of the house—a human cry. He turned back to the
house for a split second, searching for something he
could use as a weapon.

He found a broom handle on the ground. He lifted
it, held it over his shoulder like a baseball bat, and
crept silently into the dark. His eyes slowly adjusted
as shapes took form against the blanket of gray sky.
He saw a lone tree, the fence.

Had he imagined the noise?

Barney barked again. He halted, breathed. His head
pounded. The numbness had evaporated into a dull
fuzz. The pain was back. At least the cold wind eased
his aching skull.

He reached the corner of the house, peered down
the side. A garbage can, a water spigot. Below it, a
puddle of water had formed. He studied the spigot,
saw no leak. Someone had been running water.

Just then, Barney barked again. He turned back,
heard a branch snap beside him. As he turned, a
shadow dove at him. He swung the broom handle,
heard it crack on flesh as the man landed on him.
Tony fell back, slammed his head on hard pavement.
The shadow slammed him into the ground, grabbed
for the broomstick. Tony gripped it harder. The man
wore a black ski mask, had dark eyes. The two strug-

gled. Tony shoved the stick upwards, trying to knock his attacker off balance.

"Marchek," he said, remembering the name Jamie had used.

The dark eyes narrowed, the pressure increased.

Tony wedged a foot up, kicked, and hoisted the bar over his head. The man flipped over his head. Tony jumped up, spun, the broomstick still in his fists.

The dark form dropped down, barreled into his stomach. Tony crashed into the house, fell to the ground. Before he could react, the man bolted. Tony pulled himself up and sprinted after him.

The man escaped down the driveway. His legs long and lean, he moved fast. Tony dropped the broomstick, drove faster to try to catch up. His head thundered as he reached the street. A hundred yards down the road brake lights flared red in the dark. An engine roared. Tony sprinted toward it. No rear plate. Reverse lights blinded him. The engine revved, tires squealed.

Tony dove into the bushes as the van charged backwards. The car hit the curb, skidded into the dirt. The driver shifted. Tires screeched again as the car roared away.

Tony paused, watched the car disappear. He gripped his head, cursed. Then, turning, he ran back to the house.

The front door was locked. He rounded the side. He had to call Jamie. As he ducked around the garbage cans, he caught sight of a small black tennis shoe.

He halted, saw the leg. A knee. Then the other foot. Holy shit, a child.

He dropped to his knees, leaned into the bush. He found the boy's face streaked with mud. He pressed on the small neck, felt the pulse strong under his fingers. Cried out in relief.

The boy turned his head, pressed a hand to his ear, grimaced.

Tony lifted the boy from the bushes. Bits of leaf and dirt littered an overgrown Afro. "Come on, buddy," Tony said, gently pulling the boy into his arms.

The boy didn't move. Tony looked down at him, felt his own heart roar in his chest. He saw the gentle rise and fall of the boy's breath.

The boy in his arms, Tony rushed inside. He laid the boy on the living room rug and checked again for a pulse. Matted blood covered the boy's shirt. Tony sprinted to the kitchen, grabbed scissors and the phone. Fingers trembling, he dialed 911, told them to send an ambulance. He couldn't remember Jamie's address.

He dropped the phone onto the floor. Lifting the scissors in shaky hands, he cut the boy's shirt away from his chest. The blood was dry. There was no wound. He couldn't find the wound.

He touched the boy's face again.

"Come on, buddy. Talk to me."

The eyes fluttered open. Once. Twice. Then shut again.

The boy's arm twitched. His chest convulsed, and he rocked to one side, vomited on the carpet.

Tony shuddered, grabbed for the phone, and started to punch in Jamie's cell phone number as he glanced up to the ceiling.

He didn't think he could take another death. *Please don't let anyone else die.*

# 30

Jamie couldn't face Mackenzie after the lineup and had scuttled away like a roach under lights. She was a coward, but goddamn it. She had wanted Mackenzie to pick Marchek out of that line so badly, it hurt. Mackenzie had been so close. He'd spoken to her; he'd threatened her. How could he avoid being recognized? But she knew how he'd done it, the slimy son of a bitch. He'd played all the right head games, saying his lines like he was asking a question and changing his tone. And Mackenzie had never seen him. He'd never let her see him. Dark hair was all she'd gotten.

Mackenzie had been Jamie's one shot at putting Marchek back behind bars, where he would be off the streets, at least for a while. Jamie had known the chances were fifty-fifty at best, but she knew it was him, knew he was the one who beat up the rookie.

God, it killed her to let that bastard go. Jules had drawn the line on more surveillance. The current hold ended an hour ago. Nothing she could do. It was too cost prohibitive to watch him. She wondered what a future victim would pay to avoid being attacked, but she knew she couldn't think about it in those terms.

Jamie hadn't wanted Mackenzie to see how disappointed she was. She didn't want to show her despair, knew she couldn't hide it.

It wasn't Mackenzie's fault. The rookie had done

her best. That was all Jamie had asked. For that and a little bit of luck, but there was no luck in her draw. It had been a long time since luck was a friend.

In the end, she couldn't face Mackenzie. Instead, she'd asked Ann Dye to take the rookie home and Jamie had circled the block. She couldn't go back to the office now. She was too steamed to work, too damn furious. Without any evidence, she could find no avenue to pursue Marchek. Nothing infuriated her more than knowing whom to arrest but being unable to bring him in.

She pulled out one cigarette after another with the rare sensation that she'd earned them and smoked with a fervor as she walked the long block around the Hall of Justice. The weather was warm, or maybe it was the anger that made her hot enough to leave her jacket unzipped. As she moved, air caught in the wind shell and sent pockets of cool air down her arms.

She half expected to see Marchek emerge in front of her, taunting her with his freedom, but he'd probably crawled back into a hole until the next victim caught his attention.

After more than an hour of walking, Jamie rounded the Hall and stared up at the words inscribed in gold in the marble facade: *To the faithful and impartial enforcement of the laws with equal and exact justice to all.*

Faithful, she believed in. Her father had been a faithful civil servant and she was confident she had followed in his steps. Impartial? Maybe not, but damn if she didn't try like hell. The rest of it, though—equal and exact justice—these were a farce. Was Marchek getting his equal justice? What about a cockroach like Scott Scanlan or the deputy chief, who slept around on a wife of forty years? And what about Tim, who had spent three nights in prison for a crime he hadn't committed? Or Tony?

For God's sake, did anyone really get justice or was it just a notion devised by man to try to soften the dark reality? She glanced up at the words again, the commandments that she had subscribed to as a rookie. The words, carefully etched into the white stone, used to make her swell with pride.

She turned from the language, disgusted. Now the words served to mock her every effort. She sucked in the last drag of her cigarette and tossed the butt down at the base of the steps. Out of habit, she stooped to retrieve it and stopped herself. She watched the ember burn and stomped it out, leaving the blackened ash on the sidewalk. The gesture was as close to equal justice as she'd felt in ages.

Unable to bring herself to go back into the building, Jamie walked down the small street that led to the parking lot and scanned the darkness. As she reached the back of the building, she looked into the empty foyer. The metal detectors were silent, the hallways empty. Justice, or what they served of it, had definitely shut down for the night.

In the distance, she could hear the purr of trucks and cars on 280, the constant flow of traffic north and south—out and home, out and home. She leaned against the cool brick facade of the Hall and focused on the humming. She'd grown up with that sound. As a kid, traffic had been the closest thing she could remember to ever hearing a lullaby.

She didn't think she'd gone a night without the background noise of traffic until she was twenty. Now, listening to the comforting stream of engines, she wondered if she should move back to the city. She'd bought the house she was in as a knee-jerk reaction to the breakup with Tim, but maybe she should be here. She could probably afford something small. It's not like she or Barney used the backyard.

Just then her cell phone rang. She recognized an extension from inside the Hall and considered not answering. She'd had enough bad news for one day. But duty triumphed. "Vail."

"It's Hailey."

"Hey."

"Where are you?"

"Outside."

"I heard it didn't go well with Marchek."

"We let him go."

"I'm here with Chip. We've got a list of the men. You want to take a look?"

Jamie frowned. "Devlin?"

"Yeah."

"Sure."

"We're in the conference room in Homicide. Come on up."

Jamie popped some gum and rubbed lavender lotion into her hands as she made her way up to Homicide. The department was quiet when she entered.

In the interview room, Hailey sat with two cups of hot coffee in front of her. Across the table, Chip held a bottle of water.

"I poured you one," Hailey said, pushing a cup toward her. "I left it black. I don't know how you take it."

"I take it like my day. Black's perfect."

Hailey gave her a half smile, but Jamie could tell something was wrong.

Chip said hello, his face solemn.

She glanced down at the paper Hailey held pressed under her palms. "The list?"

Hailey nodded, slid it to Jamie.

Jamie turned to Chip. "I didn't think Devlin was your case."

"No, it's Anderson's, but he's got court tomorrow, so I came in his place."

"You've seen the list, then?"

He nodded. "I just went over it with Hailey."

"Any thoughts?"

He paused before answering. "I'm not sure what's worse—that she slept with all those guys, or that someone was keeping a list." His hands trembled as he spoke. He was right. It was an incredible breach of privacy, even if it was never published.

Jamie sat in the chair beside Chip and scanned the list. The names were numbered one to thirty. She recognized maybe a third of them—Tim Worley, Scott Scanlan, David Marshall, Hailey's captain. "Christ. How far back does this go?"

"Not as long as you'd think from looking at it," Chip said.

"A couple of years, I think," Hailey added.

"Who put it together?"

"Daniels."

Jamie glanced at the list again. "Well, at least he's not on there."

Hailey didn't speak at first. When she did, she said, "Neither is Deputy Chief Scanlan. Doesn't mean he didn't screw her."

"You think there are a lot of omissions?" Jamie asked.

"I'm sure IA was thorough," Chip said. "Surely Deputy Chief Scanlan was purposefully left off the list."

"But they didn't leave Scott off."

Chip nodded. "But Scott isn't known for his discretion. And his job's not on the line either."

"Not to mention that unlike Scanlan senior, Scott's not married."

No one spoke as Jamie skimmed over the names. No Ben Jules. That was a relief, but like Hailey said, what did it mean? "How did Daniels put this together?"

Hailey frowned. "I guess one of Internal Affairs' unofficial projects is to follow this sort of activity, to watch that it doesn't cause conflict of interest, probably also to make sure the press doesn't get wind of it. Especially for the higher-ranked married guys."

Jamie turned to Chip. "Did you know they did this?"

He shook his head. "I had no fucking clue."

"David Marshall?"

Hailey nodded. "Married. So are Rich Oliver, Paul Wyeth, Eric Rickens, O'Connell, White, Pilitzky . . ." She waved her hand. "More than half."

Jamie looked at the names again. "Christ. In two years, she had a new guy every month."

"And that's the ones they knew about."

Chip stood up. "You guys need me?"

"No," Hailey said. "Thanks for coming in."

"I'm heading home. See you."

Chip left and Jamie shook her head. "You have to assume there are more men like Deputy Chief Scanlan—ones they wouldn't write down. This is like the needle in the haystack—Devlin's haystack."

Hailey found another paper and slid it across the table. "I did get this."

She looked down at a report from the lab. "What is it?"

"Roger's cast of Worley's head. It looks like Tim was struck with something about an inch thick, made of a heavy polymer material. Rectangular in shape. He took one side in the skull. The corner just scratched the skin."

Jamie frowned. "Polymer? What the hell was it?"

"I don't know. Roger was on his way back to Devlin's office to look for a match."

"A letter holder or something?"

Hailey shook her head. "Not heavy enough. Had to be three or four pounds. Paper weight, maybe?"

Just then, Jamie's cell phone rang. She recognized her home number. "Hey."

Tony's voice was breathless. "Christ, Jamie. Thank God."

She halted. "What's wrong?"

"Marchek was here, Jamie. In the yard."

Jamie stood from the table. "Marchek? Are you sure?"

"Positive."

"Are you okay? Is he gone?"

"I'm fine. Marchek's gone—took off in a white van, but there's a kid here. He was in your yard—he's hurt."

She frowned, listening to the way Tony dragged his S's. "Jesus, Tony, you've been drinking."

"He's bleeding. For Christ sake, Jamie. He's hurt!"

"Is he breathing?"

"Yeah. He's breathing, but there's blood all over him and I can't find the source."

"Call 911."

"I already did, but I need you."

Jamie turned and ran from the room. Hailey started to follow. "I'll call you," Jamie told her. To Tony, she asked, "Where are his parents?"

"He looks homeless, Jamie. I think maybe he was living in your backyard."

Homeless. Christ. "How's his pulse?" She took the stairs, two at a time, running as fast as she could.

"Steady."

She heard a whine in the background.

"The ambulance is here."

At her car, she yanked the door open, shoved the key in the ignition, revved the engine. "Can you ID Marchek? Did you see him?"

"He was wearing a ski mask."

She pounded the steering wheel. "Shit."

"Don't rule it out, though. I saw his eyes."

She shoved the car in gear, sped out of the lot. She shifted into second, heart ramming in her chest. "They'll take you to Marin General. I'll meet you there, Tony. You'll be okay. I'll be there as soon as I can. Call me if you need to. Hang in there."

There was an explosion of voices in the background.

Jamie listened as paramedics beamed questions and Tony tried to respond. A kid. Christ. Why was he in her yard?

Jamie closed the phone with a snap, tossed it on the seat beside her.

Marchek had been at her house that very night. While she was out walking the streets and smoking, Marchek was stalking her house. Jamming the pedal to the floor, she sped toward home. She shuddered as she considered why Marchek had been there.

He'd come for her.

# 31

Jamie and Tony didn't speak during the ride home. The young boy sat silent in the backseat. The doctor had discharged him from the hospital with a clean bill of health. Social services had been notified, and Jamie had agreed to keep him until other arrangements could be made. The other option was to send him to the jail for the night. She couldn't do that. Wouldn't. He was only a kid. And despite the fact that she had no experience, she could manage for a night. She requested additional surveillance, but Jules had denied it. Without any hard evidence, the cost was too much to approve. Otherwise, the department would be patrolling every scumbag 24-7. She didn't like it, but she understood.

The boy looked somewhere around seven, but he was probably older. She knew from experience that homeless kids were usually small for their age. And she knew he was homeless. There was no doubt about that—his uncut lice-ridden hair, his dirty face. Plus, he ate two entire hospital dinners. Any kid who'd spent time with a family that fed him mac 'n' cheese wouldn't have touched the gray turkey and soggy green beans.

When they got home, Jamie found a pair of sweatpants and a long-sleeved T-shirt for him. "They'll be too big, but at least they're clean."

The boy held them to his chest, looked around.

"I'd like to know your name if you're going to stay here. I don't want to call you 'it' or anything."

The boy didn't break a smile. He glanced at Tony, then back to her, wide-eyed.

"I'm Jamie. And this is Tony."

The kid said nothing, didn't move. Only his gaze hopped back and forth between Jamie and Tony like the white ball in a ping-pong match. "Are you still hungry?"

Silence.

She started to back toward the kitchen and the boy watched her.

"He ate a lot at the hospital," Tony said.

Jamie nodded, remembered one of her first victims—a homeless girl of about thirteen who had been repeatedly raped and sodomized and then left for dead. She'd lived—or rather nearly died—in some discarded cardboard boxes until trash day came and the garbage men found her and called the police. After her initial exam, during which she'd had to be strapped down so the doctors could look at her, she ate her way through roughly three times more food than Jamie ate in a day. Then she'd thrown up and started again. The doctors had forced her to slow down for fear that her shrunken-down stomach would burst from the pressure. This kid didn't look as bad as she had, but Jamie thought a little more food might do the trick. Actually, what she had in mind was better than food.

She pulled open the fridge and searched for her stash of Cokes. She found two left and set them on the counter. She dug in the bottom drawer of her freezer for the emergency candy supply. Inside it were a half dozen assorted candy bars—Butterfinger, Snickers, Twix, and a couple of Reese's Peanut Butter Cups.

She emptied the bag on the counter beside the sodas, pushed the freezer closed with her backside.

When she looked up, the boy was halfway across the room. Tony leaned against the doorway and watched.

"I've only got two," she said to Tony, motioning to the Cokes. "You want one?"

He shook his head, smiling just slightly. "No, thanks. I'm going to stick with water for a while."

She pulled a stool to the counter and cracked open a Coke. Then she took a long drag on the soda, making as much noise as possible. She looked at the boy. "Oh, sorry. Do you want one?"

He hesitated, nodded, but still made no move to come closer.

She pushed the other can toward him. "Here you go."

The boy watched them both. Jamie continued drinking her soda as she fingered the candy bars.

From the corner of her eye, she could see the boy inch toward her. He stopped at the counter without touching the drink.

"It's all yours."

He picked it up and mumbled what she thought was "Thanks," then gave his full attention to the sweating red can.

She thought about his speech. Okay, so he did talk. This was good.

Using two long, dirty fingernails, the boy popped the top open and lifted it with both hands as though it were too precious to hold with just one. After his first, quiet sip, he smiled.

Jamie laughed. "Good, huh?"

He nodded and set his gaze on the candy bars.

"You can have one of these, too."

His eyes widened.

"But you have to tell us your name."

The boy frowned.

"I need to know who you are. I can't have a stranger living in my house. And I know somewhere there's someone who's probably really worried about you."

The boy looked at the Coke can and blinked, his dark eyes glassy.

"I bet your mom's missing you."

He shook his head. "No, she ain't." He straightened his back, stood proud. "She left."

Jamie nodded slowly. "Okay, then someone else. You can tell me who."

He shook his head.

Tony shifted against the doorway but said nothing.

Jamie turned to the candy bars. "I think my favorite is Twix. Is that yours?"

He shook his head quickly.

She lifted another. "Snickers?"

He hesitated, then shook his head again. "Reese's," he said, pronouncing it "Rees-eys."

She lifted the peanut butter cups, cold to her touch, pushed the package toward him. "There are two in there—one for each name. You tell me your first name, you get one. Another for your last name."

His gaze narrowed. "You going to call those folks with the foster houses?"

She glanced at Tony, then back to the boy. "Tonight you can stay here with me and Tony."

She didn't want to promise anything else. If the boy knew what a foster home was, he'd been in one. And that meant there might not be a family waiting for him.

He started to reach for the candy bar.

She pushed it toward him.

"Zephenaya."

She frowned.

The boy looked up at her, furrowed his brow. "That's my name. It's from the bible."

"Your first name?"

He nodded. "You can call me Z. That's what Shawna calls me."

"Shawna's your friend?"

"No," he said as though not knowing who Shawna was made her stupid. "My sister. You know. That's why I came here."

Jamie nodded. Now they were getting somewhere. "Where is Shawna?"

He shrugged. "Last time I saw her was with you."

Jamie frowned. She didn't remember her. Child victims weren't usually handled by Sex Crimes. "How old is she?"

He didn't answer. Instead he focused on the candy bar and took small drinks from the Coke.

Jamie tore open the Reese's Peanut Butter Cups and pushed them toward Zephenaya. "Here, Z. You can have one."

He reached in and took one of the brown cups out. Using both hands, he unwrapped it like a present.

"How old are you, Z?"

"Ten," he said matter-of-factly.

Damn, he was small.

"How old are *you*?"

Jamie laughed and Z smiled sheepishly.

"She's forty," Tony called out.

She shot him a glare. "Thanks."

"Forty," Z said. "What's that come after?"

"Thirty-nine," Jamie told him.

He nodded slowly, chewing. "Forty. I forget that one." Z glanced out at the back of the house and Jamie wondered what he was thinking about. She glanced over at Tony, but he was focused on the kid, a half smile on his face.

He hesitated then and looked up at her. "I got something to tell you."

"Okay."

"It's about your dog."

Jamie felt her stomach clench. Not trusting herself to speak, she simply nodded.

"I was here when he got hurt."

She nodded again. "What happened?"

He shook his head. "I didn't do it."

"Who did?"

"A man. A white man with a knife."

He looked over at Tony. "Wasn't him, though. Another white man." He turned to Jamie. "Wasn't the first time someone been in your yard, neither. Another time a man was looking in your windows, but it wasn't the same one as hurt the dog."

Jamie considered who might have been watching her house, suppressed a shudder. "The one with the knife, what did he look like?"

"Lighter hair than him and kinda small. He came around the house when I was getting ready for bed. It was real late. I was tired and my eyes get all itchy. I'd gone to take a—to do some business by the tree and he came around the house."

"He had a knife?"

Z nodded. "A big one—long like they have in the scary movies. He was right by the garage. I think he was going to steal your car, lady." He looked around and blinked. "Then your dog came up. The dog didn't bark or nothing, but I think just seeing that dog scared him and he jabbed that knife right into his back." He blinked hard and licked his lips. "I didn't move. I just stayed real still 'cause I didn't want him coming at me with that knife." He started to quiver.

Jamie put a hand on his shoulder.

He looked up, blinked twice.

"Then what happened?"

His gaze steadied. "He went around the house and took off in his car. Your dog followed him, but he wasn't doing too good—limping real bad and bleeding. He went up to the porch, and I didn't know what to do 'cause I didn't want you to know I was living back there."

Jamie blinked at this news. The boy had been living in her yard? For how long?

"So I rang the doorbell and ran."

Jamie stepped closer to Z, squatted down so she was below him. "You saved my dog's life."

He looked at her, nodded slowly as a smile took shape on his lips. "I guess I did."

"Thank you."

"You're welcome."

"You think you would recognize that man if you saw him again?"

He pushed out his lower lip, took it in two fingers, and pulled on it lightly. Then, dropping it, he said, "I think so. You got a picture of him?"

"Not yet, but I'm going to get one while you're getting cleaned up."

"I'm glad you're not mad at me that your dog got hurt."

She shook her head. "Not mad at all. When you see someone you don't know, the best thing you can do is to hide and keep quiet until he goes away. Or come to an adult like me or Tony."

Z finished the first Peanut Butter Cup and licked his fingers. Jamie watched him, forcing herself not to cringe at the dirt on those hands. He looked over at the second half.

"Delman."

Jamie stared, felt her mouth drop open.

"It's my last name. Zephenaya Delman."

Jamie couldn't speak. Heat burned in her neck and cheeks.

"Can I have the other Reese's now?"

She blinked hard, nodded.

Z took the candy and peeled off the dark wrapper. Jamie watched him eat. She glanced at Tony, who frowned at her. She shook her head.

She couldn't say it, didn't want to be the one to tell Zephenaya that she did know his sister. Shawna Delman had been the first cop raped, more than six months ago.

A month later, Shawna Delman had overdosed on heroin.

No, Jamie couldn't bring herself to tell Zephenaya that his sister was dead.

# 32

Hailey sat at the small round table at the far end of the main lab on Monday evening, waiting for Sydney. At least she'd have closure on one case today. By all the evidence, at approximately eight thirty on a Thursday morning, Abby and Hank Dennig had killed each other inside her parked minivan.

Hailey had spent more time than she could afford trying to imagine how two people who had once loved each other could come that far. Homicide had taught her that love and hate were often bedfellows. In the Dennig case, though, she was making educated guesses. Without a witness, there was no one to confirm her theories.

Stephanie Rusch worked in the far corner of the lab. She wore a white coat and held a small set of tweezers to separate evidence onto slides for the microscope. Hailey wondered how the night at Tommy's had changed her relationship with Scott Scanlan.

Sydney crossed the lab, sat down across from Hailey. She flipped papers, pushed them out into a halo of white on the black table. She took a long drink out of a traveler coffee mug that said "Skamania Lodge" and set it down without looking at Hailey.

Hailey guessed Sydney was a few years younger than she—maybe thirty-six—but her reddish blond hair and freckles made her look like a woman barely into her thirties. She was trim and athletic, played soccer, Hailey knew. Her husband was a soccer coach in the East Bay and they had two boys who were avid players. But Hailey didn't know much more about her. At rookie club dinners, Sydney tended to sit with the CSU techs and people like Devlin in Personal Crimes—crimes where no one died. She stayed clear of the women who worked the violent crimes, like Homicide and Sex.

Even in their close group of women, there were still divisions—by department, by class of crime. Maybe it came down to how dirty the job was.

In that case, Homicide was about as dirty as you could get, and Hailey tried not to be bothered by being a bottom-feeder in the world of police work.

The irony was that even with her line of work, the nastiest people she'd met were not the murderers but the people at her father-in-law's campaign functions. Thinking of her father-in-law made her anxious to get Jim off her back.

With the Dennig case closed, she just prayed she'd be able to put Natasha's case to bed. Things were adding up. Roger had gone out to Jamie's house and taken some casts of the footprints and tire tracks from the boy's attack. They had another warrant for Marchek's house, and she knew they were closing in on him. Once they had him, she was confident he'd spill everything he had seen the night Natasha was killed.

"Okay, let's start with hair," Sydney said, her ponytail bouncing over her shoulder as she reached for the first report.

Hailey opened her notebook, pen poised.

"We found seventeen hair samples—fifteen human, four dog. We were able to eliminate eleven of them to the victims and the children. And the dogs."

"You'll keep the others on file?"

"Until storage bursts, absolutely."

Hailey nodded. She knew the storage of evidence—

especially long-term—was a growing issue within the department. Proper preservation required dry temperatures with low humidity. Blood and tissue samples, semen, and anything living, necessitated refrigeration. The lab had a huge walk-in refrigerator, but it was already near capacity—and had been for close to three years. Even after cases were tried and convictions made, evidence still had to be held in case of appeal.

"We got forty partial prints from the inside of the car alone. Another sixteen from the outside."

That wasn't many for the outside of a car. Hailey would have expected more, especially with kids. "Washed?"

Sydney nodded. "Probably within ten days, and some rain, too, I'd guess."

Hailey nodded.

"Then there's the rest of it." She pushed the report to Hailey, who scanned the list of other items taken from the car—fiber samples, carpets, threads from another two-dozen places that had to be individually sorted and identified under the microscope.

A lab could spend months on a single case. And from the look of it, the two victims had killed each other. Hailey had found, more often than not, if it looked like a duck and walked like a duck . . .

Still, she knew better than to be rash. In a case like this, Hailey had asked CSU to run the prints for known felons. Though it was time-consuming, the process was easy enough. Technology had come a long way and prints could be scanned and compared with both California's justice system records as well as NCIC, the National Criminal Information Center, which the FBI maintained.

"No felony matches?"

Sydney shook her head. "No, but we've got a dozen partials that couldn't be matched."

"But it's like a bus—you've got kids in and out of there all the time."

Sydney nodded. "I've got some adult prints, too, but nothing comes up."

"And the blood?" The initial process with blood was to take samples to identify the blood types of the victims and rule out a third party.

"AB and O, both positive. Victims' types."

"And in the places you'd expect them?"

"The pattern of blood splatter looks consistent with the theory that they killed each other."

"And they were known for being aggressive. There had been two instances of domestic disturbance in the past."

Sydney nodded.

"What about toxicology?"

"Won't be back for weeks. The Unit's way too backed up on more pressing cases."

Hailey knew there were convicts awaiting lab results before going to trial—men and women who sat behind bars while the labs scurried to prove whether or not they were really guilty of anything. "Then we've got to close it. The Dennigs murdered each other."

Sydney gathered her notes, started to stack them for Hailey to take with her. Hailey was thankful the case was over.

She'd probably spent fifty work hours on it, enlisted the help of at least three other cops to make calls and visits to friends, neighbors, and the kids' school. The case should have been closed at that.

But because of the nature of the victims—that is, rich and high profile—the chief had pushed the lab to look through the rest of the evidence for anything else.

"How long did it set you guys back?"

Sydney shrugged. "Day and a half, maybe a little more."

Even in a case where they didn't have the assailant, CSU could test only a small sample of the evidence brought in—five percent was aggressive. It was just too much. Things were scanned with black lights for traces of blood, and then particular spots were tested. But the funds and time to test everything weren't available. "I'm glad to put it behind us."

Sydney handed the papers to Hailey, frowned.

"What's up?" Hailey asked.

"Seemed too simple, you know?"

Hailey paused, thinking maybe it was. But she knew better than to dismiss another cop's gut. "Can you think of something we should look at again?"

Sydney hesitated, shook her head. "Not a thing."

"I know what you mean. With the pressure from the chief, it would have felt better to find something more."

Sydney looked up. "But that's how it goes, you know? That's annoying, but it's not what's bothering me."

"What's bothering you?"

Sydney was quiet a moment. "I guess the fact that they had kids. Why the hell would you leave your kids without a parent?"

Hailey couldn't answer that one. The simple truth was emotion often got the best of people.

Sydney shook her head.

Hailey couldn't find anything to say, at least nothing reassuring. "If anything else comes up, call me. I'll be writing it up for a few days."

Hailey left the building with none of the sense of triumph she often had when they'd closed a case. She only hoped she'd get it from Natasha's.

Back at the Hall, Hailey rode to the top floor and wound around the busy corridors until she reached the stairwell. Then she walked down step-by-step, her black flats echoing on the cold concrete. In a decade of coming in and out of this building, the stairwells had always been the quietest spot. People were just lazy, herself included. Somehow, though, she'd thought the walk might clear her head. Unfortunately, it didn't seem to have worked.

She arrived at the fifth floor and peered down the

stairs that led back to her own floor. But she knew she had to do it now, get it over with. Buck Daniels—the name brought on a wave filled with so many warring emotions, it was impossible to sort them all. Today, frustration might have won out.

Walking toward Internal Affairs wasn't something any cop liked to do and Hailey was no exception. Everyone who got near that door seemed to skirt it as though it were surrounded by an invisible fence that shocked anyone who got too close.

With the list IA had put together, Buck Daniels was her best bet to get this investigation moving. She knew there were absences on that list.

She thought about the promise she'd made to God, the one where she'd never see Bruce if Mackenzie was all right. Maybe now was the time to end things anyway. She hesitated at the department door.

Unlike most cops, she didn't have anything specific against the Internal Affairs Department. She thought a good portion of the bad rap they took wasn't fair. They did a job and Hailey had seen enough bad cop behavior—like Scott Scanlan—to know that there had to be a system in place to police the police.

She also knew there were some cops who lived to persecute others. Some cops pegged the people in IA as the kids who had been bullied and picked on in school. As children, they'd had thick glasses or red hair, were chubby boys or girls. They didn't blend the way Hailey had, just barely staying on the fringe of normalcy. And so they'd decided to bully the ultimate bullies. Those were the ones they thought went to IA. She knew that was sometimes true, too.

She set her shoulders back, entered the office. She told the secretary that she needed a few minutes with Bruce Daniels if he was available.

The secretary told her to go on in.

When she reached Bruce's half-open door, she knocked gently.

He looked up, his eyes barely widening in surprise. She saw a smile hover just beneath the firm lips. "Inspector Wyatt."

She didn't enter. "Hi. I've got a couple of questions on the list you made, if you have a few minutes."

They both spoke in work tones, full volume as though announcing to the department that they had nothing to hide.

He nodded to the seat across from him and she considered whether or not she wanted to sit, then decided she did.

Buck stood then and closed the door before making his way back to his own chair. She didn't watch him move. It would make staying away more difficult.

She studied pictures and diplomas she'd seen a dozen times. When he was settled back behind his desk, he rested his hands on top of some papers and gave her a little nod like a high school principal. "How are you feeling?"

She nodded. "Okay."

"You talked to Vail about it?"

"Had to."

"I agree." He rubbed his face, then glanced at her. "I was scared to death," he whispered. "I don't know what I would have done."

She shook her head. "I'm fine."

"I should've come to check on you sooner. I could've stopped him—"

She bit into her lip. Closed her eyes. "Yes, you should've." She looked up at him, his eyes wide. "Christ, I was almost—" She shook her head. "It wasn't your fault. I just can't—" She waved her hand, the words caught in her throat. "I can't talk about it now."

"What did you tell John?"

She cleared her throat, studied her hands. "I made the Scanlan thing seem like more of a wrestle. Mostly, though, it hasn't come up."

"But you have bruises on your ribs, don't you?"

She shrugged, glanced up. "It was a busy weekend with Mackenzie's attack. I've been really tired."

He nodded, understanding. "Will you have time this week?"

She lowered her gaze. "I can't. Not until this is over."

He didn't respond.

"Someone saw us. Someone knows."

He nodded.

"I actually came about the case."

He straightened. "Sure."

"I need to go back, understand some things."

He sat back, slightly rigid. "Okay."

"You were the first one out at the murder scene that morning."

He nodded.

"Why didn't you stay? She's a cop. Why wouldn't IA be involved?"

He glanced at the door behind her, paused.

"You were with her," she said quietly as though by speaking the words in a low tone she could soften the blow they would have if they weren't true. But they were. She knew it as soon as they were out.

"It was a long time ago."

She felt tired then. A long time ago. "How long ago?" She drew out a notebook and flipped it open to have something to look at. Then she could avoid him, avoid the pit in her gut. They'd been together eight months. She wanted to hear him say that it had been more than eight months ago. Only she suspected it wasn't.

"Early summer."

Her heart banged against her ribs. "This summer?"

He nodded. "June."

She wrote down the word June and underlined it. They'd been together then. He'd cheated on her. God-damn it. She looked up at him, shook her head. Her

hands trembled. Anger rocked in her chest, fighting
to break loose. She clenched her eyes, thought about
how she'd almost died in his lobby. "You bastard,"
she whispered. She pushed each word from her lips
as though firing a gun.

Bruce stood.

She pointed at his chair.

He sat, defeated. "It happened while you and John
were up in Tahoe with the girls."

She struggled not to scream, told herself she had no
right to be angry. She could not have a lover and
feel any sort of betrayal when he took one. And yet
she did.

"Hailey—"

She shook her head. She wasn't going there. Not
here, not now. Damn, she wished they were somewhere private right now so she could yell at him. She
held her hands together, took a breath. She let the
fury burn through her in hopes it would smother itself,
but it only burned fiercer. She stood, turned and
paced.

"Hailey."

She shot her palm out, leaned across his desk.
"Don't you dare," she seethed.

She forced herself to sit, focused on what she
needed from him for the case. She focused on this one
thing. She could do this. "I'm the investigator on a
murder case," she said, keeping her voice low and
even. "I need to know how long it lasted."

He came around the desk, sat in the chair beside
her. "Can we talk about this somewhere else? Can we
meet later?"

"I don't think so." She felt the words slip between
her teeth, laced with anger. She looked up at him,
narrowed her gaze, tried to hold herself cold. "I don't
think we'll be meeting anymore."

He took her hand. "Please. It doesn't have to be
my place. Just anywhere other than here."

She was desperate to scream at him, to vent the anger. But couldn't. Not now. Her thoughts veered back to Natasha. She pulled her hand away. God, Natasha. Buck was with Natasha, too. Christ, was everyone? She stood up, took two steps toward the door. She wanted to get the hell out of there, told herself it was a good idea. She would end it. There was always a piece of her that wanted to stop, to come out of the shadows she was living in. Now she could. Then why the hell did she feel such a loss? Christ. "Please just answer the question."

He, too, stood and crossed back behind the desk. "It started in June, lasted until the weekend of July Fourth. Ended that night."

"With fireworks, I hope."

He didn't respond. Shrugged. He felt her anger, she knew. He wasn't used to it. She didn't explode like this. She was the controlled one. Damn him for doing this to her. "Why were you there that day?"

He paused. "David Marshall knew about us. A few people did. It's one of the reasons it ended. An IA officer and someone with her reputation—"

She nodded, couldn't look at him.

"I felt guilty, Hailey. It actually felt like I was cheating on you," he added, lowering his voice. "But then, I thought, that's nuts. You were away—with your husband."

She ignored the reference. It was different. He knew she had a husband. He knew the score with her. He had no card to play there. She focused back on the morning of Natasha's murder. "So Marshall sent you to the scene?"

"He called me first to find out when I'd stopped seeing her—that I had. Then he told me about Deputy Chief Scanlan. I already knew, so we decided I should go down there to be sure someone else from the department hadn't been there—that there wasn't something obviously harmful to the department."

Her hands trembled. "And you didn't tell me?" She lowered her voice again. "You screwed with my crime scene and you never told me?"

He pleaded with her with his eyes. "I'm sorry."

She shook her head.

"David asked me to keep it quiet. I did as he asked."

She turned to leave.

"There's something else I've wanted to tell you. I don't know if it'll help."

She didn't turn back, waited. Fury coated her skin like hot chills after a sunburn.

"She called maybe a month ago. I didn't call her back the first time. I didn't want anything to do with her, and it didn't sound like a business call."

She waited.

"She called back a few days later. She was furious. She'd somehow heard about the list we had. She told me to send it to her so she could make sure we hadn't missed anyone." He shook his head. "She had a right to be pissed."

"Hell yes, she did."

"The list wasn't my idea."

She shook her head, turned her back. "I don't care."

"That last conversation, she made a comment at the end, something that I never quite figured out."

Hailey waited.

"She asked if I had her most recent conqu-qu-quest."

"What does that mean? That the guy has a stutter?"

He nodded. "That's how I took it."

Hailey remembered Tim's comment that he'd been struck by someone who had stuttered. "Deputy Chief Scanlan?"

He shook his head. "I don't think so."

She frowned. "But you don't know."

He paused. "No, I don't."

She started to leave but paused. "Why didn't you tell me about the comment before?" Bruce didn't respond. Hailey waited, her pulse drumming. "What about you, Bruce? Do you have an alibi for the night she was killed?"

Bruce frowned. "Yeah."

She hesitated, suddenly not sure she was prepared for his answer. "You were home alone?"

"Not quite."

"You were with someone *else*?"

He nodded.

"Shit," she said, the word just slipping out.

"Hailey, you know—"

"Don't," she said, cutting him off. It felt almost comical now. "Don't say anything. Please." She shook her head, lowered her voice. "Don't fuck it up any worse than you already have."

"Christ, this is a mess. I want to talk about this somewhere else. I'm done talking here. As for your case, Marshall knows about it. He's had my alibi confirmed. I am not a suspect in this case, but I'm also not participating in the investigation of her homicide—because of the fact that we were—had been intimate."

She felt the word "intimate" hit her like a blow. Exhaled. "I'm the lead investigator. I need to know who slept with her, Goddamn it."

Buck shook his head. "Everyone slept with her, Hailey."

"So that's supposed to make it better?"

He shook his head. "I'm not talking about us right now. You see someone else. I see other people, too. Anytime you want it to change, I'm ready."

That was it. The whip had cracked and it struck hard. She rubbed the spot just above her left breastbone. She sucked in a breath, let it slide out through closed teeth. She had no right. Tempered herself. She couldn't make demands when she wasn't prepared to fulfill her end of it.

And yet she would. She knew she would. She didn't need to be with him. She could walk away. She would. It was either only her or she was done. Those were her rules. That was the upside of the affair. It was all about her. Everything else was laced with complications—kids, family, but not this.

She didn't look back at him, couldn't. "God, this place is like musical fucking beds," she whispered as she left.

She walked back through the department, head down. All she could think was what right did she have to stake a claim to him when she would let him stake no claim to her?

None.

And yet she still knew she would do just that. She would have it no other way.

# 33

Jamie arrived at the station at 8:50 a.m. to see the front of the Hall blocked by news vans. She left her car down the block, left her police parking pass on the dash, and hurried to the stairs. The newscasters were each recording their bits off to the side of the main entrance, and Jamie recognized the start of a press conference. What the hell was it on?

Her stomach knotted, she started up the stairs when the chief's press secretary walked out the glass doors. Behind him was the chief, David Marshall, and Hailey Wyatt. Chip Washington followed behind them. Hailey caught Jamie's eye and shook her head. Bad news.

Jamie stood back and waited.

As soon as the chief was in view of the camera, the reporters began shouting questions.

"Is it true that the murdered inspector had a long-term relationship with Deputy Chief Scanlan?" called one. "Is he a suspect in her murder?"

"Christ," Jamie whispered under her breath. How the hell did that get out? She watched the lines on the chief's face deepen into a scowl. Hailey looked as though she'd already taken a tongue-lashing. She stood, expressionless, and waited for more shit to follow.

"Didn't she also have a relationship with his son? The one who is on probation for beating up a college student over a burrito?" shouted the NBC affiliate.

"Is it true that your Internal Affairs Department has a full list of everyone the inspector saw in the months before she died? Is it your policy to track the sexual relationships of your officers?" ABC called out.

"Is that considered police business?" The last question came from Fox.

Finally, the press secretary raised his hand to silence the crowd. "Please, ladies and gentlemen. Quiet. Please. Chief Jackson is going to issue a brief statement on the murder case. However, we will take no questions at this time. This is an active case."

The press issued a series of moans and complaints, but the chief ignored them as he stepped forward. "Ladies and gentlemen, a member of our police force has been murdered. Natasha Devlin was a decorated inspector with a strong track record. She served this department for more than twelve years. Our homicide team"—he motioned to David Marshall and Hailey— "is doing everything in its power to uncover who did this. The list of people Inspector Devlin was involved with contains both professional and personal relationships and is standard protocol in any murder investigation. It is our job to look at each person as a potential suspect. At this time, we have not identified a suspect."

Jamie thought that was good news for Tim.

The chief nodded to the crowd. "That is all I can offer at this time. Thank you."

"Why didn't the list contain anyone from outside the department?"

"What about the rumor that the murder is tied to the series of officer rapes?"

The press secretary stepped forward and leaned into the microphone. "That will be all at this time."

The press continued to shout out questions as the group turned and disappeared into the building.

Jamie pushed through the crowd.

"Inspector Vail, is there a connection between Devlin's death and the rapes?"

"No comment."

"Isn't it true that you threatened Officer Scanlan at Tommy's Mexican Restaurant last week?"

"No comment."

"What about the rumor that the rapist was at your house and attacked your dog?"

"No comment."

Jamie reached the door and pulled it open, hurrying inside and letting it shut behind her. Finally the noise quieted. She took off her holster and slid it through the x-ray, walked through the metal detector and retrieved it.

"That's why they call them newshounds. They smell the blood."

Jamie looked up at the security guard who manned the door. "I guess." She just wondered how they'd even gotten on the scent.

She rode the elevator to Homicide and found Hailey coming out of the department. "Let's get out of here."

Jamie turned and followed her down the corridor to the stairwell. "What the hell happened?"

Hailey shook her head. "No idea, but someone got hold of it—all of it."

"When?"

"Sometime this morning—early. I've been hearing it since the six a.m. broadcast. It's unconfirmed, but it's all there—the list, the fact that she came back here with a cop, the print that links her murder to the rapist, the fact that we haven't arrested him, even the shit about Scanlan at Tommy's. It's like someone sent the press a fucking synopsis." She shook her head. "Excuse my French."

"Don't worry. It's my favorite language."

Hailey smiled. "Christ. We've got to find a quiet spot to sit down and talk this out."

"I've got just the place."

*       *       *

At the Starbucks two blocks from the Hall, Jamie ordered a grande triple nonfat latte and sat down while the one woman and two men behind the counter worked their magic. She'd heard all the complaints about Starbucks and its monopoly, but she didn't give a shit. She liked the coffee, and the characters who worked in this store were worth an extra fifty cents any day.

The man Jamie liked best was maybe five two and had been slowly evolving from man to woman over the past year. When she'd first seen him, he'd had short hair and a small goatee. Now he had long hair and breasts. Got to love San Francisco.

Jamie took her coffee to the table where Mackenzie and Hailey were already seated.

"What a morning," Mackenzie said. "I just heard."

Jamie nodded. "Quite a night last night, too." She described the attack on Z, how Tony had saved him, the trip to the hospital. "Zephenaya is at my house with Tony today. He's going to a temporary foster home this afternoon."

"This is Shawna Delman's brother?" Hailey asked.

"Who's Shawna Delman?"

Jamie told her about the rookie who'd been raped and had then overdosed.

"Does the kid know?" Hailey asked.

Jamie dropped her gaze, shook her head.

No one spoke for a moment.

"Christ," Hailey whispered.

"I'll tell him. It just felt like he'd been through enough."

"He have other family?"

Jamie shook her head. "I don't think so."

"I hate the foster system," Hailey said.

"Maybe someone will adopt him," Mackenzie added.

No one responded. Adoption for a ten-year-old

homeless black boy was about as likely as Marchek walking into the station and confessing.

"So was it Marchek who attacked him?"

Jamie shrugged. "Tony thinks so, but he couldn't pick him out."

"With the ski mask, it would be tough," Hailey agreed.

"He saw him take off in a van, though," Jamie added. "But it had no rear plate. I've got him on the Internet, trying to match the van to a year and make." It felt like having Tony search for a needle in a computer haystack. "Unfortunately, it also means Marchek now has a car, which makes him mobile and means his kit could be stored anywhere. We've got an APB out on the van, but we're not likely to find it."

Jamie took a breath. "In better news, Zephenaya picked out Scanlan for the attack on my dog."

Both women were silent.

"That takes balls," Hailey said.

"Guy's an asshole," Mackenzie said.

"We can all agree on that," Jamie agreed. She thought back to the press conference. "We know how the press was notified?"

"E-mail, supposedly," Hailey said. "The computer lab is trying to track it, but it's a random Hotmail account. Get this—the address is sanfranpolice @hotmail.com."

"But the information had to come from an officer. No one else knew that stuff." Jamie turned to Mackenzie. "I know your husband works for a paper."

Mackenzie shook her head. "Alan didn't know most of what was in the news report. I haven't told him much and some of what came out, I didn't even know."

Jamie watched her.

"It's not that I don't trust him, but it's better to avoid the temptation."

She nodded. "Yeah, temptation can be a bitch."

"Speaking of temptation, I've got something new," Hailey started.

They watched her.

"Bruce Daniels slept with Natasha, too."

Jamie examined the inspector's face. She didn't look at Jamie. Jamie knew why. Her lover had cheated on her. Man, that was screwed up.

"It was last summer, but she called him last month. She knew about the list and she was pissed. Asked if Bruce knew about her most recent conquest. Only she said 'qu-qu-quest.' "

Jamie frowned. "A stutter?"

Hailey nodded. "Remind you of anything?"

"When Tim was hit that night—" Jamie started.

"He mentioned that he thought the man had a stutter," Hailey finished.

Jamie nodded. "I can't think of a single person in the department who stutters."

"And how does Scott Scanlan fit in?" Mackenzie asked.

Jamie considered Scanlan. "He may be guilty only of the dog thing." She looked at Mackenzie. "No possible way he was your attacker?"

Mackenzie shook her head. "No way. He's smaller and shorter than the guy who attacked me. Plus, after the night at Tommy's, I would have recognized his voice."

Jamie nodded.

"So maybe he's involved peripherally." Hailey paused. "Or maybe he's covering for someone else." She glanced at Jamie.

"You mean like his father?" Mackenzie said.

Jamie shuddered. God, she hoped Devlin's murder didn't lead to the deputy chief of police.

Just then her cell phone rang. She looked down and recognized Tim's cell phone number. He'd probably heard about the press fiasco. She pressed the button to silence to call. She'd call him later. She was momentarily surprised to realize that she actually planned to return his call.

Immediately, her phone rang again. She stared at the Hall number, wondered if it was Tim calling again. "Vail."

"It's Klein."

"What's up?"

"I'm at 113 August Aly. Looks like your guy was here."

Jamie sagged against her chair. "Shit."

"He got a woman coming out of the building at about five fifteen this morning, dragged her into the trash room in the back. She's en route to General now."

"How bad?"

"He did her good, Jamie. I've never seen one like that—two black eyes, a broken jaw, arm, ribs. Her face was a balloon."

"Was she conscious?"

"Barely. She did say the guy told her she wasn't the one. He was waiting for someone else. Kept saying 'You're the wrong one' or some shit."

Jamie halted. "The wrong one? What would that mean?"

"Hell if I know. You sure know how to pick them."

She frowned. "Thanks, Klein."

"No problem. I'll finish up here if you want to go on to General."

She pulled her notebook out of her pocket. "I will. What was that address again?"

"113 August Aly."

She shook her head. "I've never heard of it. You got any ideas?"

"Not a single one. He's your crazy."

"113 August Aly. Okay."

A cup fell with a loud pop, coffee splashed across the floor. Jamie looked up, saw Hailey drop to grab it. "You okay?"

Hailey's head reappeared, her complexion pale. "What was the address?"

Jamie looked up, met her gaze. "113 August Aly."

"It's right off Washington Park," Klein said.

"Off Washington Park," Jamie repeated.

Hailey stooped to soak up the coffee.

Mackenzie ran to the counter for more napkins.

Jamie hung up with Klein, stared at Hailey. "Are you okay?"

She nodded.

But Jamie knew she wasn't. "You know that address?" She met Hailey's gaze. "The guy said he had the wrong one. Maybe he was looking for someone else at that address."

Hailey paused, squeezed her eyes closed.

Jamie felt the dread pool like hot tar in her middle. "How do you know it?"

Hailey stood slowly, hands trembling. "Bruce Daniels lives there."

# 34

Emily Osbourne couldn't have been happier to get the hell out of work on Wednesday. It was 4:02 when she exited the lab building. Usually, she had to stay later—an hour at least to get things finished up, findings recorded, her station cleaned. Paul, who worked in the financial markets, always managed to be finished before she was. Often he'd be home an hour or more before her. But today her work was done at ten to four so she could walk out at four. She didn't care that there were dozens of items that needed processing—not today, anyway. And she had no plans for the night. Nothing but a quiet dinner and maybe a movie—something stupid and funny.

The drive across the city was quiet at this hour. She crossed to Franklin and then turned right, heading north to Greenwich, then across to Laguna Street. She stopped in front of the white Victorian duplex where she lived. The whole thing took about forty minutes. It was still light, and she considered going for a walk. The weather was cool and comfortable and a walk might make her feel better. A little, anyway.

She thought about what her therapist had said at their meeting the day before, how she needed to focus on how she was feeling. Get it out, talk through it. Make notes about her reactions, keep a journal of the process so she could eventually record her progress.

There would be progress. She touched the small spiral notebook she had tucked in the back of her bag. She'd run the gamut this week—anger, fear, self-pity, self-disgust.

She'd also told Sharon, her therapist, about Paul—how cold he'd been in the car, how he hadn't called since the trip from the airport. They hadn't gone more than a day without talking since last Christmas when she was back East with her family. And they had been dating for only three months then.

"How does that make you feel?" Sharon had asked.

Emily had started to cry. She felt disgusting and dirty and she hated herself and him all at once. She'd been raped and he'd stopped calling. She knew she was supposed to be angry—really angry. Instead she felt ashamed that he no longer wanted her.

On the plane trip back to California, she'd fretted over how she would handle it when he wanted to have sex. She didn't know if she could, if she would be ready. But now he didn't want anything to do with her. Who would want to have sex with her after what had happened?

She cupped her hand over her mouth and ran up the short flight of stairs to her front door. She pushed her key into the lock, turned it, wiping her cheeks as she pulled open the creaky door and stepped inside. The door creaked closed again and she shivered.

"I'll oil that," a voice said.

Emily spun around, slammed into the row of mailboxes attached to the foyer wall. Standing on a short ladder was a man near her age in overalls, painting.

He put down the brush, started down the ladder.

Emily didn't move. Her heart jumped around like a rabbit in her chest. She wanted to leave, to be outside. But he was closer to the door.

"I didn't mean to startle you. I'm Kyle."

She shook her head, but like an idiot, she couldn't say anything.

"I sent a notice around that I'd be painting this week and maybe part of next." He put his hands up, like he was surrendering. "Are you okay?"

She shook her head. Her heart still jackhammering, she ran for the door. As she bolted outside, something yanked her back. He had her bag. She whirled around to fight when she saw him standing back, staring. The strap of her bag was caught on the doorknob.

"Oh God," she cried out.

She spun around to loosen the strap from her shoulder, abandoning her bag on the door as she sprinted to the street.

When she reached the bottom stair, she sank down and burst into tears. What was wrong with her? What the hell was wrong with her?

She held her head in her hands when she felt someone beside her. She looked up.

"I brought you this." Kyle handed her a can of Coke. "It hasn't been opened."

She took it, the metal cool against her fingers. Even in the cold air, the metal felt good. She fiddled with the top, popped it open. The fizz tickled her nose. She drank, mostly so she wouldn't have to talk.

"Are you all right?"

She nodded. "A little skittish."

"I think it's understandable after what happened."

She frowned.

"Kim told me. I'm sorry. I figured it was you when I saw the—" He motioned to her face, to the bruises.

Her cheeks flamed up and she took another sip of Coke. Damn her roommate.

"It happened to my sister, too—in college."

Emily didn't respond.

"She says the most important thing is that you talk about it and give yourself time to get over it." He paused. "She's married now, has two little girls." He kept talking, like he was stumbling. "She does rape counseling. Out in Virginia."

They sat in silence for a few minutes; then he stood. "I'll get out of your hair. Sorry again for startling you."

She shook her head. "It's okay. And, thanks, uh—" she said dumbly.

"Kyle," he said.

"Thanks, Kyle."

He opened the door with his key, set her bag on the porch, and went back into the building.

Just when she had gathered the courage to go back inside, Paul's Jeep Cherokee pulled to the curb in front of her building. She watched him get out of the car and lift a box off the passenger seat. He came around, carrying it. He didn't spot her until he was almost at the stairs.

When he did, he jumped back a step. "Hey." He shifted the box in his arms. "I didn't know you'd be home yet."

She stood up on the step and dusted the dirt off her butt. She peered into the box—one of her old T-shirts lay on top. She lifted it, stared down at her stuff—a few CDs, a book, an extra hairbrush, a bottle of red nail polish she'd bought and worn to a wedding over the summer. He was returning her things—bringing it all back when he thought she wouldn't be there.

Dropping the T-shirt, she turned and walked up the stairs to the door without a word.

"Emily," Paul called, but she didn't answer. Let him come after her, the bastard. Or better yet, let him be a coward and leave her stuff at the door.

Her key shook in her fist as she shoved it in the door and turned it. Without a backwards glance, she grabbed her bag off the step and stormed past Kyle and into her apartment.

"You okay?" he called after her, but she didn't risk answering. She was not okay. She was not at all okay.

The front door banged shut. Paul had a key. It was

probably somewhere in that box with the rest of the stuff he was giving back, now that he was dumping her.

She let herself into her apartment and slammed the door behind her, securing the chain before crossing to the smaller of the two bedrooms.

She locked the door and dropped face-first onto the bed. She screamed into her pillow, tried to get it all out—the anger, the hurt, the fear. Then, turning on her side, she pulled the pillow into her arms and cried into it, wishing she'd never come back from Connecticut, that she'd never come out to San Francisco at all, and certainly that she'd never dated that asshole Paul.

When the doorbell rang, she sat up and wiped her face. No way would she let that jerk see her cry.

When she got to the door, she heard talking.

"I don't think she wants you around, man."

She peered through the peephole and saw Paul turn to stare at Kyle.

"Who the hell are you?" Paul asked.

"Kyle," he said as though it answered everything.

Emily actually smiled.

Paul looked furious. "You don't know shit, buddy. Why don't you get lost?" He knocked on the door again, and Emily jumped away from the door.

"I think you should leave her alone," Kyle repeated. "She didn't seem that thrilled to see you."

Paul spun around, walked toward Kyle. Kyle didn't back off.

"I told you to get lost," Paul said.

Kyle shook his head. "I don't think so."

Paul charged Kyle, but Kyle was ready. He shoved Paul across the foyer.

Emily yanked the door open, heart pounding.

Both men turned to look at her.

"This asshole—" Paul started, pressing his palms against his shirt as though to iron it with the heat of them.

"Just leave, Paul."

Paul's mouth dropped open. "What?"

"You heard her, Paul."

"You bitch. You were cheating on me? With a handyman?"

Her stomach clenched. She opened her mouth to stop him from going, but instead she just crossed her arms and shrugged.

Furious, he turned to the door. Then he spun back, finger raised. "You owe me a cell phone, Emily."

She shrugged again. "Bill me."

With that, he was gone.

The momentary rush she felt emptied like water from a cracked vase. She'd let him go, she thought to herself. He was going anyway, another part of her said.

Just then she looked up and saw Kyle, still standing on the other side of the foyer.

He motioned to the door. "I thought maybe he was the one who—"

"He's my boyfriend." She forced a smile. "Was."

Kyle studied the floor. "Jesus, I'm sorry."

She shook her head. "Don't be. It was over anyway." She hesitated, not sure what to say. "Thanks again," she added as she went back into the apartment.

"Emily?"

She turned.

"I know it's too soon, but would you like to get a coffee sometime?"

She frowned. "It's—" She searched for the words. Too soon. It was too soon.

"It's too soon."

She nodded. "Yeah."

"Shit, I'm such an ass. I'm sorry."

"No, I mean yes. A coffee would be good. But slow, you know?"

He grinned. "A slow coffee?"

She smiled back. "Yeah."

He nodded and she saw a glint in his blue eyes she hadn't noticed before. "A slow coffee, it is."

With that, she returned to her apartment, closed the door, oddly more at peace than she had been since the attack.

# 35

Jamie stood over the bed of the latest victim and watched her chest rise and fall in a drugged sleep. Around them, hospital machines whooshed and beeped. They dripped fluids, measured her heart rate, controlled her breathing. Her right arm was covered in a bent cast, her left was heavily bandaged. Bruises covered her skin like flowers on wallpaper. Her face was the shade of a plum, her eyes barely lines in the swollen mass. Goddamn.

Jamie sank into the chair, dropped her head to her hands.

Hailey had come and gone. They'd met with the victim's husband. He'd shown them a picture of his wife from his wallet.

Jamie had heard the quick intake of breath from Hailey's lips. The woman had brown wavy hair, cut in a bob, brown eyes. She was attractive, athletic-looking. There was no doubt that she and Hailey had similar features. Looking back at the woman in the bed, Jamie pictured Hailey Wyatt.

The only good that had come from this was that the captain had approved additional surveillance on Marchek. A team had been dispatched to him already. She had no doubt he'd behave until the surveillance was called off again. She also had no doubt that she had to catch him before that time. The escalating violence had almost left a woman dead. She could not let it get to that point.

Just then Jamie heard the door behind her open. She stood, expecting the woman's husband and saw Bruce Daniels.

He nodded to her, walked to the bed. Shook his head. "Christ."

Jamie turned without a word and crossed to the door.

"Vail."

She looked back, hand on the knob.

"If you need any support on this—any at all—you call me. We've got to get this guy."

She watched the glassy passion in his eyes. He, too, saw Hailey Wyatt in the woman in the hospital bed.

She stood outside in the cold and smoked a cigarette, trying to calm herself before she got in her car to drive home. Her cell rang and she answered it with a curt voice, tired of all the shit. "Vail."

"It's Roger. I'm down at the lab. I've got a match on the dirt from Marchek's boot."

"You matched it to the soil from my yard?"

"No."

Jamie frowned. "What then?"

"There are some similar elements, but the soil from your yard was much richer in sulfites, commonly found in potting soil. The dirt from Marchek's boot was nearly five percent clay."

"Clay?"

"It's consistent with landfill. It contains more unnatural elements than other soils. I confirmed it with the ph, which is 5.2, too low for potting soil."

"Landfill," she repeated

"Right. And where do you find landfill in San Francisco?"

"Anywhere there's dirt, I'd guess. But there isn't

much of that in the city. It's mostly cement." She paused. "And I'd guess the park's dirt would be more consistent with potting soil."

"Right. Anywhere else you'd find landfill?"

Jamie thought for a moment. "Roger, if you know the answer, why don't you tell me?"

Roger laughed. "Because it's more fun for you to get it. Plus, it confirms my reasoning."

"So you've ruled out undeveloped land."

"Right. There's nothing anywhere near Marchek's apartment that's not developed."

"How about a renovation?" Jamie thought out loud. "If someone was taking a house down in the area, they'd hit landfill." Jamie gasped. "The crawl space."

"That was my guess."

Jamie turned and paced. "Shit. That's genius. He's hiding stuff under his building." She started to hang up. "You're the best, Roger. I've got to get a car out to his place."

"Call me if you find it and I'll send someone out."

"Will do."

"Oh, one more thing, Jamie."

"Yeah?"

"We matched the polymers on Tim's head wound."

"What was it?"

"It's the plastic they use in making the bases of trophies. The company is out of Ohio—Dayton Trophy Company."

"Do you know if that's where the trophies came from the night of the awards dinner?"

"It is. I left a message for Hailey Wyatt, but I thought you'd want to know, too."

She nodded. "Yeah. This is good, Roger. Thanks."

"No problem."

Jamie hung up and dialed Hailey's line. She answered on the second ring. Jamie quickly told her about the soil sample from Marchek's boots.

"Meet at his place?" Hailey said.

"I'll be there in twenty. And you heard about the trophy?"

"Yeah. Mackenzie is getting together a list of who won an award that night. I'll have her meet us at Marchek's."

Jamie headed for her car. Her cheeks flushed, adrenaline rushed around her brain. For the first time in longer than she wanted to consider, Jamie felt close.

Marchek had screwed up and they were going to nail him.

Please, God. Let them nail him.

She couldn't bear the thought of him on the street one more day.

Jamie arrived at Marchek's and parked behind the patrol car they'd sent to handle surveillance. When she got out of the car and flashed her badge, the officers walked toward her.

"No sign of your guy. We've been waiting for him."

"He's not working today?"

"No. According to the store, he's off today and tomorrow."

Jamie nodded, felt the sick sense of dread rise in her gut. "Keep an eye out. I'm going inside."

The officers nodded and returned to their vehicle.

Jamie made her way into Marchek's apartment and began to look for access to the crawl space. She checked the closets and searched for any hidden doors, but there didn't appear to be any access from inside. As she came out his front door, she ran into Mackenzie and Hailey.

"Find it?" Hailey asked.

"Not yet. There's nothing from his place."

"In our building, the crawl space is just off the garbage room," Mackenzie offered.

Jamie nodded. "Let's try that."

Down the hall from Marchek's front door, they found the disposal room. It was a tiny space, filled by two huge flip-top garbage bins. A metal vent hovered above one where people on the upper floors could dump their trash. It would slide down the vent and into one of the cans.

"How about that?" Mackenzie said.

Jamie followed her gaze. Behind one of the cans was an opening, maybe two feet wide by sixteen inches high. Hailey and Mackenzie pulled the trash can aside and Jamie shone her flashlight into the dark hole.

"It's the crawl space, all right."

Jamie got down on her knees and climbed through the hole. On the other side, the space was large enough to stand. "You guys coming?"

She heard Hailey groan, but soon the other two women were inside. Each using her flashlight, they scanned the space for anything Marchek had hidden. They split up. Jamie went left around a thick cement pillar she guessed was footing for the stairwell. She could see the other lights flickering behind her.

"Scream if you see anything," she called out.

The space was cool and moist and the thought that Marchek might be there gave her the chills. She shook them off, returned to the hunt. A mound of dirt blocked her view of the far corner. She had to crawl across it to continue.

Just then she heard one of the others call out.

She turned back and scrambled across the dirt, half crawling, half running.

When she reached them, Hailey and Mackenzie stood over an old metal meat locker. Padlocked closed, the locker had been mostly buried. Only four inches stood above the surface.

Jamie motioned Hailey and Mackenzie back and, using the backside of her Maglite, she smashed the lock. It didn't break. She drew her gun and aimed it at the lock. "Stand back."

Hailey and Mackenzie moved behind her. Without

any other eye protection, Jamie slipped her sunglasses on and fired at the lock. The steel dropped open.

She found a pen and used it to remove the lock and lift the top of the locker.

The inside was neatly organized. A pile of straps lay carefully coiled beside a box of powder-free latex gloves. There were towels, a pair of heavy work pants, tennis shoes, and a dark sweatshirt. Jamie lifted what looked like a pillowcase and found a hood. Jagged eyeholes stared back at her and she imagined Emily Osbourne's fear.

"Oh my God," Mackenzie gasped.

Jamie turned.

Mackenzie pointed at the open lid. There, taped to the surface, was a series of photographs and personal items. Jamie recognized a candid of Shawna Delman coming out of the police station. Beside it was one of Jill Muhta in her police car. But the one she knew Mackenzie was fixed on was a photograph of Mackenzie herself sitting on the steps of her apartment, a drink in her hand. Beside it was a card that read "Café Baby Cakes Frequency Card." On the card were four small daisy-shaped punches. Next to each photo was a similar memento. A Blockbuster card with the name Jill Muhta, an insurance card issued to Shawna Delman.

Jamie looked up at Mackenzie.

Tears streamed down the rookie's cheeks. Jamie placed her hand on Mackenzie's arm and said nothing. Hailey, too, remained silent. There was nothing to say that would erase the fear that Marchek had instilled in his victims.

Taking him off the streets would help. That, at least, would be a step.

Baby steps. At least she was moving forward. That had to count for something.

# 36

Hailey and Mackenzie had agreed to stay with the evidence while Jamie initiated the search for Marchek. Roger would come to start processing the locker, but they all knew it was plenty to make an arrest. Jamie wanted to be there when they brought him in. Takedowns were rare and when they came, she savored them. Jamie also didn't like the fact that her surveillance team hadn't seen Marchek in the eight hours since they'd called in additional surveillance.

Besides, there wasn't much to go home to. Tony had taken Zephenaya to Sacramento to meet his temporary foster parents. They'd even taken Barney along for the ride. For some reason, Jamie didn't look forward to going home to the empty house. She didn't consider that it would soon be permanently empty again. She'd have Barney, she thought.

On a whim, Jamie decided to work one last piece of the puzzle before turning in. She knew she could bring Zephenaya in to ID Scanlan as the man who had knifed Barney, but she might be able to get confirmation without having to drag Z through more crap.

She called the main desk and was relieved to get her favorite clerk, Shirley.

"It's Vail."

"Hey, you. How's it going?"

"I've got a question about Scott Scanlan."

Shirley grumbled. "I got ten minutes before dinner. Don't ruin my appetite."

"Don't worry. I'm looking to nail him."

"Then I'm your woman."

Jamie laughed. "What can you tell me about his partner?"

"Hell. I thought you were going to make it tough. Hang on."

Jamie heard the phone drop to the desk, then the background noises of Shirley working. Shirley had never mastered the hold button. She came back a minute and a half later. "Name's Dave Priestley. He came out of the academy in June."

Someone spoke behind her and Shirley paused. When she returned, she said, "Teresa says he's the youngest of three brothers. They're all in blue."

Three cops. That was a good thing. "You have a number for him?"

"Sure do." Shirley rattled it off and Jamie wrote. She thanked Shirley for the help and told her to grab dinner a few minutes early.

"If only I worked for you, Miss Vail," she said, laughing.

Jamie dialed Priestley's number and immediately heard the recording of his voice. After the tone, Jamie said, "This is Jamie Vail. I'm an inspector in the Sexual Assault Unit. I have reason to believe you were on my property at 129 Payne in San Rafael last Saturday night with Officer Scott Scanlan. I'd like to speak with you about that evening. I don't believe you were committing a crime, and I'm confident we can straighten this out if you call me directly."

She left her cell phone number, paused, and added, "If you decide not to call me back, you'll be treated as an accessory in any investigation I conduct." The threat sounded full of wind. It was. She wouldn't be conducting any investigation. It wasn't in her jurisdiction, for one. For two, she didn't do that kind of investigation. That would be someone like Bruce Daniels, if the deputy chief didn't nip it in the bud.

But since Dave was a new cop, with family pressure, he might just call and come clean. It was worth a try, anyway. Worst case, she'd get scolded by Captain Jules and she'd have to bring Zephenaya into it.

She glanced up at the clock and tried to decide whether to stay. It was almost eight and she was tired. When the call came, she'd see Marchek behind bars— that was all that really mattered. The warrant was in process, and she'd put in a request to release an APB on Marchek.

She drove home slowly, smoked. She blew the breath out into the dark, clear sky and listened to classic rock on KFOG. Sang out loud. The sense of redemption at nailing Marchek was almost as intoxicating as a drink of scotch. She sang along with Mick and Sheryl Crow and Norah Jones and pulled into her driveway at a quarter-past nine.

A patrol car sat in front of her house. There was one at Mackenzie's house and Hailey's as well. They weren't taking any chances. Jamie rolled her window down and waved. The officer waved back.

The house dark, Jamie opened the garage door and pulled inside. The light clicked on and she scanned the garage for signs of anything strange. Saw nothing.

As she started to get out of the car, her cell phone rang. It was Chip Washington confirming that the warrant for Marchek had been signed and delivered and that the APB was out. This was it. She finally had enough to hold the son of a bitch. Bail would be too high. He'd sit in jail. They'd get a conviction.

This was a good moment. Rare. It didn't always work out like this. She opened her phone again to call Hailey, but decided against it. They'd talk in the morning.

The light on the garage door opener clicked off and

Jamie cracked her car door open. Using the car light, she gathered her things. She swung her holster over her shoulder, scooped up her laptop and notes and backed out of the car. Her holster caught on the emergency brake. She leaned forward but couldn't free it. She shifted her computer and notes to the other arm, let the holster fall from her shoulder onto the passenger seat. Her hands were too full to grab it. She'd have to come back.

She maneuvered her way through the dark to the back door, flipped the light switch with her elbow. Nothing happened. The bulb had blown. "Damn it."

She stepped toward the door, heard a crunch beneath her feet. Her heart stopped when she realized it was broken glass. She dropped her pile. The laptop clattered to the ground beside her feet. She dove for her car. Too late.

Heavy hands snatched her from behind, gripping her shoulders like steel vises. He rammed her, headfirst, into the door. She heard a sharp crack—wood or maybe her skull. She saw red in the blackness. Her hands swam in front of her, struggled to make contact with something she could use for support. It was all air.

She grabbed for one of the hands that held her. They were sunken into her flesh like anchors. He yanked her backwards. Her hand struck the doorknob. She stretched for it, seized the cold metal in her fist. She twisted as he shoved her head toward the wood again. The door flew open. She catapulted into the laundry room, the man behind her.

His hands vanished from her shoulders. She spun onto her back, raised her legs to kick. She got only one leg in the air before he came down on top of her. She pinned her foot against his chest. Steely eyes, dark hair. Marchek.

"Help!" she shouted, kicking, but she knew the officer

couldn't hear her from the street. Her effort barely budged Marchek. Too heavy. Panic corked her throat. She popped it free. "You almost killed a woman."

He grinned, his teeth clenched. His chin mottled with drool. A day's growth of beard looked like a smear of grease on his chin.

She fought to hold him back.

"I wanted the cop this morning, waited all night for her. She never came back to that building. I thought I had her until I got that woman into the back. Then it wasn't her. I was very disappointed. Could you tell?"

Her leg began to tremor.

Marchek bared yellowed teeth. Grinned. "The other one, she was too sweet for a cop. She's lucky I didn't have more time. But now there's you and we've got all night." He spit as he spoke. "This isn't my first time out here. I've been watching you, waiting for the right time. I've been looking forward to tonight."

Jamie forced his words from her head. He would not win. She counted to three, let her leg buckle momentarily, and then forced it straight with all she had. She shoved him free, moved.

He descended on her again. A giant hand clamped onto her arm. The other one wrenched her leg beneath her. She tumbled onto her back.

Tears stung her eyes.

She swung her hips right. She didn't want to be pinned on her back. Couldn't let him have her.

She screamed.

He backhanded her and threw her down like a doll. Before she could shift, he was on top of her. His hips pinned hers.

Panic descended like water, choking, drowning her. She screamed out. Twisted. Shoved. Used her elbows. Her fingernails. Heard one finger snap like a toothpick in his grip. Moaned.

His left fist burst into her peripheral vision. She

flinched as it flew toward her face. She reached down, grabbed for his balls.

His fist struck her face first, knocked her back. Her head slammed against the floor. Red stars and white spots exploded in the dark. Then blackness again. She blinked hard, fought off dizziness, nausea. Her hand sought the soft spot between his legs. He began to rock against her, his erection a gun aimed into her belly.

Then he began to grope. She wriggled to reach down enough to hurt him. Felt like she was trapped under a car.

Suddenly she felt rough sandpaper skin on her flesh. His hands grazed her stomach, grabbed her breasts. He pinched her right nipple hard, twisted it. Cupped her breast, kneaded it in his fist like bread dough.

She screamed, flailed beneath him. She twisted left, then right, couldn't free herself.

Trapped. She was trapped. Tony was gone. The cop couldn't hear her. No one was coming. Her weapon was in the car. Even Barney was gone.

He tugged at the waist of her pants. The button popped off and suddenly she couldn't breathe.

She was nauseous and blind. Her vision dulled. She sobbed. It came upon her without her control. She was pinned too hard. She couldn't reach him. He brought his face toward hers. She saw teeth first, like the fangs of a wild cat.

Breathless, she clawed at the socket of his left eye. The ball was hard, deterring her at first. She jabbed into the soft spot in the corner of his eye, dug at it.

Marchek howled and moved back, grabbing her hand.

She snapped it from his grasp, mauled his neck. She stabbed her finger into the small hollow spot at the base of his throat, fought to tear the skin off. She battled with every drop of strength.

He dropped her other arm, clutched his neck. She rounded her back, reached for his crotch with her right hand. Seized the soft sack as tight as she could. Gripped her fist tighter.

Marchek roared, raised his hand to snatch hers. She poised her arm over her face to protect herself, squeezed harder. Clenched her teeth to bare down. He shifted back, caught her hand, struggled to loosen her grip. She bent one knee, nailed it hard against her hand.

She felt wiggle room, a tiny bit of air, and twisted as hard as she could. He fell off. Pulse frantic, she scrambled to her feet. Shoved open the garage door. He latched on to her foot. She pitched forward, landed on her hands. She smashed her chin on the cement floor, felt the hot sear of her tooth tear through her lip.

She didn't stop. Kicked. She gasped, kicked again. She rushed to her feet, grappled for the handle of the car door.

"Where do you think you're going?" he said, his voice a menacing growl.

She yanked the car door open, climbed halfway in. He shoved the door closed on her. Air streamed from her lungs. Metal gouged her ribs. Her breath blistered in her chest. She struggled not to breathe. The pain let up momentarily as he opened the door. Sobbing, she crawled farther into the car.

Her fingers made contact with her holster as he tugged on her leg. She fought to kick free, but the grip was too tight. She caught his leg with one kick. He cursed. She clambered toward the gun, caught the leather holster in her fist.

She felt his whole weight on her. Agony ripped through her as he punched into the small of her back.

She collapsed, smashing her chest on the emergency brake. She let herself go still. Clung to her weapon. Every move was torture as she struggled to free the gun from the holster. She gasped for air, fought against the pain—in her ribs, in her chest, in the small of her back. Her eyes teared. She blinked to clear her vision. Felt them tear again. Finally, the gun snapped free. She gasped, cradled it to her chest.

Marchek yanked her out by her legs. Dragged her by the hips. Letting herself be pulled, she slipped and slid across the seat until her knees touched the cold cement of the garage. She cradled the gun to her chest.

He growled in anger, clutched a fistful of her hair. He wrenched her head back. She heard the shearing whisper of hair ripping from her scalp, the pain like scalding water.

She cried out.

Marchek laughed. "Why don't we do it right here in the garage, then, copper? As good a spot as any."

He jerked her back. Still clasping her hair, he shoved her toward the floor. She put one hand out as though to resist. When he let go of her hair to push her down, she dropped flat to the floor, spun onto her back.

Panting, aching, she held the gun straight out above her.

Marchek halted. His mouth formed a small O as he lifted his hands into the air.

Jamie pushed herself up slowly, using her free hand to scale the garage shelves until she was sitting. Her heart pounded in her ears as she watched the rise and fall of Marchek's chest, his own breathing labored. His last breaths, she thought.

"You can't shoot an unarmed man," he said, taking a step backwards. He smiled slowly. "Officer."

Jamie stared. Tried to clear her mind, to think. But the rush of anger and pain clouded her brain. Like the sky of a burning sunset, red was all she saw.

Marchek took another step backwards.

Jamie blinked quickly, aimed with two hands. She pulled the trigger.

The first shot hit just behind the zipper of his pants, where he kept the weapon he'd used to rape at least five women.

She fired again left, at the heart, then right to be sure. Unlike in the movies, there was no change in Marchek's expression. He didn't look down at the wounds or stagger around. All Jamie saw was his legs crumbling as he dropped to the ground just before the blood began to pool.

She didn't move for several seconds—maybe it was more. The gun still out in front of her, she held it until her arms began to shake.

"You weren't unarmed, Marchek. Not now, not ever."

Then she rose slowly, shivering, and limped inside to call for backup.

# 37

Mackenzie had called Alan to pick her up from Michael Marchek's apartment. Her car was at the station, but at that moment, she didn't care. She shivered hard, the image of her photograph on Marchek's rape kit stamped in her mind. They'd gotten the call from the hospital. Marchek's latest victim had died in the OR from internal bleeding. And Marchek was AWOL.

She pictured him in front of her house, photographing her. How close she'd come. She kept expecting an onslaught of tears, but none came. Instead, she just felt cold. So cold.

Alan had come from the paper, still wearing his white dress shirt and suit pants. His tie was gone, as was his coat. She glanced at the way the pants creased across his strong legs. He didn't always dress like that. In Montana, he never had. He looked nice dressed up. It felt like a strange thought to have.

Michael Marchek was a rapist. He had raped five women, attacked another four. Killed one. Mackenzie had almost been raped, a woman was dead, and she was thinking about how cute her husband was. It had been like that since she'd emerged from Marchek's basement. A series of disjointed thoughts flooded her. She couldn't string a sentence, couldn't focus on one thing. Except that every time she closed her eyes, she imagined the moment she'd been thrown down.

"I've been thinking maybe we should move back home," Alan said.

She glanced over at him, tongue catching on her chattering teeth. She'd lived her whole life with freezing winters and snow and had never felt as cold as she did now, inside the car with the heat blasting. It was late, she thought. She didn't know how late, couldn't get her eyes to focus on the yellow digital figures on the radio. Didn't care.

"What do you think?"

She shrugged. She tried to close her eyes, but found it made her nauseated the way too much liquor made a room spin.

"I could work on the book there," Alan said.

Montana. How badly she'd wanted to go home a week ago. Now nothing felt right. The woman who had looked like Hailey Wyatt was dead; a rapist was on the loose.

Her cell phone rang and she stared, feeling nothing but fear. She couldn't possibly take any more news. She turned her head to face out the window.

Alan lifted the phone and she heard the little beep as he answered. "Hello," Alan said. Then "She's here. She's really beat. Can I give her a message?"

Mackenzie didn't look at him. She wasn't beat. She was so far beyond that. She was done, fried to her very core. But not in the way she felt when she'd finished the mountain run—20 miles and 9600 vertical feet. That had been a good sore, like pushing her body to its very limits. No, this was something entirely different. This was like being ripped apart and left to die. She blinked hard, waiting for tears. None came.

"Jesus," Alan said.

She cringed. What now? She didn't want to, but she had to look at him. "What?"

His eyes met hers. They were wide and she saw fear—stark and black. He wanted to take her home where she'd be safe. He blamed himself. He'd brought her here—for his job, his career. And she'd almost been killed.

She shook her head, tried to tell him without speaking that it wasn't his fault. She had wanted to be a cop. She could have tried for a thousand other things. This wasn't like Montana. There were millions of jobs here.

"It's Hailey," he whispered. "You want to call her later?"

Mackenzie shook her head and took the phone from his grip. He hesitated, held on a little too hard. She shook her head again. "It's okay." She pressed the phone to her ear. "Hello."

"Mackenzie."

"Yeah," she repeated, the word catching in her throat. She cleared it. "I'm here."

"Listen, I wanted to let you know. I just got a call—" Hailey stopped and Mackenzie felt it in her bones.

The word came out as a plea. "Jamie?"

Hailey's voice cracked, too. "She was attacked tonight—in her house, but—"

Mackenzie grabbed Alan's arm. "Stop the car," she commanded.

He looked over, frowned.

"Stop the car, Alan! Stop it."

Alan moved slowly, used the blinker, stopped at the curb.

He reached for her, but she pulled away. "God, no," she whispered. She tugged the door open, tumbled onto the sidewalk.

"Mackenzie," Hailey said again, her voice more urgent. "She got away. He didn't get her."

"Was it him—Mar—"

"Yes."

Her knees buckled and she locked them so she wouldn't fall. "Did he assault—God." She couldn't get the question out. Since her own attack, she'd been thinking how lucky she was that he hadn't raped her, how horrible it would be to live through that, to face each day knowing that some man had—

"No," Hailey said firmly. "He didn't assault her. She got away. She shot him."

"He's—"

"Dead, Mackenzie. He's dead."

She exhaled and closed her eyes. Faced heaven. Thank you, God. Thank you. "Where is she?"

"She's at General. She doesn't want visitors. Go home and get some rest. Call me when you get up."

Mackenzie nodded. "She's going to be okay?"

"She'll be sore, but she'll live," Hailey said.

Mackenzie nodded. They'd probably never be okay—not any of them. She stepped back toward the car, pressed her hand on the cool glass. "Devlin?" she whispered.

"Nothing new. We'll work on it tomorrow. You get the list of awards?"

"Yeah. They gave out thirty."

"Get some sleep now and call me in the morning."

With that, Mackenzie pulled herself back into the car.

Alan stared at her, his mouth a flat line. "You're going in tomorrow?"

She watched him, not sure how to answer.

"I don't think you should go back there."

The chills vanished. She turned the blower down and adjusted the vent toward the middle of the car. Calm washed over her. "I have to," she said. "Marchek's dead."

Alan didn't move the car. "How many more times do you need to put your life in danger before you realize this job could get you killed?"

She didn't respond, but an answer popped into her head immediately. At least one more, she thought.

She wasn't quitting until they caught Devlin's killer.

# 38

Jamie walked out of the hospital the next morning through the same door she usually entered to interview victims of people like Marchek. And now she was the victim—almost. Almost, she told herself. Not quite. Marchek hadn't gotten her—at least not in the way her victims suffered.

And yet she realized with sudden clarity that the act of rape began way before penetration. Rape. She could have gone home last night. She hadn't broken anything. She was bruised—everything was bruised. But there were no cracks in her ribs. Even slamming the door on her, that bastard hadn't broken anything except for one finger. But when she closed her eyes, she imagined him coming down on top of her. She blinked hard, forced the image away.

She stopped outside the hospital door, lit a cigarette and sucked it until her lungs could draw no more smoke. She held the breath, the buzz burning away her headache. Let it slowly out. Without moving, she repeated the motion until the cigarette was gone.

Marchek was dead. She'd finally gotten him. She thought about the reports that would have to be filed, her gun removed and tests performed, the interviews Internal Affairs would conduct, the time expended on a full investigation of the incident. She'd be on probation until she was cleared of any wrongdoing. At that moment, though, even the bureaucratic bullshit seemed worth it.

Jamie shook another cigarette from the pack, noticed her trembling fingers. It worsened as she lifted the lighter, spun the metal wheel, and heard the flame whisper.

As she took the first drag, she saw her beat-up Subaru pull to the curb. The last officer she'd interviewed with had said someone was coming to get her and take her home. He didn't say who; she didn't ask. After three separate interviews and more than two hours of questions, she had been done talking. But she'd hoped it would be Hailey or maybe Mackenzie. This would be harder.

She watched Tony step out of her car. He wiped his palms on his pants as if he were picking up a date for the junior prom. She didn't move toward him. It took all she had not to turn back into the hospital, not to run.

When he reached her, he touched her cheek, skimming his thumb over one of the nasty bruises Marchek had given her.

She flinched.

He reached his arms around her, pulled her to his chest. "When they called, I thought you were gone," he whispered and she felt his hands in her hair.

She let out a moan as he tightened his arms around her chest. He loosened his arms, not letting go. "Shit. Are you okay?"

"I ache. Everything aches."

"God, I'm so glad you're okay."

She leaned against him, stayed there. Closed her eyes.

"Did they give you anything?" he asked.

"A prescription for Vicodin."

"You want to fill it?"

She shook her head, stepped back. "Too tempting."

"I'd be okay."

"I wasn't talking about you."

He nodded. "You ready?"

"Did you see it? What's it look like?"

He frowned. "What?"

"The house—the garage?" She pictured the blood everywhere.

"It's clean. I cleaned it up. Installed the washer and dryer, too." He shrugged. "Couldn't sleep."

It was gone. The blood would be gone. She'd still see it, of course. And him. It would all still be there for her. But at least it was physically gone. "Thank you."

They turned to the car.

There was silence, but she knew what was on both their minds. The subject would come up eventually. She knew it was time.

Tony opened the car door for her, waited while she sat. She fastened the seat belt across her chest and moved the chest harness behind her back. She didn't want it to tighten across her aching ribs.

Tony drove without a seat belt. She thought about telling him to put it on but couldn't find the words. She wanted to start, to get it over with. She owed him an apology—they all did. Already she knew that. She understood more than ever.

She said nothing for twenty minutes. The car was silent. He'd shut off the radio she'd had playing when she'd driven home the night before—celebrating her victories. Christ, what a lot had changed.

She knew that's how it happened. Things turned upside down in a matter of moments. That's how it had been for them all those years ago.

Now or never, she thought. She watched him until he looked over at her. He smiled nervously and studied the road over his left shoulder to change lanes.

The bright orange pillars of the Golden Gate Bridge emerged in the distance against the brilliant sky.

He didn't want to hear it, she knew. He would have asked. He knew what she was thinking.

But suddenly, she had to speak. "I don't think any-one realizes how hard it is."

He didn't ask what. He knew. He didn't even look at her.

"I'm sorry. I should have done something back then."

She saw the slow tremor in his hands work its way up his arms, but she didn't stop—couldn't.

"When he was on top of me," she said.

Tony shook his head. "Don't."

Her own shoulders quaking, Jamie gripped her hands together to fight off the trembling. She shuffled through the pile of stuff between the seats in search of her cigarettes. She found them, fumbled with the pack. It fell onto the floor, cigarettes spilling.

She wanted to reach it, but couldn't imagine leaning down to pick it up. She let it go, turned to Tony. "I have to. I have to talk about it. Please. We never talked about it."

He clenched the steering wheel, sped across the bridge. "Jamie, no."

She stooped again for her cigarettes, couldn't reach them. She shifted in her seat. There was no outlet for the anxiety that coursed through her. "He's dead, Tony. He's dead and I still can't close my eyes without seeing him on top of me, coming at me."

Tony jerked the car to the slow lane, swung off the bridge into a small vista. It had a name, but she couldn't remember it.

He spun the car into the nearest parking spot and yanked on the emergency brake. Then he pushed the car door open and tumbled out.

Jamie moved more slowly. Followed. The sky daz-zled, the blue flowing right into the color of the bay. The city buildings stood like a row of pencils in the distance. She thought for a moment of 9/11, of the buildings across the country that had been standing one minute, gone the next. She thought of Mick, but mostly she thought of Tony.

A few cars were parked in the lot despite the cold weather. A Japanese tour group stood a few yards away, cameras aimed at the cityscape across the water.

Tony headed for a quiet corner.

Jamie limped behind.

When he reached the railing, he hung his shoulders. "Don't do this now. Not after all this time."

But Jamie didn't stop. "I always blamed myself, Tony. I should've stopped him. I always thought he was creepy. I always hesitated to take his candy. But that day, when we were in the back, when he locked that door—" She shuddered, imagining the man who had worked in the small corner grocery store. Tall and thin, he stood partially stooped over as though always eyeing the floor for a nickel someone had dropped.

He'd been a quiet man with round hazel eyes and a soft, round face. Not like her father and Pat, who were always scruffy; this man didn't have facial hair.

Whenever Tony and Jamie had gone alone to the store—usually sent by Pat or her father to pick up milk or bread—he'd always offered them a piece of candy from a tin behind the register. Sometimes it was butterscotch, sometimes chocolate. Her favorite were the little rolls of tart candies. Tony used to go in for baseball cards, too.

That day the man had told him he had some extra packs of cards in the back. He'd locked up the store, walked to the storeroom.

Jamie had hesitated, but Tony had gone ahead. "No big deal," he'd said.

She remembered the musty smell of the room, the damp floor. She saw rows of boxes piled up against the walls, threatening to fall at any moment. It had felt like a maze of cardboard and steel shelves. She shuddered. "I thought he was coming for me. I was sure of it."

He backed from the railing, pushed past her. "No."

She grabbed on to him as he went, his motion sending agony through her. She bit back a cry of pain but didn't let go.

People stared. She didn't care.

She clutched his arm, forced him to face her.

She kept her voice low. No one could hear. It was just them. "I thought he was going to rape *me,* Tony."

Tony shook his head. Tears streamed down his cheeks, eyes pleading with her to stop.

She didn't let go. She couldn't now. "I never thought it would be you."

Tony reared his head, a painful cry exploding from his throat.

People stared. Jamie waved them away.

Tony dropped to his knees. "God, no. Jamie. Why did that happen?"

She fell too, tucked her head into his shoulder as he gripped her. Felt herself let go. All those years ago. All those years of hiding it, of pretending it hadn't happened—of Pat and her father ignoring the blatant pleas for help.

"I don't know, Tony. I'm so sorry."

"God," he choked, sobbing.

They stayed there, embraced until she felt the rocking of his chest still. Even then she didn't loosen her grip, didn't wipe her own tears. She let them remain where they'd fallen, long overdue.

Finally, she spoke, "I'm here now, Tony. It's over. It's over for both of us."

And, she thought, maybe for once she was telling the truth.

Maybe they could finally start to put that horrible day behind them.

# 39

When Jamie arrived in the conference room, Hailey and Mackenzie were already waiting.

Mackenzie rose from the table and stepped toward her. Her brown eyes were wide and wise. She looked older to Jamie, more mature. Shit, the rookie had grown into a full-fledged cop. Mackenzie hesitated for only a fraction of a second before she wrapped her arms around Jamie. "I'm so glad you're okay." She squeezed gently.

Jamie closed her eyes for a moment. "Thanks."

Hailey nodded, pushed a chair toward her. "You sure you want to be here?"

Jamie forced a smile. "And let you guys be Charlie's Angels without me?"

Mackenzie laughed, swiped at a tear.

"We're some sad-looking Charlie's Angels," Hailey said.

"Hey, speak for yourself," Jamie said, hobbling toward the chair.

Tony had been surprised that she was coming in today. Jules had tried to deter her. But no one was going to forbid it. Not after yesterday.

Jamie had waited until most people would be gone for the day. She wasn't ready to answer questions just yet, but she needed to stay in the game. She felt close and didn't want to lose ground. Or maybe it was because at home alone it was too easy to remember what had happened. She wasn't prepared to face it all yet.

She and Tony had spent a quiet day in the house. He'd made grilled-cheese sandwiches for lunch, burning both of them. She didn't mind. He'd spent as little time learning to cook hot foods as she had. They had talked little, but most of what needed to be said was already out. And mostly she was relieved at the comfortable silence.

Tony had intended to start his rehabilitation this week, but since her attack, it hadn't come up again. And she was thankful. He'd stayed with her last night, sleeping in the bed beside her. It had been decades since they'd shared a bed, but it felt the same as always. Tony was her brother, the closest thing she'd ever have to a sibling—the closest for either of them now.

Every time she stirred, he woke beside her. She hadn't thanked him. She knew she didn't need to. They'd been apart for years, but they'd found each other. He'd found her. Thank God for that.

Tony had driven her through the city, dropping her at the building at almost six in the evening and telling her he'd be back at nine. They had planned to grab dinner on the way home—take-out, probably. She couldn't see sitting at a table and dealing with the stares she'd get with the cuts and bruises on her face. Plus, sitting too long hurt.

Mackenzie and Hailey waited until Jamie was seated. Neither commented on how long it took her or on the bruises on her face. Mackenzie's were turning greenish. Hailey probably had some, too. But Marchek was dead now. No more women would suffer at his hands.

Hailey spoke first. "The medical examiner called on the autopsy."

Jamie knew Hailey meant Marchek's. She was thankful not to hear his name out loud.

"He had an explanation for the aspermatic samples we got from his victims."

Jamie took a slow, measured breath, tried to listen analytically.

"Seems he had an anatomical anomaly called retrograde ejaculation. It's rare and probably congenital in his case. Instead of exiting through the urethra, the sperm is passed in retrograde fashion into the bladder."

Jamie listened. "So there would be DNA sample in his urine but not in his semen."

Hailey nodded.

"He probably figured it out after his first arrest." She paused. "Or maybe not." We'll never know now, she thought. Thank God. "How about Devlin?" she asked.

"We're focusing on the list of awards," Hailey said. "Roger tested Natasha's trophy for transfer evidence and confirmed she wasn't hit with her own."

Jamie nodded. "Good. So the killer probably hit her with his. Who else is on the list?"

Hailey slid a piece of paper across the table. Jamie turned it around and scanned the names.

Someone had made a small hash mark next to David Marshall's name. Jamie looked up, raised a brow. "Your captain?"

Hailey shrugged.

She returned to the list. Cameron Cruz had received an award. Captain Linda James. She recognized most of the names but none stood out. "You have the other list?"

"There are no other crossovers," Hailey said. "Just Marshall."

"The only other person who touches both lists is Devlin herself," Mackenzie added.

Jamie frowned. "What do we do about Marshall?"

"I had his trophy sent to the lab."

"Does he know?"

Hailey shook her head.

Christ, she hoped the captain of Homicide wasn't Devlin's killer. Jamie stared at the list again. She scanned the titles on the names—captain, lieutenant, sergeant. "This is the whole list?"

Hailey nodded.

Jamie frowned. She pulled her phone out of her pocket and dialed the lab's number. "Roger, please," she said when someone answered,

Hailey and Mackenzie exchanged a glance.

"Roger here."

"Roger, it's Jamie."

"Hey. How are you?"

"I'm alive."

"Yeah. I heard about what happened. Your gun's down in ballistics," he added awkwardly.

"Roger, I'm calling about something else."

"Sure." He sounded relieved.

"You won an award at the banquet, didn't you?"

"Uh, yeah. I used it to test against the mold of Tim Worley's head injury."

Jamie nodded. "That's what I thought. Thanks, Roger."

"Is that it?"

"That's it." Jamie shut her phone and set it on the table. "That's not a complete list."

Hailey frowned. "It's only police."

"Right."

"You think we're looking at someone from criminalistics or administration?"

She shrugged. "Natasha's list includes a guy in the lab, doesn't it?"

Hailey nodded. "And another from administration."

"I'll get the rest of the names together now," Mackenzie offered.

"I've got to finish up some things before I can head home," Hailey said. "We'll talk in the morning?"

Jamie nodded.

"You going to be okay?" Hailey asked.

"I'll live."

Nodding, Hailey stood when there was a knock. She pulled it open and a young man stood at the door, looking terrified.

"Hey, Dave," Mackenzie said.

The officer looked at her, wide-eyed. "Hey."

"What are you doing here?"

He scanned Hailey and Jamie and seemed to stumble on his words. "I'm looking for Jamie Vail."

Jamie knew exactly who he was. "David Priestley."

He nodded.

She waved him in.

Hailey looked at her and motioned to the door, but Jamie shook her head and explained, "Officer Priestley is Scott Scanlan's partner. He's going to tell us about the night he was at my house."

Priestley glanced at them, then studied the floor.

Hailey shut the door behind him.

He focused on his hands as though there were something written there that he could use to get him out of this.

"Just tell us what happened," Jamie prodded.

Priestley glanced at the others in the room.

"They're staying," she said firmly. "We're all involved." She nodded at him to tell his story.

He hesitated and then, shoulders sinking, he began to talk. "Scanlan said he wanted to play a trick on someone who'd been giving him a hard time. He made it sound like a joke." Priestley looked up at Hailey and Jamie but avoided Mackenzie's gaze.

They'd been in academy together, Jamie figured. He was embarrassed. She didn't care.

"He said he was going to let the air out of a couple of tires—that's it." He shrugged. "I didn't want to go, but shit, I didn't want to get into a thing about it. It was our lunch break—or dinner break, I guess, because of how late it was. So we drove up there. I knew it was going to take longer than an hour, but he promised not much—" He stopped, stared at the white wall, continued.

"When we got up there, he told me to wait in the car. He just got out. I stayed. I didn't even see the knife until he came back.

"He got a T-shirt out of the trunk and wiped it off. That's when I saw the blood. He said a dog tried to attack him—that he was just defending himself. I freaked out. I didn't know what to do." He shook his head. "He knew it, too. He made me swear not to say anything. He said it was lucky he got to the dog first because it probably would've killed some kid." He looked up then. "I've been trying to figure out a way to get a new partner, to transfer. He's such a prick, but his father's—" He stopped then, silent.

Hailey nodded to Jamie.

"You can go," Jamie told him.

He looked up, relieved. "Really? Are you going to—"

"No," she interrupted. "But don't say anything about this yet. I'll call you."

He nodded, avoiding Mackenzie's gaze, and left the room.

Hailey spoke first. "We should start by telling IA and the DA's office."

Jamie nodded. That probably made sense.

"I'll talk to IA," Hailey offered.

Jamie nodded. "I'll go talk to Washington. Call my cell and we'll touch base. I'll be here until nine—at my desk or on my cell. Tony's picking me up."

As she made her way up to Chip Washington's office on the eighth floor, Jamie prayed one of these leads would end in an arrest. They had to be close. She just hoped they weren't somehow looking at Devlin's murder all wrong.

Chip's secretary was gone and she considered for a second that he might be, too. She knocked on the door, but no one answered. She started to turn when she heard it open.

Chip emerged, wearing his coat and carrying a bulky leather attorney-style briefcase with a brass snap at the top.

"You heading home?"

He nodded. Yawned.

"You okay?"

He nodded to her bruise. "I should be asking you that."

She touched her cheek.

"I'm sorry about what happened."

"Thanks."

"Come on in." He turned back, carried his case to his desk, and set it down. He shrugged out of his jacket, bent down.

She heard the click of his bag opening as she moved into the office, shutting the door behind her. "I'm here because of another Scanlan incident."

He looked up, frowning. "What now?"

Jamie told him about David Priestley's confession. Chip shook his head. "That kid is a menace."

"He wouldn't be here if it weren't for his father."

"His father's a menace, too." He lifted a yellow legal pad and began to make notes. "Let me get the specifics."

Jamie repeated the date and time of the attack, gave him her vet's name and number. As she spoke she glanced over at his shelf, scanning the pictures of his wife and daughter she'd seen dozens of times before. She started to ask about the girl when her eye caught an award at the end of the shelf. "What did you win that night?"

Chip stared at his notepad without looking up. He continued to write. "Oh, case records for the year. It's no big deal." He shifted in his seat, kept his head down. He seemed to be writing faster now.

Jamie pictured him in the meeting with Bruce Daniels and Scott Scanlan. He'd been uncomfortable. Just like Daniels and Captain David Marshall. She stepped toward the award, her heart drumming.

Bruce Daniels and Captain Marshall had known about Deputy Chief Scanlan's affair with Devlin. That's why they had been uncomfortable. But Chip? She couldn't see the deputy chief telling a district attorney.

She lifted the award and ran her finger across the corners. One was chipped.

She felt her mouth drop open, reached for her gun.

"Don't," he said. "Put your hands up."

She turned slowly, the air seeping from her lungs like from a punctured inner tube. "That morning in the meeting about Devlin's murder—you knew about her and Deputy Chief Scanlan."

He didn't respond.

"But not because anyone had told you. You knew because you caught them together that night."

Chip leveled the gun at her.

"Right before you killed her."

# 40

It was almost eight and Hailey had been in the office for eleven hours without a break. For lunch, she'd eaten a stale muffin from a vending machine and since then, all she'd had were two Diet Cokes.

When her cell phone rang, she'd thought it was going to be Mackenzie or Jamie.

"Yeah."

"It's Stephanie Rusch at the lab."

"You're there late."

"Yeah, I guess. Listen, Sydney asked me to call. She said you should get over here as soon as you can. Are you home?"

"No. I'm at the Hall. Is everything all right?"

"Uh, yeah. There's just someone here you need to see."

"Can it wait until tomorrow?"

"Uh, I don't think so. It's a guy from the sheriff's department up by Lake Tahoe."

"Okay. I can be there in fifteen minutes."

Hailey started to ask more, but Stephanie cut her off. "I've got to get back."

Hailey grabbed her coat and headed out of the station. John called on her way out. "Another late night?"

"I'm sorry, babe."

"Be careful, okay?"

She told him she would and started to promise it would be better one day. She couldn't promise that. It would be a lie and she told enough of those already.

The streets were quiet. She made it into Hunters Point in less than fifteen minutes. She showed her badge to the guard, wound down the road to the lab. As she pulled into a parking spot, she thought about all that had happened since the day she'd been assigned Natasha Devlin's murder. What to do about Buck Daniels entered her mind. She shoved it out. Now was not the time to figure it out. Soon, though, she thought.

When she entered the lab, both Sydney and Stephanie were at work behind microscopes. A man Hailey didn't recognize was cutting apart a big piece of carpet with a box cutter.

Another man sat at the table where she and Sydney had been just days before, working on Abby and Hank Dennig.

Sydney turned and stepped toward her, looking at the man as she pointed to Hailey. "This is Inspector Wyatt."

The man rose from his chair. He was short and stout. A pair of black elastic suspenders clipped from his jeans and ran over his shoulders. He laughed as he put out his hand. "Sorry. I was expecting a man."

She smiled. "No apology necessary. I think my mother was, too."

He laughed.

Hailey shook his hand and waited for someone to explain why she was there.

Sydney didn't speak.

Stephanie and the other tech continued to work.

"My name's Carl Watson. I'm a deputy with the Placerville Sheriff's Department."

"What can I do for you, Deputy Watson?"

"Please. Call me Carl."

She nodded.

"We had a suicide up there that we thought may interest you."

Hailey frowned. "A suicide?" She scanned her memory for any questionable death that had recently been deemed suicide. She came up empty.

"Deceased is named Colby Wesson."

"Wesson?"

"As in the gun maker. This guy's the grandson or great-grandson. Still in the business—or was."

A tank sunk in her gut. Leaning against the table, she crossed her arms and dropped her shoulders. He was there about the Dennigs. They hadn't killed each other. If there was another victim, it meant the Dennigs had been murdered. "Wesson," she whispered.

The man nodded. "Right. He's somewhere down the line from the original gun maker."

She glanced at Sydney, who gave a tiny nod. "When did this happen?"

The man fingered his mustache, frowned. "Three weeks ago—three and a half now, I guess."

"How'd he commit suicide?"

"Car in the garage."

She waited.

"We didn't think anything of it until we found some traces of a drug in his system. Took us two weeks to get the tox reports back. Once we had 'em, we re-opened the case and looked into the possibility of homicide. That's when we got the state lab involved. They linked it to a double homicide you worked recently."

"Abby and Hank Dennig," she supplied.

"That's the one." He motioned to Sydney, who crossed the room to where Stephanie worked. "I brought down some evidence from that case—the thing that links them."

Sydney lifted a small plastic bag off the counter beside Stephanie. Even as she made her way across the room, Hailey knew what it was. She'd been the one to enter the pin's description into NCIC, to be certain she wasn't overlooking something that related to a series of other crimes.

Through the plastic bag, Hailey read the words, "Wage peace, not war." It was identical to the one they'd found in Abby Dennig's minivan.

Hailey closed her eyes, held them closed. "Christ."

"It's got a clean print," Sydney said.

Hailey jerked her eyes open. "You get a match?"

Sydney nodded but didn't look happy.

"Who?"

"Nick Fredricks."

She shook her head. "I don't know—" But then she stopped. She did. "The lobbyist."

Sydney nodded. "Right. Anti-gun, anti-NRA."

Hailey frowned, dragging her memory for something. "But I thought he was—"

Sydney nodded again. "He is. Dead."

"Could it be an old print?" Hailey asked. "Some sort of joke thing they gave out a long time ago?"

"We don't think so," Carl cut in. "It was a brand-new car. Wesson had it for only a couple weeks before he died."

"And Fredricks' is the only print on the button," Sydney added.

Hailey realized she'd screwed up big-time. She'd missed something on the Dennigs. There was a third person, had to have been. "What about the button from the last scene? Was there a print on it?"

"We're running it again. It was only a partial. We didn't have enough to get a match the first time."

Stephanie crossed the rooms, rolling the gloves off her hands. "Under the scope, it looks like the same print. You can see the tented arch in both."

Hailey shook her head, stared at Sydney. "You were right."

Sydney didn't acknowledge that. She merely said, "We'll send the buttons out to be sure."

Hailey nodded as her phone rang.

"Hailey." It was Mackenzie's voice, breathless.

"What? What's wrong?"

"I just got the full list of awards."

"Who's on it?"

"Chip Washington."

"It can't be Washington—he's—" She stopped herself. What? He's an attorney? Was that a defense?

"Jamie's not answering her cell phone and he's not in his office," Mackenzie continued.

"Maybe her battery died," Hailey said, not at all reassured by her own words.

"I'm going down to her office now," Mackenzie said. "If I can't find her, I'll go to his."

"Mackenzie, wait."

"I can't. This place's empty. Why wouldn't she answer her cell phone?"

Hailey turned back to Sydney. "I've got to go."

Sydney nodded as Hailey ran for the door. "I'm at the lab, but I'm leaving now. I'll meet you there. Don't go anywhere until I get there."

"Hurry!"

Hailey sprinted across the linoleum and up the few steps to the gravel parking. Her feet kicked up dirt as she dashed to her car. Breathless, she yanked the door open, jammed her key in the ignition. She revved the engine and threw it in reverse, tires spinning on the gravel. She tried to tell herself it was nothing. Jamie was in her office, had turned off her phone.

As she sped up the road out of the naval station, she fumbled with her phone to dial the department's main number. When it was answered, she asked for Chip Washington's line. Thirty seconds passed and she heard his voice mail. She hit end and dialed the main number again.

"This is Inspector Wyatt. I'm trying to reach one of the assistant district attorneys—Chip Washington. Do you have a cell phone number for him?"

"Sure. Want me to connect you?"

"Please."

Hailey listened to it ring as she raced through the streets toward the Hall. She hit a yellow light, flattened the accelerator to the floor.

The phone rang once, twice, three times. Then she heard a click and a woman's voice. "Hello."

"Jamie."

"No, I think you have the wrong number."

"I'm sorry. I was trying to reach Chip Washington. Did I dial wrong?"

"No. This is his cell phone."

"My name is Hailey Wyatt. I'm an inspector with the SFPD. Is Chip there?"

"This is his wife. He's not here. I think he's still at the office. He left his cell phone at home."

Hailey shook her head. "Is there another number I could try?"

"You tried the office?"

"No one answered."

"He might be on his way home then. He always has his cell phone, but his car got hit last week, so it's being worked on."

Hailey held her breath as she sped around another corner. "Mrs. Washington, can I ask you something?"

"Call me Pam."

"Pam?"

"Sure."

Hailey thought about Tim Worley. As she turned right onto Third from 25th, she asked, "Does Chip stutter?"

"Oh, Lord, no."

Hailey exhaled. This was all wrong. Thank God.

"I haven't heard him stutter since law school. Well, once in a while when he's really upset."

Hailey couldn't bring herself to say anything else. She punched the end button and dialed Jamie's cell phone again. There was no answer.

Her heart racing, Hailey called the main number and told them to get some officers to start combing the building for Jamie Vail. She called Mackenzie. The rookie didn't answer.

She dropped the phone onto the seat beside her and gripped the steering wheel with both hands.

Tried to bargain with God again. Please, save Jamie.

She pressed the accelerator to the floor and prayed she made it there in time.

# 41

Jamie moved slowly despite the gun Washington had jammed in the small of her back. It was her backup gun and she knew it was loaded. He held it in a Lysol wipe he'd pulled from his desk drawer—the same kind he had used to wipe down Devlin's desk after he'd killed her.

Washington had left his own gun in his office and taken hers. She knew why—this was going to look like a suicide if he had his way. She was a perfect candidate. Even she thought so.

"I almost dumped the stupid thing," he said softly, nodding to the trophy. "But the department is always encouraging us to show them off, like some fucking award makes the public feel more confident about our abilities. I thought it would be too obvious if it was missing, so I left it. What a mess."

"What happened, Chip?"

"God, she was such a whore!" He tensed, aggravated, and he shoved the gun into her spine.

She let him talk, trying to think of a way out. Nothing came to her. She was trapped. *Think, damn it.* All that came to mind was: not twice in two days.

Cracking the office door, he peered out. Pushed her into the hallway.

"You didn't mean to kill her," Jamie whispered.

"God, no. I came to see her, to congratulate her on

her award." He breathed heavily as he urged her forward. "We'd been together for a few weeks. Only a few times. But when I saw her with"—He moaned—"that old man. I was so disgusted. I was so angry."

She considered running. She ached, could barely walk, and the gun was too close. She didn't doubt he would shoot. He had everything to lose.

She considered a bullet. She could take one, but not in the back—not if she ever wanted to walk again. Panic gripped her. She fought to stay calm.

Chip held her arm as they passed through the empty hall. He stopped at the stairwell, motioned her to open the door. She did, praying someone would be just inside. Empty.

They were eight floors up. She had to believe there would be people. It was the Hall. Even at night, there were always people. Just be calm. Distract him. Her heart jackhammered in her chest.

"She was fucking an old man right there on her desk."

They walked slowly down the flights. "Why didn't you leave?"

"I was frozen. I was so appalled, so humiliated. And then I got angry. I was so angry."

"Deputy Chief Scanlan left."

"Yeah. He hiked up his pants and walked out, shining like a sweaty pig. And when she saw me, she had the nerve to ask what I was doing there. That bitch." He thrust her toward the stairs. "You're all bitches."

Jamie stumbled, grabbed the banister, pain rocketing through her rib cage. She tripped, caught the rail. Tried to swallow the pain. Tears pressed in her throat. "She just used you. She used all of you."

"No. It was different with us. At least until that night."

"Bullshit. She fucked you the same as the others."

"No." Chip launched himself at her. Her hand slipped from the banister. She fell forward as he slammed the gun into her skull. The crack hit her just above her right ear. She toppled to her knees on the concrete stairs. The room spun.

She hung her head, fought the urge to vomit. Her vision cleared, she thought to roll. As she went to move, the gun was right back on her. Too slow. She was too slow.

"It was different. You don't know. I'm not like those others—like Worley or Scanlan. She wanted to be with me, but she let the others have her. I thought it was over until I came in and saw them.

"She acted like the whole thing was funny, like it was no big deal. She'd had too much to drink and she started to egg me on. She made fun of me and we fought. I pushed her. That's all. Just one push. She tripped on her goddamn shoe.

"She fell backwards and hit her head. That's how she died. It wasn't my fault. It was an accident. I'm not going to jail for it. If she hadn't been such a whore, it never would have happened. She should have been loyal. I was loyal to her."

"Loyal? You're married!"

His frown deepened.

They reached the fourth floor. Still no one. She dragged a breath, changed her tactic. "I'm not the only one who knows."

"Your partners, Hailey and Mackenzie? I know about them, too. It's a big mess, but it's not my fault. I just have to clean it up; then it'll be over. I can forget about that whore and get back to my life."

Jamie remembered. "You told the press about her list."

"Sure. I wasn't on it. It gave you idiots an entire list of folks to chose from, men she'd screwed. Put a little pressure on, get the case closed fast. But you couldn't handle that, could you?"

She stopped midway between the second and third

floors, bracing the steel rail as she lifted her head. She blinked at the white spots.

"Move," he commanded, thrusting her forward. She stumbled, wondered what time it was. Was it almost nine? Would Tony be waiting for her? Would he come after her?

"Where are we going?"

"Just go."

She stepped down the next stair. Pain resonated through every inch of her. And still, her mind turned the pieces of it, trying to get it to all fit. She looked at him, forced her back straight. "You killed her, Chip. Even if it was an accident, you left her there and she didn't deserve that."

He let out a growl, kicked into the backs of her knees. She collapsed, pitched forward. She tumbled down the stairs, crumpled on the landing. She could barely lift her head. The pain was like a vise on her skull. She moaned. When she opened her eyes, he stood above her. "I didn't kill her. I pushed her, that's it. I hit Tim Worley that night. I just hit you. He's alive; you're alive. It was bad luck. That's all. And it wasn't my fault."

She tasted blood, swept her hand across her mouth.

"G-get up!" he shouted, the vein in his neck like a rope along the skin.

Let him shoot, she thought. "N-n-n-o."

He hoisted his foot to kick her again. She closed her eyes, stiffening against the blow. But instead he gripped her hair. He jerked her head up. "That's enough. I'm in control here, not you."

Blood trickled down her chin like dribble. She looked at his brown eyes, at the way his lips snarled as he spoke. He and Marchek were two of the same. Two beasts. At least she'd gotten one. "Fuck you, Chip."

He dropped down and shoved the gun in her neck.

Their faces were inches apart. She could smell his breath, the scent of sweat.

His hand still gripped her hair at the base of her neck. He used it to drag her to her feet as he rose.

The gun was warm against her neck, the metal stealing the heat in her body as it would soon steal her life. The scent of gun oil mixed with the copper scent of her own blood.

She thought about the fight with Marchek, the adrenaline rush of escaping him. She had known she wouldn't die. She had known she could get away. She'd had her weapon. She'd just had to get to it.

But now, her own gun clenched in Washington's fist, she wasn't so sure.

For the first time in her life, Jamie considered that she might die.

# 42

Still clasping her hair in his fist, Chip held her at the final landing. He drove her face to the wall as he opened the door. She heard voices. She opened her mouth to scream as he shifted the gun from her head to the hollow of her cheek. The door clicked shut again.

"Don't do it. I'll kill them all."

She closed her mouth, blinked back tears.

When the voices passed, he opened the door again. Peered out. He shoved her into the hallway, moving quickly behind her. He held the gun at her side and out of view.

She tried to slow him, to stall, but he shoved the muzzle into her ribs. The pain urged her forward.

The hallway was empty. With her in front, they walked through the back doors and into the quiet parking lot. She had prayed somehow Tony would be there, waiting. But the back lot was deserted.

Terror surged through her. She couldn't let him reach his car. She couldn't get in. This was her best chance.

He moved quickly now, his fist in her hair driving the momentum.

They turned the corner into the dark lot. She heard a tiny cry escape her lips. It was too close. There was no way out.

He pushed against her. "Not a sound." He stopped by a white Volvo and she heard the double beep of doors unlocking. He took her arm, steering her toward the driver's side when light exploded in her eyes.

He backed up, dragging her.

She blinked hard, waved her arms.

Headlights. A car's headlights shone on them. She squinted to see the driver.

"Move," Chip commanded.

The car engine revved as the lights came toward them.

Chip ducked behind the Volvo, dragging her with him.

Jamie wrenched free. Threw herself into the line of the car.

They were separated. She stood and ran, tripped. She fell and crawled on, scrambling to get up again.

She turned back to see Chip raise his weapon and fire at the car. The car revved but didn't move.

Then she heard gunshots from the other side of her. Three quick blasts.

She dropped, then rolled toward a cement post. A cry of pain burst from her lips as she tried to stand. A muscle tore against her ribs. She swallowed a scream.

Silence. She waited, listened. She stared into the headlights. Then looked for Washington. She saw him lying huddled on the ground, still.

A car door opened. Shoes scraped on the pavement. She heard voices.

Someone bent over Washington, rolled him onto his back. She saw her gun in his hand. He didn't move.

It was over. She closed her eyes, dropped her head to her hands.

Then she heard her name, felt hands.

Hailey and Mackenzie stood over her. Mackenzie still had her gun out.

"Good shooting, rookie," Jamie told her.

Mackenzie nodded.

Then came other voices, men shouting.

Time seemed to fade in and out. Through her fog, Jamie heard the onslaught of questions, felt Mackenzie try to help her up. She just shook her head. Didn't want to move.

"Jesus Christ, it's Charlie's Fucking Angels again," a familiar voice said.

Jamie opened her eyes, stared at Scott Scanlan, ready to let him have it.

Hailey raised her hand. "Save your breath," she told Jamie, pointing at someone walking toward them.

Bruce Daniels emerged from the dark with two other officers. Jamie recognized them from her own IA experience way back when. Daniels gave Hailey a quick nod, turned to Scanlan. "Officer Scanlan, you need to come with us."

Scanlan looked around, befuddled. Then he settled an angry gaze on Jamie.

Jamie smiled at him, the same shit-eating grin that he'd given her that first night when IA had come to his rescue. It wasn't as satisfying, though, because even smiling hurt like hell.

As Scanlan was led away, she leaned back and listened to the whir of an ambulance siren, saw the spinning lights. Paramedics jumped out of the cab and jogged toward her.

She insisted she didn't need to go to the hospital but they loaded her up anyway. She spotted Tony in the crowd, heard him say he'd meet her at the hospital.

Hailey climbed up into the back of the ambulance first, then offered Mackenzie a hand. They both sat down, waiting for the paramedics to load Jamie in.

"Only one can go," one of the paramedics told them.

"We're both going," Mackenzie stated, leaving no room for argument.

The paramedic looked at his partner for support, but the other man shrugged.

Jamie smiled and lay back on the gurney, thinking she might just take the Vicodin prescription this time. Or maybe not.

The women were silent as the ambulance bounced across the parking lot. The men up front spoke softly, the radio crackled.

Jamie knew they were all thinking about how close she'd come. She blinked hard and tried to think of something amusing. Scott Scanlan was going to get it. That helped. And Chip Washington was gone. And Marchek . . . No, she couldn't think about that. Not yet.

She focused back on Scanlan, his cockiness. He was the easiest. Charlie's Angels, he'd called them. Jamie looked up at Mackenzie and then over at Hailey. Hailey smiled at her, the way a mother might smile at a child. It was soothing. She tried to smile back.

"Maybe we could sell the story rights to Hollywood—" Jamie whispered.

Hailey frowned. "What?"

"Sell the story to Hollywood, make a million dollars. Retire."

Mackenzie laughed and Hailey shook her head. "We can be stunt doubles."

"God, no," Jamie croaked. "Let's just consult."

Mackenzie grinned. "Who's going to play you, Jamie?"

"Probably Lucy Liu."

Hailey laughed.

Jamie glanced from one of them to the other and said, "After all, she looks the most like me."

She heard them laugh—big belly laughs—and she did, too. She stopped because it hurt too much, but at least she could. She could laugh and feel and breathe.

It was like she told people about her victims—she might never be okay, but she was definitely going to survive.

# EPILOGUE

*Twelve weeks later*

Jamie glanced over at Z. His gaze was glued to the basketball court fifteen rows below them, his eyes shifting only enough to move up and down the court. And every time a player named Antawn Jamison made a move, Z launched out of his seat like a rocket. Tony wasn't much better. They'd been jumping in and out of their seats throughout the game though the Warriors were beating the Spurs forty-seven to twenty-three.

Jamie sat back and drank her second Coke. Or was it the third? Her pants were fitting better. She was probably going to have to start monitoring what she ate before she outgrew them. Or maybe she'd just buy new ones.

She paid more attention to the boys than the game. To her, they were infinitely more interesting. All she needed was some cotton candy. How could a professional team not offer cotton candy? They'd eaten everything else—hot dogs, pretzels, nachos.

The third quarter ended and Z jumped up. "Can we get some popcorn?"

Tony's mouth dropped open. "You've already had two Cokes, a hotdog, and nachos."

"And a pretzel," Jamie added. She smiled at Z. "But no popcorn yet."

Z grinned back at Tony. "Yeah, no popcorn yet."

Tony laughed, rubbed Z's head. To Jamie he asked, "You want anything?"

"No thanks."

Tony led Z out of the stands and she watched them disappear into the crowd. Jamie scanned the people, watching as the group on the court launched T-shirts into the crowd using giant rubber bands and gave away free pizzas to whomever could make the most noise.

She was just content not to be running the chaos. She still dealt with plenty of it, but not tonight. Her caseload was heavy, but the stress was nothing like it had been with Marchek. She and Mackenzie and Hailey had attended Chip Washington's memorial services the Saturday after he died. His death had been treated as an accidental shooting. The department had promised Washington's wife and the press that a full investigation would be conducted, but she knew there would be no investigation.

Devlin's murder would remain officially unsolved. Hailey would get no credit for cracking it. The result was better for the department. Chip Washington's family received death benefits, which was better for them, too. After all, Devlin's death *had* been an accident.

Jamie had taken two weeks off to recover and had now been back at work for more than two months. She'd been talking to a therapist, something she never thought she'd do. And she was trying to quit smoking. She had a patch and she chewed a lot of gum—packs and packs of it—but she figured it was better than smoking. Every once in a while, though, she ripped the patch off and had a cigarette. Baby steps, she thought.

Lately she'd been doing a lot of things she never

thought she'd do. She'd let Tim take her out to a
movie. And she hadn't shot anyone, so that was something. Tim was assimilating back into the department.
He complained about the way some of the other officers looked at him. Some of his old friends were no
longer so friendly. All the charges against him had
been dropped and he had received an official apology
from the department as well as full pay and comp
time for his days spent in jail. It didn't relieve the
embarrassment, and nothing would restore his reputation. Jamie knew all about that. She remembered how
things had changed after she'd shot at him and Natasha. It would probably get easier eventually, she told
him. Probably.

Jamie wasn't the only one breaking new ground.
Tony had been out of rehab for three weeks and was
still sober. He went to his AA meetings religiously,
sometimes every day. Z was settling in to his second
foster home. The first one hadn't gone too well. Tony
didn't think this one would, either. But Tony picked
him up every weekend for an overnight at Jamie's.
Tonight—the game. Last week, Tony and Z had
rented *Men in Black* I and II and they'd done a dou-
bleheader that would have been torture for anyone
who had taste in movies. Thankfully, Jamie wasn't one
of them.

Tony was also teaching Z how to use the computer.
They'd started by searching for Z's name and found
Zephenaya, spelled Zephaniah, was a book in the
Bible. Tony said that was news to him. To Jamie, too,
though they'd both been raised Catholic.

The three of them sat by the computer and looked
up the book of Zephaniah. Tony read from Zephaniah
1:3, where God preached for the people to have patience and mercy. God promised that the wicked
would be punished for their sins and revenge would
come to them.

Z had listened intently and made Tony repeat it.

Then he had looked up, his small brow furrowed, and asked, "Does that mean God will punish whoever hurt Shawna?"

She'd seen Tony's eyes grow glassy, had to glance away herself.

Tony had wrapped an arm around Z. "I think it does." Then he'd met Jamie's gaze over Z's head and she'd considered how hard it was to answer a child's questions. Maybe her father and Pat hadn't done such a bad job after all.

After that night, Tony had decided to pay for weekly grief counseling for Z. Tony still worried that Z didn't talk enough about Shawna. Jamie assured him that sometimes it took decades to work through that kind of grief. She thought Z had a big head start with Tony on his side.

Tony was also pushing to get approval to become Z's foster father. Though Jamie moved a little slower on the idea, she was amazingly open for someone who never thought she'd have a family.

Jamie still spoke to Mackenzie and Hailey every few days. Hailey was already in the middle of a new high-profile murder case, thanks to her father-in-law, and Mackenzie had gotten her cast off and was back to her beat. The rookie already had her name down on the lists for Sex Crimes and Homicide, though she was years away from being eligible for either. It didn't look like she was going back to Montana just yet.

Jamie had heard through the grapevine that while she was recovering, Scott Scanlan had been dismissed from the department. In the course of the investigation, he had confessed to logging into Jamie's chat room using her ID. He wouldn't be tried for any of his crimes, but he was no longer a cop, probably wouldn't be one again. That was enough for Jamie.

According to the rumors, he'd also moved out of state. Tonight's tickets had been a gift from Deputy Chief Scanlan. She'd been getting a number of things

from Deputy Chief Scanlan recently. He'd paid her
vet bill and sent a three-hundred-dollar gift certificate
to a restaurant called Boulevard, where she'd taken Z
and Tony. They had eaten expensive food, declined
the wine list and cocktails, and decided next time
they'd rather go to Chevy's at Embarcadero. Three
weeks later Scanlan had sent another restaurant gift
certificate, and she'd sent it back. He'd sent tickets to
the game instead. Hailey and Mackenzie were receiv-
ing similar treatment.

Jamie knew there were strings attached. Deputy
Chief Scanlan wanted to be sure she didn't talk to the
media. That wasn't her style, but she hadn't told the
deputy chief that. Not yet. He could sweat a little.
Lord knows she had.

She saw Tony and Z hiking back up the stairs. Tony
held a big tub of popcorn and another soda. She wondered if any of them would sleep tonight and figured
it didn't matter much. There was always tomorrow.

Both boys were grinning.

"What did you guys do?"

Tony nodded to Z. "Show her."

Z pulled his hand out from behind his back and
handed her a bouquet of pink and blue cotton candy.

"Where'd you get this?"

Z smiled proudly. "We bribed it off a vendor who
had some in the back."

She smiled. "You're a tricky one, aren't you?"

Z nodded very seriously. Then he slid into his seat
and turned to her. "Since I was so tricky, you're gonna
share it with me, right?"

Jamie laughed out loud. "Maybe a little," she
said, winking.

"Half," Z said.

"Thirds," Tony cut in, leaning in with his hand out.

Jamie ripped it open and they all tore at it, shoving
big strands of pink and blue fluff into their mouths.
This was one of the good things, she thought.

She met Tony's gaze over Z's head and he winked, the gums around his front teeth blue. He nodded as though he understood.

Maybe he did. Maybe better than anyone, Tony understood.

She thought she did—better now than ever before.

# Monkeewrench

## by P.J. TRACY

"FAST, FRESH, FUNNY, AND OUTRAGEOUSLY
SUSPENSFUL...THE DEBUT THRILLER OF THE YEAR."
—HARLAN COBEN

People are dying for the new computer game
by the software company Monkeewrench.
Literally. With *Serial Killer Detective* out in
limited release, the real-life murders of a jogger
and a young woman have already mimicked the
first two scenarios in the game.

Now Grace McBride and her eccentric
Monkeewrench partners are caught in a vise.
They can go to the police and risk shining light
on things in their pasts they'd rather keep
buried. Or they can say nothing—and let
eighteen more people die.

"A KILLER READ." —*PEOPLE*

0-451-21157-X